LITERARY PRAISE FOR *OL' SPLIT TOE:*

"A powerful, lyrical meditation on wilderness, myth, and memory. Ellens has created a tale that feels ancient and urgent at the same time."
—**William Gibson**, author of *Neuromancer* and *The New York Times* bestseller *Agency*

"In this wise, deeply moving modern legend, a majestic deer is chosen by the spirits to travel across time while staying in place—his birthplace, one small corner of Michigan—and to witness the ceaseless changes on Earth by glacier, fire, flood, plants, and animal, ever more clever and numerous humans, and Mother Nature's unhurried, even-handed remediation. Spanning time from the end of the Ice Age to the climax of the Industrial Age, *Forest Legend*, a story for all ages, brings to vivid life the question on which our survival hangs: Can humans ever conquer and replace nature? Should we even try? Can we relearn that we are a part of her, and corral our technological powers within the reverence and respect of our Indigenous ancestors?"
—**Annie Gottlieb**, author of *Do You Believe in Magic?*, co-author of *Wishcraft* and *The Cube*, critic and commentator in *The New York Times*; *O, the Oprah Magazine*; *Vogue*; *The Nation*

"*Forest Legend: The Tale of Ol' Split Toe* provides a unique perspective on the natural world and humanity's place in it. Through charming storytelling and deep reverence for Mother Nature, the book both entertains and inspires a fresh look at the world that surrounds us."
—**Mary Radcliffe**, self-described forest enjoyer and frequent hiker, chairperson of Data Science at State Navigate

"Dan Ellens has written a novel of impressive quality, gleaned from 2,500 solitary nights spent in a remote forest sanctuary of his own design. Within the midst, the author's spirit blends with that of Ol' Split Toe, a timeless forest presence since the last glacial recession and a giant force, purveyor and critic of mankind's clever ways, with an imposing survivalist storyline fortified by a strong didactic undercurrent. *Forest Legend* bridges an immense readership gap, from the adventurous needs of young adult readers to the varied callings of serious-minded adults."
—**J. August Lithen**, author of *The Road to Marion Town: The Settlement of Osceola County, State of Michigan*

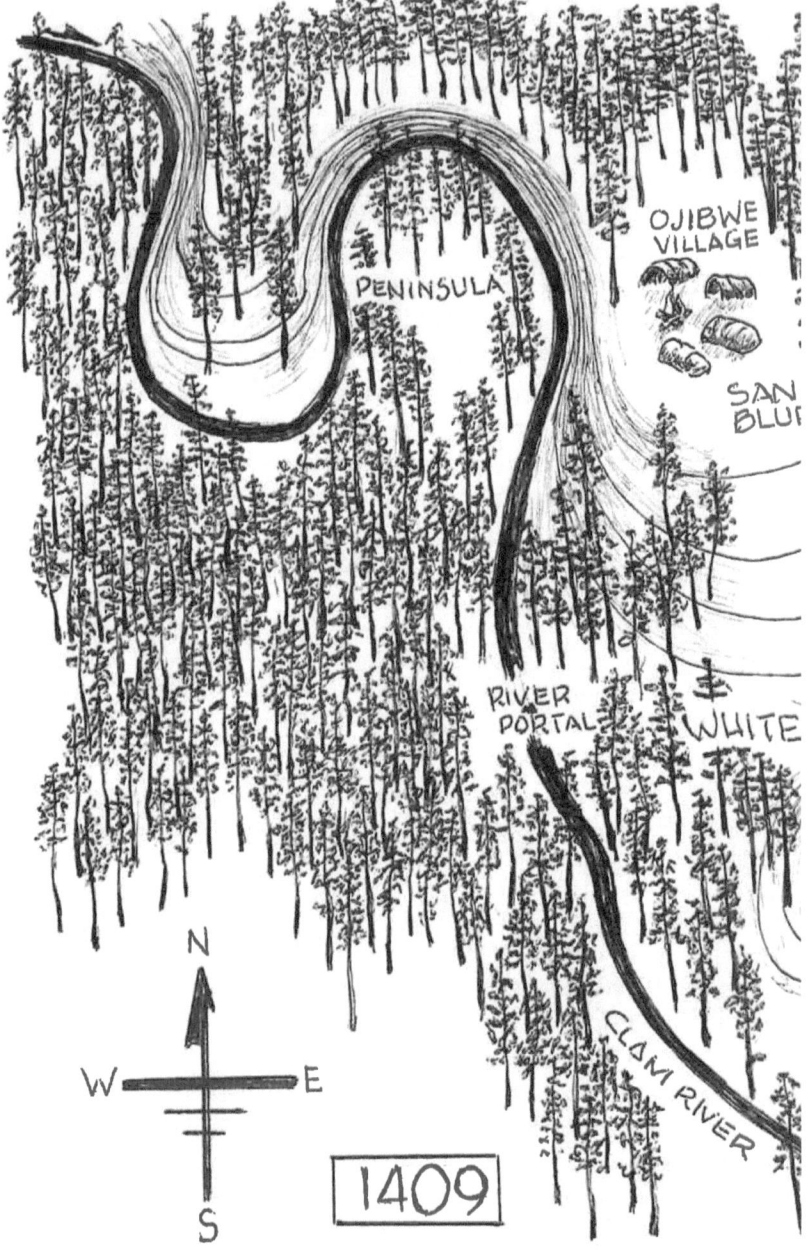

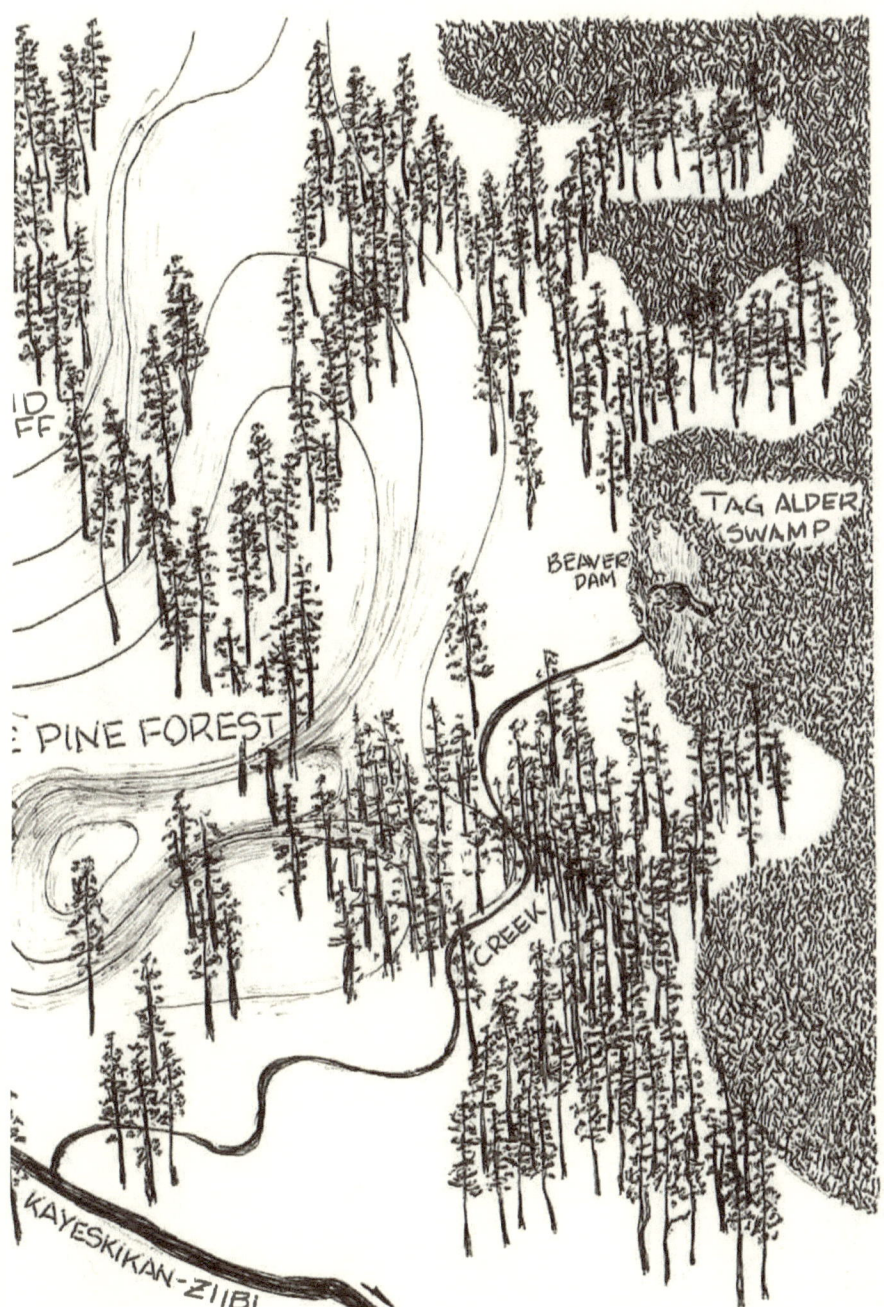

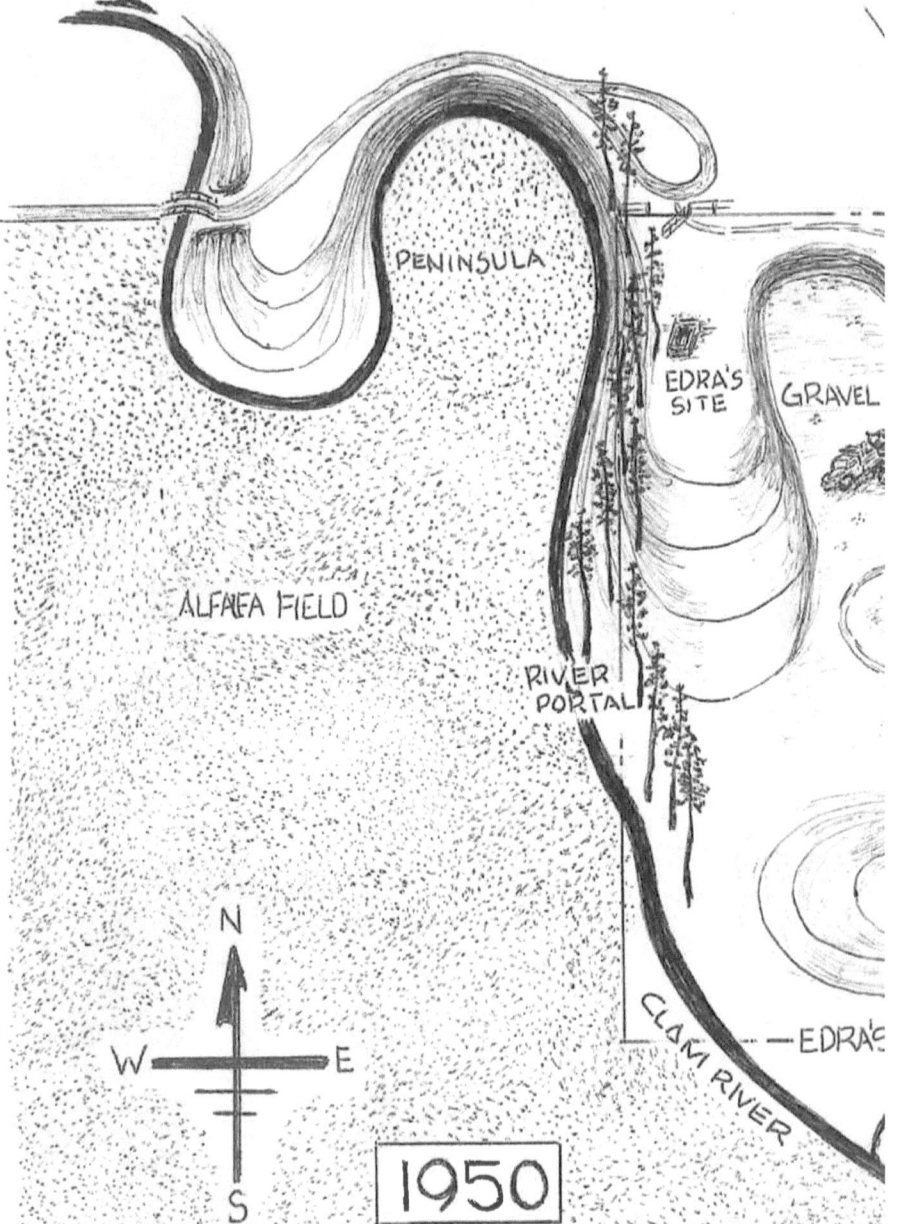

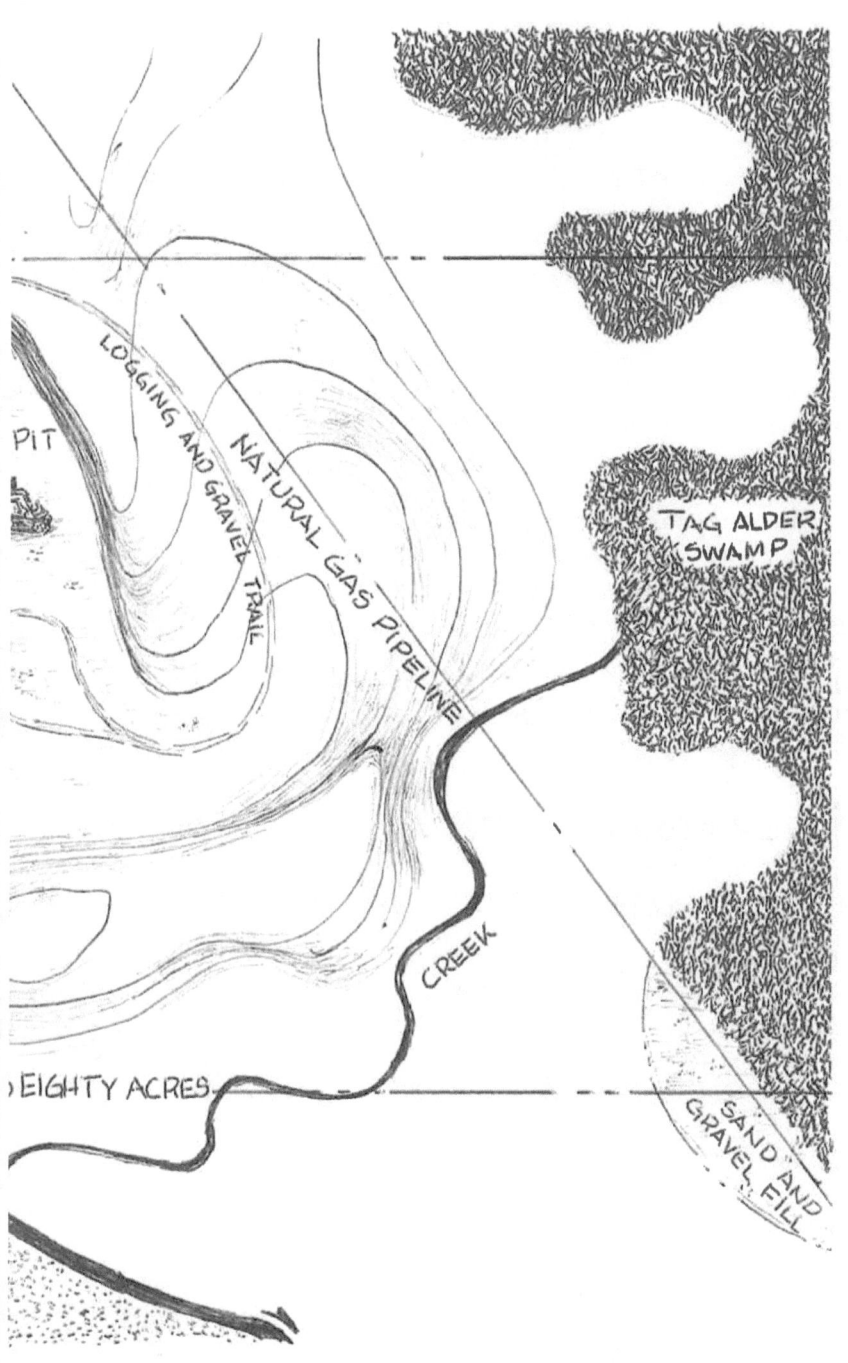

Copyright @ 2026 by Daniel S. Ellens
Copyright Registration Number: TXu 2-478-929
Effective Date of Registration: March 15, 2025
Title at the time of registration: Ol' Split Toe: The Forest and a Deer
All world rights reserved.

This is a work of fiction. Names, places, and incidents are the products of the author's imagination or are used fictitiously. Any resemblance to actual events or locales or persons, living or dead, is entirely coincidental.

No part of this book may be reproduced, stored in a retrieval system, or transmitted in any form or by any means electronic, mechanical, photocopying, recording or otherwise, without the prior consent of the publisher.

Readers are encouraged to go to MissionPointPress.com to contact the author or to find information on how to buy this book in bulk at a discounted rate.

Mission Point Press

Published by Mission Point Press
2554 Chandler Rd.
Traverse City, MI 49696
(231) 421-9513
MissionPointPress.com

Preface page pen and ink art by Dan Ellens — Whitetail deer

Hard cover: ISBN: 978-1-968761-07-3
Soft cover: ISBN: 978-1-968761-08-0
Library of Congress Control Number: 2025921435

Printed in the United States of America

FOREST LEGEND
— THE TALE OF —
OL' SPLIT TOE

DAN ELLENS

M·P·P
www.MissionPointPress.com

For Kevin, who has seen Ol' Split Toe.

CONTENTS

PREFACE		1
Chapter 1 — AD 1409	**THE OJIBWE**	4
Chapter 2 — AD 1409	**THE TAG ALDER SWAMP**	11
Chapter 3 — AD 1409	**MANY WAYS FOR A TREE TO DIE**	18
Chapter 4 — AD 1409	**DANGER ALL AROUND**	33
Chapter 5 — AD 1409	**THE SACRED CIRCLE**	43
Chapter 6 — AD 1409	**THE RIVER CROSSING PORTAL**	57
Chapter 7 — 8500 BCE	**ARCTIC TUNDRA**	61
Chapter 8 — 8500 BCE	**DIRE WOLVES**	77
Chapter 9 — AD 1870	**LOGGING**	88
Chapter 10 — AD 1874	**EDRA**	104
Chapter 11 — AD 1878	**DYNAMITE**	112
Chapter 12 — AD 1880	**PIONEERS**	120

Chapter 13 — AD 1885	**THE RAILROAD**	130
Chapter 14 — AD 1885	**EDRA'S CABIN**	136
Chapter 15 — AD 1911	**THE LAST WHITE PINE**	143
Chapter 16 — AD 1911	**THE FAMILY FARM**	148
Chapter 17 — AD 1911	**THE GATHERING**	153
Chapter 18 — AD 1911	**EDRA'S FOREST WORLD**	158
Chapter 19 — AD 1911	**JAKE'S VISIT**	169
Chapter 20 — AD 1918	**THE SPANISH FLU PANDEMIC**	176
Chapter 21 — AD 1950	**COMMUNITY INFRASTRUCTURE**	182
Chapter 22 — AD 1950	**THE RUT**	190
Chapter 23 — AD 1950	**HUNTING FOR SPORT**	197
Chapter 24 — AD 1960	**HUNTERS BUY THE EIGHTY ACRES**	201
Chapter 25 — AD 1974	**SPLIT TOE IS SHOT**	208
Chapter 26 — AD 1974	**THE BOY**	214
Chapter 27 — AD 1974	**PBB**	218
Chapter 28 — AD 1986	**THE BOY BUYS THE EIGHTY ACRES**	222
Chapter 29 — AD 2020	**SO MANY DEER**	232
Chapter 30 — AD 2020	**CORPORATE FARMING**	238

Chapter 31 — AD 2020	**THE GRANDFATHER TREE'S WISDOM**	243
Chapter 32 — AD 2020	**WINTER CROSSING**	255
Chapter 33 — AD 2080	**SPLIT TOE UNDERSTANDS**	260
Epilogue: Split Toe Returns — Forty Years Back in Time — AD 2040	**THE OLD MAN'S DREAM**	281

AUTHOR'S NOTE   298

ACKNOWLEDGMENTS   301

REFERENCES   303

ABOUT THE AUTHOR   305

These sightings, taken across cultures and languages, are the story of Ol' Split Toe.

Dan Ellens – 2025

CHAPTER 1
THE OJIBWE

AD 1409

When the doe blurted her warning, Split Toe froze, every sense intensely alert. They all waited: Split Toe, the doe, and the Ojibwe. Neither Split Toe nor the Ojibwe wanted to give away their position. Split Toe didn't dare move his head to search for the Ojibwe. But the Ojibwe had been watching the large, dark shadow of the deer for some time as it slipped silently through the thicket. Just a few more steps and the deer would reach the opening.

Split Toe stood just inside the edge of a large tag alder thicket, his antlers blending with branches that surrounded him. On one side of the thicket was the marshy wetland where he was born and spent his fawn months. Tall grasses, wild rice, and cattails blew in the breeze. On the other side was the vast white pine forest.

The path where Split Toe stood was ancient. Between the tag alders at the thicket's edge, generations of deer and other animals had worn down the knee-high grass into a dark, wet trail of rich soil.

The doe warned him of danger. But where was this predator? What was this predator?

Further in the thicket, shallow pools of water surrounded each tag alder clump, clumps close enough together that their branches mingled tightly. Their roots connected below the thick bed of decaying leaves and fallen stems, forming a mucky bottom in each pool, built up through many seasons in the cycle of growth.

If Split Toe could make it further into the thicket, he would be safe. The predator was unlikely to follow him deeper into the swamp.

Tag alder stalks grow for decades, crisscrossing each other in a dense tangle that even Split Toe could not easily navigate. Then, rarely more than two inches in diameter, they often die off one by one, making space for newer stalks sprouting from the same root system. Some of the stalks might reach sixty years in age, but most surrender earlier, each stalk gently collapsing, until the whole thicket is like a battlefield of fallen soldiers lying below a live network of tag alder cousins. The fallen pieces all eventually break down and return to the soil from which they were born.

Split Toe breathed in slowly, searching for the predator's scent. Damp, warm air pulled in through leathery nostrils at the end of his long snout. A breeze blowing through the thicket carried with it the musty aroma of decay. Fallen leaves. Stagnant water and rotting wood. But something else was there too. Was it the hint of smoke humans carried with them from their campfires? Or the dried blood that always clung to a cougar's pelt? Perhaps the stale, sweaty scent of a wolf? What had the doe seen?

The edge of the swamp concealed both predator and prey. It was a precarious place.

Split Toe was not really his name—at least not yet, in 1409. For now, the few humans who had seen him, with the massive antlers adorning his head, simply called him *Waawaashkeshi*: deer.

European settlers of another age, perhaps around 1900, called him *Ol' Split Toe*. Truth be told, these humans did not know enough about Split Toe to understand that he was only one deer. For them, he was a lineage of deer, each with a set of antlers larger than any other. Each one, they called *Ol' Split Toe*.

As the remarkable lineage continued, an Ol' Split Toe appeared in the hunting dreams of the European settlers' offspring. He was their legendary King of the Forest, who had survived the dangers of the wilds to become the largest and heaviest buck in the woods. Enormous antlers. A huge body. Each deer extraordinarily smart. Almost impossible to take. He slipped past them year after year, outfoxing all their hunting strategies. They knew when Ol' Split Toe had passed in the night because he left a mark of two front toes split wide apart, followed by two rear points so far from the toes that a human hand could not cover the print.

A lineage of large-antlered deer certainly existed. But these fellows did not know and would never believe the real Split Toe was truly just one deer, a real deer—*the* Split Toe. Those who saw him were unaware of Split Toe's movement from one age to another through a natural time portal, *the river crossing*, which only opened under the shadow of an eclipse. Split Toe's highly developed instincts always drew him back to the crossing, with the spirits of nature guiding him on a journey toward understanding.

If humans had known he was truly just one deer, they might have thought he was immortal, protected from death. It would have seemed so, for there were many times when Split Toe was lucky to still be alive.

But here, standing on an already-ancient trail at the edge of the tag alder thicket in 1409, he was *Waawaashkeshi*. And he was in mortal danger.

Waawaashkeshi remained still, his eyes unblinking, hidden only a few feet within the thicket, his antlers blending with the branches he peered through. His nose twitched—though the smell was faint, he was now sure a human was around. Hiding.

The Ojibwe was patient. Mud smudged his buckskin shirt and leggings, and a bit of grease broke up their tan color. It covered his face and hands too. The Ojibwe had even rolled the buckskin in a pile of decaying tag alder leaves to disguise his scent. Though he was young—just fourteen winters—and still gaining the experience he would need in life, he already knew how to blend in, how to wield his patience as a weapon against the extreme stillness of a deer.

The doe Waawaashkeshi had come here to meet finally detected something—a silent, subtle blink.

The Ojibwe had tried his best to resist this tiny eye movement. The doe blurted a warning—*shhhh, shhhh*—and the boy knew the chase was over. He'd lost his chance.

Her warning surprised the Ojibwe. His attention had been so fixed on the dark shadow of the large deer that he hadn't noticed she was waiting nearby. The buck was still just out of reach, and the Ojibwe knew the large-antlered deer, senses alert, would not emerge from the thicket.

The Ojibwe was frustrated that he'd let the doe catch him by surprise, but he didn't mind letting Waawaashkeshi get away. He knew Waawaashkeshi was special, likely immortal, for to an Ojibwe all things in nature are connected—and where does life really begin and end? What is one life? Does it exist only within one creature, or is it shared between many bodies, like the trees of the forest, that all seem to connect with each other below the forest floor?

The Ojibwe removed the flint-tipped arrow from his bow and closed his eyes. He felt the power of his ancestors. He felt the approval of his grandfather, who also knew of this special deer, for his grandfather spoke reverently of Waawaashkeshi many times at the sacred campfire, passing down the story from his father before him.

Without disturbing the moment, the Ojibwe first bowed respectfully to the doe, and then to Waawaashkeshi, and then to the deer's refuge, the thicket. Finally, the Ojibwe turned around and bowed to the deep white pine forest behind him. The tall trees—many so wide that three people could not reach their arms around them—formed a dark, cavernous realm. The thick canopy blocked sunlight, and branches below the canopy could not survive the darkness. No understory grew in the perpetual darkness at the forest floor.

When the Ojibwe put away his arrow and nodded respectfully to his quarry, Waawaashkeshi lowered his head in return, then turned and, in one massive ball of muscular movement, leaped back down the trail from where he had come. Instantly, the doe dove deeper into the thicket; two spotted fawns, who mysteriously seemed to appear from nowhere, bolted in opposite directions to escape. The deer instinctively knew they would soon rendezvous deeper in the swamp.

The Ojibwe boy was brave. Tall, strong, and a good runner, his band thought of him as an up-and-coming hunter with great promise. He was old enough that the village didn't worry when he slipped away into the forest for a few days without returning home. He'd already brought in several young deer for meat and buckskins. Other animals too. A raccoon. Rabbits. Three turkeys. A duck, which he took out of the air with an arrow.

But he really captured everyone's attention when, at just twelve years old, he returned to the village dragging a full-grown black bear. The bear was not huge, but it was certainly an adult. Seeing the boy bringing it back surprised the whole village. No other child his age would have dared go after an animal so large and powerful. The older men of the village rubbed the boy's head and patted his back for his brave deed. His mother quickly skinned the bear to make a robe for him to curl up under when winter set in.

Yet most of the village believed it must have been a lucky shot. Few adults had a black bear to their own credit.

The boy, however, knew the truth—he alone had tracked the black bear, and his arrow had struck exactly where he intended.

The whole village named the boy *Mukwoh*—bear. His parents wanted to call him *Makoons*—bear cub—but everyone in the village thought it so incredible that he went after a full-grown bear and then dragged the bear all the way back to the village without help, that they insisted on calling the boy Mukwoh. It was a kind of graduation. They all thought Mukwoh was fearless. They were proud of him, but it worried them, too.

With his bow stowed, the boy turned to head home. The forest opened up into pleasant terrain, clear enough for Mukwoh to circle back easily between the giant trees as he made his way to his small village of dome-shaped bark shelters. The shelters circled a central fire ring on a large sand bluff above the river. This time Mukwoh returned with no contribution to his band's food supply. He was not disappointed. There would be other chances.

CHAPTER 2
THE TAG ALDER SWAMP

AD 1409

Waawaashkeshi's trail followed the edge of a shallow depression in the terrain that formed the tag alder swamp. Its dense entanglement of complicated thicket seemed as though it had always been this way. But in truth, a receding glacier had carved out the low area ten thousand years earlier as the Ice Age gave way to warmer climates. At that time, the land was barren, covered in deep deposits of sand, gravel, rock, and clay—a winter desert empty of plant life. But with open water and wet seepages caused by the vast melting glacier, vegetation from warmer equatorial regions slowly pushed northward, plant by plant, expanding wherever climate and soil permitted.

Eventually, a small bird—blown off course by a strong wind during a day of exploration—left its calling card on a soft fossil projecting from a moist seepage in the depression. The excrement contained a tag alder seed which the bird had ingested that morning, half a day's flight to the south. The waste surrounding the seed provided natural fertilizer, giving the seed a good start. With the next rain, the seed washed into a narrow, moist crevasse and sent out its first, tentative rootlet. When it sprouted, it soon turned into a sparse young bush.

This first bush produced berries of its own after eight years. Nearly a decade later its first stalk snapped off in a strong February wind. It took another decade for the stalk to decay naturally, but in that time a few berries from the bush found their way to other moist cracks in the ground and began to sprout. The real blessing for these bushes was the thin layer of soil that developed from their decaying branches and fallen leaves. Thin as it was, it still retained moisture and contained nutrients that benefited new plants as they took hold.

When the tag alders thickened into a large grove and grass began to inhabit the soil forming over sand and gravel between each tag alder bush, a family of beavers moved in, turning the depression into a swamp. Beavers gnawed off several of the bushes and dragged them to a spot where water perpetually trickled along the ground. They also brought in rich soil that had built up for decades under tag alder clumps. By weaving together layers of branches, grass, and soil each night, the beavers soon built a low dam that stopped some of the water runoff.

During the day, water accumulated until it found a low spot in the dam to flow over. In the night, the beaver family gnawed more tag alder bushes, brought more grass and mud, and expanded the dam to stop flow at the spot from the day before. Over time, the entire depression filled with shallow water, with mounds of rich soil protruding through puddles at the base of each tag alder clump.

Within ten years, tag alders trimmed by the beavers developed new shoots from the same root systems. Debris from the beavers' logging efforts composted into additional rich soil. A small overflow, which the beavers finally tolerated, trickled over the top of the dam, forming a creek of clear water, tea-colored from decades of tannins produced by the tag alders. The creek wound a path to the river not far downstream.

The glacier left several high spots within this wet swamp—four peninsulas and five small islands. Many from the Ojibwe band knew the islands existed because they could see a few groups of hemlock trees reaching above the tag alders far off in the swamp, but they never went there. The islands were simply too difficult to get to. And once in the thicket, spotting the taller hemlocks could be impossible. Mukwoh imagined he could walk in circles for hours in that wet tag alder swamp and never find an island. Perhaps never find a way out.

Waawaashkeshi headed toward one of these islands. His instinct and sense of self-preservation drew him there—a force shaped by all his life experiences so far. For Waawaashkeshi, self-preservation was a seamless blend of smell, taste, touch, sight, and memory. And it included something deeper that had saved his life many times—guidance from the natural spirits.

They were spirits that inhabited the tag alder swamp, the river, and the white pine forest; the spirit of every rock and tree and being that had ever existed in this place; the moon, the sun, and the clouds—all coming together as a single current that flowed through everything. It was a combination of everything, the contribution of everything. Waawaashkeshi tuned into a singular sense that included all these things. When its force tugged at him, he surrendered to its pull.

Waawaashkeshi followed the trail that skirted the edge of the swamp, always within cover of the thicket, until he reached a wisp of a trail that went inside. The doe, who had not lost track of Waawaashkeshi after the Ojibwe encounter, followed close behind. She stopped briefly to look back. Her twins, though distracted by a myriad of things to nibble on, followed behind in a playful, wandering sort of way. Once in the water, the trail was invisible. It was more a narrow tunnel than a trail, leading along a watery passage through tangled branches, winding around ancient tag alder trunks and fallen limbs.

This, too, was an old trail, well known to the small group of deer that inhabited this swamp. For when in danger, it became their refuge. And while the islands were small, each offered grass and leaves for food and a dry place where three or four deer could curl up and sleep for several days. The deer could hole up there for long enough to outwait a wolf or bobcat—predators that, like humans, avoided entering water. A few tried, but the water slowed them down and prevented them from moving silently. Deer on the islands always had ample warning of an approaching predator.

After the doe and fawns settled into comfortable dry spots beneath the hemlock trees, Waawaashkeshi bent his knees and curled into his own nest, softened by layers of fine hemlock needles and decaying tag alder leaves. Waawaashkeshi kept his head erect, alert to his surroundings. He saw the twins, no bigger than a pair of young coyotes, each blending into the foliage behind them. Pale spots still covered their backs. One fawn had two buttons on its forehead, the beginnings of antlers that would start to grow later in the fall.

Was Waawaashkeshi the father of the twins? He drew in a deep breath and exhaled slowly, glancing at the doe resting nearby. Biologically, he did not know. He certainly could be. But Waawaashkeshi knew that being a father was more than a matter of blood. And fawns accepted most bucks in the herd in a fatherly way. All grown deer looked after the young as parents would. The herd was one big family. Mature deer all trained the newborns—protected them, cared for them, and often sacrificed their own safety to ensure the safety of the herd's offspring. Yes, to the twins, Waawaashkeshi was a father.

Waawaashkeshi liked this swamp island. It reminded him of the hidden spot that his mother had discovered for his birth. The grass was tall and protective. Off-trail far enough to avoid stray predators.

Waawaashkeshi remembered the moment he first opened his eyes. Cool spring air greeted him, welcoming him to his surroundings. He saw his mother standing over him—four long legs that looked much like the surrounding saplings. The sky was dark, but only briefly, for Waawaashkeshi was born just as a solar eclipse reached its peak. He blinked the mucus from his small eyes and saw an orange glowing ring in the sky beyond the dark form of his mother's body.

Sky? He did not know what "sky" was—only that it was a simple two-dimensional surface directly in front of him. How long did it take him to understand depth in his vision? Not long. Waawaashkeshi was a quick learner.

Perhaps it was the auspicious timing of his birth that caused the natural spirits to choose Waawaashkeshi for a special life. Perhaps he was chosen for his extraordinary perception and the flawless memory the spirits knew he possessed. Or maybe the spirits knew that Waawaashkeshi would pay attention and demonstrate humble respect for the natural world around him. From the many deer in the forest, the natural spirits chose Waawaashkeshi for a lifelong journey of special knowledge and understanding: *to know, to feel, to understand the whole life of the forest and the natural workings at play in the forest's survival.*

It took time for Waawaashkeshi to realize he was not the same as the other animals in the forest. He lived, grew, and foraged like one of them. He was vulnerable—fighting, suffering, surviving—just as they did. He grew to be a bit stronger than the other deer. A bit faster. When he fought, he won. He traveled a little further than others in the herd, crossing rivers they could not. He endured hunger a bit longer and escaped predators that others would never know. He lived where others perished.

As time progressed, Waawaashkeshi slowly began to understand that he was born for a purpose—that the natural spirits often placed unusual, even extraordinary, situations in his path. He began to see his string of experiences as a purposeful education, guiding him toward a deeper understanding of his forest world.

Though patient, Waawaashkeshi was eager to learn. He understood that the natural spirit's instinctive pull was a call to learn—one that he must follow. Waawaashkeshi lowered his head. His large antlers rested on the side of his belly and on the ground. Waawaashkeshi knew they were safe on the island in the swamp.

CHAPTER 3
MANY WAYS FOR A TREE TO DIE

AD 1409

Rain had fallen for three continuous days. Waawaashkeshi rose from his resting place, stretching his neck and shoulders in both directions. The doe was already on her feet, watching over her fawns. The little twins wandered around the edges of the water, nibbling on tag alder leaves. Waawaashkeshi motioned to the doe with his nose and let a stream of air escape through his nostrils.

"Keep the young ones here for a few hours," he seemed to say. "I will be gone for several days. I have a place to visit that is far away—somewhere the little ones should not follow. There is still plenty to eat on this patch of dry ground, and the youngsters can wander into the water without much risk. It will be good for them. They will learn."

The doe curled her neck while lowering her head, as if to say, "I understand."

Waawaashkeshi turned to follow another tunnel-trail away from the island. The fawn with buttons on his head pranced forward several steps, eager to follow. Waawaashkeshi turned back, lifting his foot from the water and stepping toward the small deer.

The fawn looked longingly into Waawaashkeshi's eyes. Waawaashkeshi glanced at the buttons on the fawn's forehead. He brushed the fawn's spotted back affectionately with his snout, then nudged him back onto the island with his nose.

"Not this time, little one," Waawaashkeshi's eyes told the small buck. "There is a place I must go. Far away. I have an important question to ask at this place. You still have some growing to do before it is your time. The world out there—beyond our tag alder swamp—is dangerous."

Waawaashkeshi started down the trail into the wet swamp. He took several steps before pausing to look back. The doe stood confidently, watching him leave, flanked by a fawn on each side. They all gazed stoically. Waawaashkeshi nodded his antlers in a fatherly bow and disappeared into the swamp. Waawaashkeshi knew this trail led to where the white pine forest began.

A grassy dry stretch that was its own kind of habitat formed a bridge from the wet swamp to the dark forest. Sunlight reached down upon the grass—one of the few sunny spots in the area—where native grasses grew abundantly. It supported the whole food chain. Some were predators; most were not. Waawaashkeshi always felt the voice of the old white pines warning him in this place.

"Look around, Waawaashkeshi. Trust what you feel. Take care. Don't stay in the open for long."

Waawaashkeshi was alert. Most animals who survived in the wilds possessed a single sense like his, one that grew stronger with time, experience, and a deepening relationship with the natural spirit current. Waawaashkeshi took his surroundings in, his ears twitching as he scanned the area.

He understood the feelings of anticipation, caution, occasional surprise, and always an urgent need to survive. Waawaashkeshi understood pain and tried to avoid it. A porcupine quill in his nose. A bee sting near his eye. A long, barbed thorn buried into his shin or hoof. He did not experience fear; it was not in his nature. But he was always ready to escape. Always ready to fight back.

Today, Waawaashkeshi sensed this grassy stretch was safe. He cautiously stepped into the open.

Waawaashkeshi saw a large snapping turtle ambling across the trail, returning to the old beaver dam where, each spring, she laid her eggs along its side. Waawaashkeshi and Mukwoh called her *Mikinaak*. This turtle had lived for more than 150 years in a pool where runoff from the beaver dam flowed. As far as Waawaashkeshi knew, she was the oldest creature in the area. She spent much of her time underwater, her nose buried in the muddy side of the creek. She did not need to worry much about danger; she carried her protection on her back and looked just intimidating enough to be left alone. Though slow on dry ground, she could whip her neck around in a flash, and the power of her jaw was only surpassed by the cutting capabilities of her sharp, bony beak. All the creatures of the forest watched her with curiosity when they could, but none dared to mess with Mikinaak.

The beaver dam had long been abandoned by its builders. Now, it just filled in part of the forest terrain—an earthworks that became permanent over centuries, and which formed the natural definition of the west edge of the swamp. To Waawaashkeshi, the rise offered an important semi-dry place where the ancient trail followed the swamp's edge, winding through heavy thicket while still providing cover.

Today, Waawaashkeshi embarked on a journey to an ancient place he had visited several times in his extraordinary life—a large circle where trees were different from the white pines, and old in their own right. It was one of Waawaashkeshi's favorite places, where the spirit pool's voice sang clear and true.

In another age—more than a thousand years ago—humans had constructed the circular rise. It was not unlike the beaver dam, though its shape was nearly a perfect circle. The Ojibwe called the people who made it *Aanikoobijiganag*—Ancestors. This place had weathered hundreds of seasons. Generation upon generation had visited this sacred ground. Its history stretched beyond memory, so far back that the Ojibwe were not certain whether the builders were their own ancestors or a people who had come and gone long before.

Waawaashkeshi and the Ojibwe both knew the circle was a sacred place. The spirits of the aanikoobijiganag and the great trees came together there, where the collective spirit pool that existed everywhere could be felt with powerful intensity. Waawaashkeshi felt compelled to make this trip. A slightly nervous, unsettled feeling urged him forward; perhaps it was instinct, or perhaps the pull of the natural spirits. It was an unexplainable urge he could only resolve by following the invisible force tugging at him.

There was a question Waawaashkeshi wanted answered—a question for the natural spirits. He did not know exactly how to form the question, but he hoped that, along the journey, a respectful way to ask it would come to him.

Waawaashkeshi reached around with his neck, baring his teeth as he dug into the fur on his hip. He felt a flea biting him. He could not get ahold of the flea, but he could gnaw at the skin where the flea bit, providing some relief.

"Get off my back!" he thought, nibbling in frustration at his fur. "Why are you doing this?"

The flea bit again, taunting. "This is what I do. You are so big and powerful. Don't you think you should be able to catch me?"

"Get off! You know I can't catch you. I have a long way to go and don't want to take you along." Waawaashkeshi's teeth dug deeper into his pelt.

The insistent flea, craving its bloody meal and unable to resist tormenting Waawaashkeshi further, bit once more. "Forget it, Waawaashkeshi. I'm coming along and there is nothing you can do about it."

Frustrated, Waawaashkeshi acknowledged the point and continued on his way, hoping he could rid himself of the pest at the nearest river.

The adventure ahead and the promise of delicious food at the circle excited Waawaashkeshi. He could hardly keep his tail from twitching. He would see the deep parts of the white pine forest again, pass by some of the most interesting trees, and perhaps discover something new. A trail did not guide Waawaashkeshi through the forest. He simply knew the direction—and he knew to follow the force that tugged him.

Waawaashkeshi slipped quietly into the dark forest, each long step silently disturbing the thick bed of pine straw covering the forest floor. The disruption was subtle—just enough that a skilled tracker could follow if they came before the needles dried out and settled back into place. Waawaashkeshi walked freely but frequently looked over his shoulder.

He enjoyed the forest of tall white pines. He rarely entered this part of the world, as there was not much for him to eat. He needed grass, or the low green leaves of saplings and tag alders. He needed fruits like wintergreen berries or haws of the hawthorn trees or nuts. If all else failed, Waawaashkeshi could eat bark from young trees or dark green moss that grew hidden from sunlight on shady surfaces. Many times he simply took what he could get.

Waawaashkeshi's gaze followed a large tree's tall trunk from the forest floor up to the canopy.

"There's a place for you," he told the flea. "Up there at the top."

The tree grew straight, reaching for a spot of sunlight far from the ground. Evidence of the many branches that once grew out from the long trunk absorbed long ago into thick, fractured bark that formed the tree's outer skin. Live branches made a tuft at the canopy above, where smaller branches extended from each large branch, and then twigs extended from the smaller branches. There, near the top, an eagle perched, its sharp eyes locking with Waawaashkeshi's in a silent exchange of respect.

Waawaashkeshi continued on his way, admiring the sea of soft green needles encircling every twig and shimmering in the breeze at the canopy. The needles overlapped each other in dense layers, sunlight sifting through one to the next, until the forest below became a dark, endless grove of columns—each tree supporting the vast, living ceiling above.

The mature forest's deep shade prevented new saplings from surviving. Only when a storm toppled one of these giant trees or a decaying limb fell did enough sunlight reach the forest floor for a fresh batch of white pine children and grandchildren to spring up. Even if they survived into childhood, the going was slow. Each year brought only a small gain in height. If a seedling happened to take hold where the sunlight struck it directly, it grew faster. But those that grew slowly at first—focusing on core strength and root structure rather than height—were often better off in the long run.

Waawaashkeshi liked the majesty of the old white pines. The tall, strong columns tapered off in girth as they reached up to mingle with their siblings and cousins high above the ground. They were a family that stayed together as a group and seemed to work together. To care for each other. He felt their energy.

"The trees would make such great companions for you," Waawaashkeshi mocked the flea. "Why don't you stay here?"

The pesky flea acknowledged Waawaashkeshi's thought with a quick bite. "You know, Waawaashkeshi, you're no better at trying to give me to another home than you are at making insulting remarks. Give it up."

Waawaashkeshi flicked his tail in frustration at the flea.

The white pine forest was a comfortable place that stretched for days across the landscape. Shade from the canopy perpetually cooled the ground. A pleasant pine aroma filled the air. When Waawaashkeshi needed to sleep, pine straw covering the whole forest floor made a thick mattress softer than his favorite spots among the tag alders.

There were few young saplings here. With vegetation so sparse—only in sunlight openings—the small trees had to miraculously survive the food chain at the forest floor. Waawaashkeshi ate them from time to time, though they were generally not worth the trouble for him to find. There were never enough saplings to satisfy his hunger. The crushing paw of a bear might do them in; hungry, desperate mice would eat bark from the base; even a family of insects might select a fledgling tree as its host and consume it from the inside out.

There are many ways for a tree to die.

Fortunately, when a small tree's root system began to develop, the trees around it made a lifeline to the sapling. While performing photosynthesis to remove carbon dioxide from the atmosphere and release oxygen back into the air, they could also transfer some of the carbon they collected to the nearby fledgling tree through a complex network of roots and fungi. The small tree, hidden in shade and unable to perform much photosynthesis to generate its own carbon, would get a boost from older trees surrounding it.

Photosynthesis and carbon dioxide were terms unknown to Waawaashkeshi, but he already knew trees connected soil to the air in a natural way. Waawaashkeshi would never understand exactly how that happened, but the spirits showed him these things worked together in an important, life-sustaining way.

When Mukwoh found the deer tracks leading into the deep forest, the prints were already two days old. Mukwoh was intrigued.

He crouched to inspect them—there was no mistaking the size, the depth, the spacing.

"Waawaashkeshi," he murmured reverently. "Why are you going into the dark forest?" Mukwoh was genuinely curious.

Mukwoh gathered his thoughts. "Perhaps …"

Mukwoh was young, and though he sensed that this deer was better left alone, he couldn't help but imagine the campfire stories after bringing this deer home. The whispers in the village about him being a lucky hunter would finally cease. It was skill—not luck—that had brought down the black bear he was named after.

A damp morning fog hanging like a cloud over the tag alder swamp was just beginning to burn off. Morning fog often meant a hot day ahead, especially in autumn, as the world prepared for winter. The white pine forest would be a cool place to spend the day. A cool place to track down this deer.

With the bow over his shoulder and a handful of arrows, Mukwoh began to work out the trail. He picked up his small bag of survival supplies and settled in for an easy trot, moving silently across the blanket of pine needles.

Waawaashkeshi wandered through the mature forest, pausing now and then to look up at the trees. He saw a decaying snag standing like a skeleton among healthy trees. He knew a deep hole high up in the snag's trunk was at one time home to a large pileated woodpecker. The woodpecker had discovered insects while burrowing into the tree, earning a meal as it opened a hollow large enough for its own nest.

Waawaashkeshi felt the flea bite. It made him twitch.

"Now that's what you need, flea," he snapped back. "A woodpecker to carry you around. Just think of the places you could go. Try it. I insist. You know I'll be rid of you one way or another. Besides, you'll be much safer there than if you stay with me."

The flea, enjoying his warm spot on Waawaashkeshi's hip, did not respond.

Perhaps, a squirrel would someday occupy the woodpecker's hole. But for now, squirrels did not spend much time in this forest because only white pines grew here, which did not produce much food for a squirrel. When a sunny spot opened up, a squirrel might discover the hollow nest in the snag and bury a beech seed nearby. If it survived, the growing beech might provide nuts to sustain the squirrel's offspring. But that would be a long story, told over many generations of squirrels.

Waawaashkeshi remembered when a lightning strike killed this tree. Already 500 years old, the tree had stood for fifty more years with the same majestic posture. But lightning ignited the fuse, and there was no turning back. It left a fissure in the bark down to ground level, a fissure soon discovered by a small insect. Before the tree released enough sap to seal the opening, the insect laid its eggs in the fissure. During the next season, when the eggs hatched, the insects began using the tree.

Not long after, a ladder-backed woodpecker arrived, pecking at the tree in search of an insect dinner. It made a hole the size of its own body. Several years later, having lost the protection of its outer bark skin, the slow process of rot set in. As rot spread, grubs, termites, and countless microscopic organisms burrowed into the softening wood. The tree hung on, life continuing to flow up and down its veins despite the festering injury. Eventually, a raccoon discovered the grubs, and easily hollowed out the decaying, punky wood from the trunk.

The tree weakened structurally and biologically. Though doomed, it lived on for another thirty years. The hollow base had plenty of space for the raccoon to raise a litter of her own and to protect them through their most precarious months. Now, twenty years after the last live needle fell from its upper branches, generations of raccoons have made the hollow their home, with each parent eventually surrendering the dry, protected space to one of its children or grandchildren.

As the tree crumbled, it would become home to countless microorganisms that, given time, would compost the tree's skeleton into fertile forest soil, permitting a new batch of white pines to take root. Many trees began the race. Over its 500-year lifespan, the tree produced tens of millions of seeds, each striving to start life. Yet, of those millions, only one was likely to live to full-life maturity, claiming its parent's place in the forest as another majestic, mature white pine.

Waawaashkeshi thought about how much longer the process

of dying took for the tree than for a typical deer or human. Perhaps only Mikinaak lived long enough to understand life in these terms.

By nightfall, Mukwoh could tell he was catching up. He saw the spots where Waawaashkeshi had stopped for one reason or another. He bent to one knee when he found the matted impression where Waawaashkeshi spent the first night. When he reached the second night's impression, he placed his hand where the deer had slept.

"Getting closer," Mukwoh told himself. "Two sleep spots in one day. Yes, getting closer."

He noted the fresh saplings Waawaashkeshi had nibbled on.

"Waawaashkeshi will be getting hungry if he cannot find more food than this."

Mukwoh resumed his trot. Later that evening, when he found the spot Waawaashkeshi had slept on his third night, he knew he would find the deer soon.

"We will meet again tomorrow," he told himself.

Walking between the huge trees, Waawaashkeshi felt unsettled. Was it the pull of his instincts? Was he was being followed? Or perhaps the spirits were trying to speak to him. Though their voice was distant, he felt they wanted to show him something—to teach him something. So he followed their voice.

"Can you feel the ancestors here?" Waawaashkeshi asked the flea.

"Aanikoobijiganag drifting among the trees," the flea bit softly. "I feel them, and the spirit of old trees that also drifts on the wind. Even the spirit of trees that already lived and died in this forest. They are all here. I feel them." The flea crawled across Waawaashkeshi's hip.

Waawaashkeshi wanted to gnaw at the flea, but he resisted.

Waawaashkeshi passed a tree skeleton lying on the forest floor. Not the whole tree—only the top half. The main trunk still stood close by. Sometimes a spinning wind would single out a tree like this, twisting it off above the ground. Waawaashkeshi thought of it as pruning the forest. How the wind selected the tree it wanted was a mystery to Waawaashkeshi. Size did not matter. This was one of the trees so large that three humans linking arms could not reach around it. A spinning wind had raced above the forest one year ago and reached down to take only this tree. Now, though its needles hung brown and drooping, they still clung to its fallen branches. The trunk looked solid from the ground up. It would take many years for this one to return to the soil.

"There are many ways for a tree to die," Waawaashkeshi told the flea.

"I know. I know," the flea bit back impatiently. "What's the big deal?"

"Pay attention, flea. There is plenty you don't know. Plenty to learn in the forest."

Bite. Bite.

Rarely did the wind rush down to pluck a single tree from the forest. Most often, the trees worked together, resisting the wind's great force as one. When the strongest gusts roared through the forest, one tree could catch its neighbor at the canopy, and together they could withstand the wind. They worked together above the ground just as they did below it, where they sent signals to each other through their root networks about dangerous diseases and predator insects.

Communicating below the ground was something forest fungus taught the trees to do, helped them to do. Below-ground fungus attached to each hair of a tree's root and assisted in connecting pathways from the roots of one tree to the roots of another, pathways through which one tree could also send nutrients to another tree close by.

Just a few days ago, a spinning wind crashed through the forest, accompanied by pounding thunder and flashes of lightning. It toppled one of Waawaashkeshi's favorite old trees, a mighty giant that had bifurcated when it was 200 years old, growing upward as twin stems from its midpoint to the canopy. First, the wind split off one of the twin trunks, toppling it to the ground. On its way down, the limb tore through the canopy branches from the tree next to it and the tree beyond that. Then the wind uprooted the whole tree, leaning it against a line of trees that kept it from falling clean to the ground.

This tree knew its fate. It could not survive. It would continue to perform photosynthesis for a decade or so—perhaps longer—but it had already begun its soft descent. Even when its spirit finally left the shell to blend in with the voices of the ancestors, the tree's nearby cousins would continue to support the shell lovingly in their arms. They would hold it off the ground for as long as they could.

"I feel good knowing that both twins came down in the same storm," Waawaashkeshi told the flea. "It's comforting. Now they can continue their journey of decay together."

"You've got a sentimental side, Waawaashkeshi," the flea responded with a taunting bite. "Where did that come from? What happened to the stoic old Waawaashkeshi?"

Waawaashkeshi grunted. "I'd almost forgotten why I didn't want you around."

It would not be long before forest animals found this tree and made new homes in its cavities. Both trunks would soon be on the forest floor together. Soon, that is, in the lifetime of a tree.

CHAPTER 4
DANGER ALL AROUND

AD 1409

Waawaashkeshi now sensed that he was being followed. It made him uneasy—tentative. Nothing around him justified his concern. He simply knew. His acute perception told him, just as surely as it warned him of rain before storm clouds gathered. Life in the natural world had honed such instincts. Waawaashkeshi did not like the feeling of being trailed.

The voices of the spirits pulled him east through the dark forest for three days. Only his instincts provided the direction.

Nearing a small stream, Waawaashkeshi looked at a tree's trunk and asked the flea, "Do you see the deep claw marks where a tall bear reached up and scraped bark from the trunk? Do you think this is another way that a tree can die?"

His nose warned him that the bear was still nearby. But to Waawaashkeshi, a bear, preferring berries for food, saw him as just another animal inhabiting the forest and posed no more danger than a squirrel.

"What is the bear doing out here where there are no berries to eat?" Waawaashkeshi wondered.

The flea bit hard. "Maybe it's just trying to get away from fleas. Or it could be following its instinctive pull."

Waawaashkeshi winced as he studied the stream. At first, he wondered how this stream had escaped the work of the beavers. The water flowed clear, pooling along the far bank. He dipped his nose into the stream. The water was fresh, fed by a continuous flow. He lapped up a bit. Cool. Thirst-quenching. Eventually, the thought occurred to him that there were no small trees or grass in the darkness of the forest that beavers could use to build a dam. The stream moved freely here, carving out a deep ravine that meandered through the heart of the forest.

As he crossed the stream, Waawaashkeshi thought of the river it flowed into, and then the larger one beyond that, each gathering water from the one before. All of them were far from the tag alder swamp, where a single raindrop, once fallen, became part of a small, muck-bottom pool—a collective of raindrops. If enough raindrops accumulated, they would trickle from pool to pool, then spill over the beaver rise, joining other swamp-borne drops to form a thin creek. That creek meandered to the small river where the Ojibwe built their village. The *Kayeskikan-ziibi*— Shell River. (Centuries later Waawaashkeshi heard European settlers call this the Clam River.) His raindrops would gather from farther away and merge with raindrops from other tributaries, all swimming as a group to the Muskegon, a much bigger river that collected water from other creeks and rivers as it flowed south and west across the land known to the Ojibwe as *Mishigamme*— what would one day be called "Michigan."

It took his swamp raindrop fifteen days to finally reach the huge gathering, Lake Michigan, where trillions of raindrops dissolved into one congregation, including raindrops that traveled down other great rivers: the Kalamazoo, the Grand, and the Manistee.

To Waawaashkeshi, the spirits of the trees and of the ancestors and of all natural things were each like drops of rain that became part of a river. Its current flowed through his own veins.

"Interesting," Mukwoh noted, pausing at a tree scarred by a bear's claws near a forest creek.

He needed to be cautious now. This area was unfamiliar, and he couldn't be sure what animals might be lurking nearby. Bears weren't the only dangerous creatures in a forest like this.

Not far back he had lost Waawaashkeshi's trail briefly, but after considerable searching, he picked it up again near the marked tree.

"So, you saw it too, my friend. We will meet soon."

Waawaashkeshi was hungry. Nearly four days had passed since he'd last eaten when he finally saw a heavily traveled deer trail cutting through the trees. He could tell the tracks were recent even before he saw the steaming pellets of fresh deer dung. His nose picked up the scent of several deer traveling together. Two sets of tracks were large, though still only half the size of his own. These were not the tracks that worried him; it was the large paw marks of a cougar that caught his attention. He detected the scent of dried blood. Cougars often carried that smell on their pelts after a meal. Was the large cat waiting for him?

Waawaashkeshi knew the heavy deer trail meant that grass and other food was close by, but he worried about the predator in the area. He looked up toward the canopy. No branches were low enough for the cougar to lie in wait.

The canopy hid a sizable nest made of branches the same diameter as Waawaashkeshi's ankle. A large bird watched him from high above—Waawaashkeshi recognized it as the eagle from before. With its huge white head and shiny white tail, the bald eagle swooped down between the trees as if to warn Waawaashkeshi. From its new perch, the eagle observed all the animals in this part of the forest, watching as they each planned their next moves.

On the third day of his chase, Mukwoh paused to rest on a flat rock. Removing the bag of food and supplies slung across his shoulder, he peered inside. It was nearly empty. He approached the point of no return. Even if the hunt was successful, it was unlikely he could carry both the meat and the hide all the way back to the village.

What is the point of this hunt if I cannot bring you home? Mukwoh wondered, beginning to reconsider the wisdom of this journey.

What if he made a wrong turn and lost his way back? Mukwoh did not worry about being truly lost—only delayed. He could always find the big river and follow it to where the waters of his village's smaller river converged with it. But that would make for a much longer and more difficult return trip.

Mukwoh was young, and though he was beginning to hear the spirits of the natural world, he did not always listen. Were the spirits now urging him to return? Perhaps he should consider it. But his desire to see what lay beyond the shadow of the next tree, to glimpse the great antlered deer again, to smell the pine forest, urged him forward. He began a slow afternoon trot following the now-fresh trail.

Waawaashkeshi proceeded cautiously, alert for the cougar.

He felt the flea bite. Waawaashkeshi quickly slapped his tail to one side.

"Stop that," Waawaashkeshi silently scolded the flea. "This is no time for your antics. If you can't behave, get off me."

Waawaashkeshi felt the flea move on his hip, then stop, as if it intended to heed the instruction.

Waawaashkeshi paused after each step, scanning for the animal he knew was nearby. Several times, he used a familiar trick to draw out his adversary: he stomped his front foot and waited, then stomped again. When he felt certain that he had waited long enough, Waawaashkeshi stepped onto the trail and followed it to the edge of a large, shallow pond that filled a depression in the forest floor. The pond looked newly formed. It was still in the shadow of the forest canopy and flooded the bases of nearly fifty mature pines. No thicket or grass grew at the water's edge. Waawaashkeshi spotted a recently constructed beaver dam at the low end of the pond. Perched on the dam was the cougar, crouched over a small, lifeless deer, one deer leg in the water and the rest of the body draped down the dam's slope. The cougar tore into the deer's belly, eager to consume its heart, liver, and lungs first.

Waawaashkeshi froze in place watching the cougar tear apart the young deer. He felt a kinship with all deer and wondered about the loss the deer's mother might be feeling. But all deer knew how the food chain worked. Waawaashkeshi knew the doe would understand her loss and stoically accept it. Waawaashkeshi wondered if the young deer had been old enough to understand what role it played in the natural system.

Waawaashkeshi knew he, too, was in danger and had no time to dwell on the young deer. Dwelling on it distracted his instinct for self-preservation.

From the tree branches, the eagle watched everything that was happening: Waawaashkeshi waiting cautiously, eyes fixed on the cougar. The cougar, complacent, gorging on the small deer and paying no mind to Waawaashkeshi. And the Ojibwe, slipping from tree to tree, drawing ever closer to Waawaashkeshi.

Mukwoh watched a large shadow pass between two trees not far in the distance, certain it was Waawaashkeshi. He slowed from the steady trot he had maintained for some time and shifted into a silent, deliberate walk.

"Be patient," Mukwoh told himself.

The shadow moved again. This time closer. The large deer stood on a heavily trodden deer trail, sensing impending danger. Waawaashkeshi seemed alert.

How does this deer know I am here? Mukwoh frowned, puzzled by the thought.

Knowing Waawaashkeshi had highly developed senses, Mukwoh moved carefully as he slipped through the trees. Mukwoh considered himself a stalking expert, more skilled than the older hunters in his band. That he, with his finely tuned stalking skills, had triggered Waawaashkeshi's alarm astonished him. Mukwoh knew Waawaashkeshi was on guard. But he misjudged the reason.

Waawaashkeshi stood perfectly still. The cougar was not particularly close, but with no cover between the tall pines, Waawaashkeshi felt exposed. Surely the cougar must have detected his scent by now. But as he watched and waited, it remained fixed on devouring its meal.

Occasionally, its eyes flicked sideways, avoiding direct contact with Waawaashkeshi. It let out a low, menacing growl.

Perhaps the cougar already had enough to eat with the small deer. Most forest creatures were like that. They took only what they needed when they needed it. But you could never be sure about a cougar.

Perched high on a branch in the pines, the eagle watched the scene unfold with sharp eyes.

Mukwoh quietly slipped from tree to tree, bow in one hand, arrows in the other. He stepped across the well-used game trail that skirted the beaver pond. His moccasins padded silently over the soft ground. Stopping behind a large tree, Mukwoh saw Waawaashkeshi's dark form standing broadside. The deer was motionless, his attention focused on something in front. Waiting.

Mukwoh took one step. He slowly set down all but a single, well-crafted arrow and lifted his bow. One more step. The deer remained still as a statue. What was his attention focused on? Mukwoh stepped closer. Nearing the edge of the pond, he was finally able to follow Waawaashkeshi's stare. His breath caught in his chest. He saw a large cougar baring its teeth. Gnawing its prey.

Mukwoh considered this for a moment. The deer might be an easy target because of its focus on the cougar. But taking the deer while the cougar was so close could be a problem. He began to question the wisdom of this venture. He was far from the village. Would he be the cougar's next meal?

The eagle glided to a new perch between the cougar and Waawaashkeshi.

It knew Waawaashkeshi was waiting for the right moment to bolt past the predator. Turning, its keen avian eyes watched Mukwoh nock an arrow, draw back on his bow string, and wait.

Waawaashkeshi stood with the leg that faced Mukwoh—his front leg—in its backstep, protecting his vitals from a clean arrow shot.

Mukwoh knew Waawaashkeshi must eventually step forward. That would be the moment he would let the arrow fly, slipping it just behind the leg and into Waawaashkeshi's lung and heart.

Waawaashkeshi watched the cougar, waiting for a chance to make his escape.

Mukwoh could not hold the bowstring back for much longer. "Just one step," Mukwoh whispered to himself.

Suddenly, the eagle let out its chilling screech.

The cougar stopped, glancing up at the eagle.

In a flash, Waawaashkeshi's neck tightened, his body crouched, and in a powerful leap, he dashed down the trail past the predator, ready to race to safety.

Mistaking the movement for the forward step he expected, Mukwoh instinctively let his arrow fly. Waawaashkeshi's crouch saved his life. The arrow skidded across his back, taking a crease of deer hair with it.

The cougar simply lifted its head, bared its teeth, and snarled in annoyance.

Mukwoh's eyes darted to the cougar as Waawaashkeshi's white tail raced away. Now Mukwoh had a problem. Everything had gone wrong—an unsatisfactory end to a long hunt. The thought crossed his mind that Waawaashkeshi truly was immortal. Before leaving, he felt compelled to find his arrow to discover what happened to the deer. He needed to be sure that there was not blood on the arrow. That it was a clean miss. But he first must wait for the cougar to leave before looking for the arrow. Only then would he return to the village.

Why did I take the shot? Mukwoh asked himself. He should have known better—he did know better. If he ever met Waawaashkeshi again, he would let him pass. The deer seemed to live under some kind of natural protection, and it was wiser to cooperate with that force than to fight it. Mukwoh thought about what happened. He closed his eyes and halfheartedly bowed to the cougar. Then, out of respect, he looked up and bowed to the eagle. Finally, he looked toward the trail where Waawaashkeshi disappeared, took a deep breath, and he bowed deeply.

"Go well, my friend," Mukwoh whispered.

CHAPTER 5
THE SACRED CIRCLE

AD 1409

Waawaashkeshi plunged down the trail. He knew food could not be far. An opening in the canopy letting in enough light for grass to grow must be close by. How else could beavers here find the branches and grass to construct that dam? Waawaashkeshi wanted the grass.

"We were lucky," the flea bit hard.

Waawaashkeshi stopped briefly to scratch at the flea on his hip.

"I should have left you with the cougar," Waawaashkeshi mused. "He would make a better partner for your bloodthirsty ways."

Following the trail, Waawaashkeshi soon stood shoulder-deep in giant ferns lining a muddy flat along the edge of a large river: the Muskegon. A narrow island broke the water a short distance from shore, tall grass covering its downstream half. Waawaashkeshi bent his head to lap up the sweet, refreshing water from the river's edge. Dipping his snout deeper into the liquid, he washed the sweat from his face. Rejuvenated, Waawaashkeshi placed one foot into the cool, swift current. The distance to the island's shore was not far, but the water was deep. With one leap,

Waawaashkeshi was in the water swimming, and then walking ashore in deep grass.

After four days of traveling in the forest and foraging for small bits of this and that, Waawaashkeshi was delighted to find a thick patch of island grass—something substantial to fill his stomach and quell his hunger.

The eagle, continuing to circle overhead, acknowledged its approval.

Waawaashkeshi spent three days bedded down on the island, basking in the sun's warm rays. He studied the poplar, birch, cedar, willow, and maple trees that lined both banks of the river. These trees were the source of the beavers' sticks. He noticed a nearby birch still standing despite the large cavity gnawed from its side. Waawaashkeshi lay curled in the grass. When he lifted his head, his antlers looked like the willows growing on the upstream half of the island. The willow thicket was just dense enough to hide three or four deer.

While resting on the island, each evening after sunset, Waawaashkeshi stood and stretched his body—first his neck and rear legs, then his front legs and back. He often wrapped his neck around to chew at the flea under his fur.

"This island is a good place for you, you annoying pest. Maybe you can latch onto a half-drowned mouse, or some other creature more your size."

The flea bit again. Hard.

Waawaashkeshi spent a few hours eating buds from the ends of tall grass stalks and later eating the blades of grass, growing green and tall. He ate continuously. It relaxed him. He stopped only briefly from time to time to let the food settle. Before sunrise each night, he ate until he was satisfied and then curled up in a hidden spot to sleep until daylight. Though he felt restless, Waawaashkeshi was in no hurry, and he knew he was not likely to eat well again until he reached his destination: the ancient circle deep in the forest. Though he rarely visited the circle, he held it firmly in his memory. Waawaashkeshi felt closer to the natural spirits at the circle than at any other place. The natural spirits always found their own way to speak with him there, and Waawaashkeshi would listen. He knew he could ask the spirits for guidance at the sacred circle. He always left the sacred circle having learned something important.

Several hours before daybreak on the fourth day, with a large moon still hanging high in the sky, Waawaashkeshi stood nibbling on the grass, watching the moon shift toward the western horizon. The force pulling him toward the circle tugged at him from inside, hard at his gut.

"Okay, flea, this is where you get off." Waawaashkeshi shifted his hips. "I'm serious. I've got to swim across this river, and you're likely to drown. Get off now. I'm not kidding."

The flea latched on even more tightly.

Waawaashkeshi felt the flea's grip. He knew the flea was taking his blood.

"Your choice, my friend. The island or the river. I can't wait any longer for you to decide. I hope you enjoy the river ride. It is an end you really deserve."

Waawaashkeshi took two steps onto a sandbar that stretched out like a long tongue below the water's surface at the downstream tip of the island. Moonlight glinted off the deep pool where the sand ended, a place where the strong current had deposited a thick layer of sand as the river curled around the island and rejoined the water that raced around the opposite side. One more step toward the river's center and he would be up to his belly in cold water.

Waawaashkeshi, with an almost imperceptible crouch, leaped across the pool and landed knee-deep in the river where a gravel bottom was irregular but firm. A swift, cool current wrapped around his legs, beckoning him further downstream. Each step brought him into deeper water. He aimed for the bank but there was no easy place to climb out. Where the river made its natural bend, the current undercut the bank, leaving only a tangle of cedar roots hiding a cave in the rich, dark soil.

Waawaashkeshi felt water coming up to his hip where the flea gripped his flesh. He needed to walk farther downstream to find a way up the bank. One more step.

The river bottom suddenly slid from under Waawaashkeshi's hoof. He instantly thrust two hooves downward, trying to step back toward the gravel bottom near the river's center. He spun, reaching for higher ground with his front hooves, but the current caught him and swept him downstream.

Waawaashkeshi had crossed rivers many times—he knew what to do. Still, it was not ideal for a deer. Not like the beaver, with its paddle-like tail and webbed toes, or the otter, who slipped beneath the surface on one side of the river and emerged upstream minutes later on the other side. Waawaashkeshi's hooves had no webbing. They churned the water clumsily, offering little to propel him forward. He knew to keep his nose above water, and now, it was only his head and massive antlers that moved along the surface.

Waawaashkeshi knew he was in trouble. He breathed in rapid gasps as his heart rate accelerated. Sweat forming on his neck disappeared into the swift current. The current pulled him much too close to a large, uprooted cedar that lay in the river. The cedar's tip bounced on the surface as current rushed around the tree. It was not just one tree, though. Branches and limbs of other trees piled up in the cedar's branches as they drifted downstream, creating a messy logjam. Waawaashkeshi needed to get around this obstruction. His legs paddled and his head bobbed as he felt the current relentlessly pull him downstream. He did what he could to turn so his left shoulder would hit first. Perhaps he would simply bounce off.

His massive antler's fourth tine slipped into the crotch of two large limbs, jerking his neck. His lungs bellowed an unexpected exhale, and a wrenching pain shot from beneath his jaw to his shoulders as the current twisted his body beneath the log. Waawaashkeshi thrashed, but the cedar held firm, flexing only slightly. His feet kicked in desperation. Droplets flew through the air and dissolved into the current as Waawaashkeshi struggled to escape.

As his neck stretched, pulled, and contorted, his legs bucked frantically below the surface, hoping to find something solid. Waawaashkeshi flopped over, the current pulling hard. He rolled from one side to the other, twisting again and again, calling on his powerful neck muscles. Now he was on his back, with his neck nearing the breaking point, straining to its limit and twisting unnaturally while his legs splashed water into the air. The piercing pain that spasmed through his body became meaningless, replaced by a singular drive for survival. Waawaashkeshi wanted only to live.

He reached deep into his soul to find a final trace of energy, a flicker of strength. His rear hoof suddenly landed against the cedar's main trunk. He pulled his other leg close to the first and placed them firmly together. He crouched. With all his remaining strength, Waawaashkeshi made one desperate push, a powerful leaping movement, pushing his massive, sweating body horizontally against the current across the water's surface. Waawaashkeshi felt his antler's tine snap. And then, miraculously, he drifted free, the current carrying him along with a nest of river debris.

On the downstream side of the logjam, behind the cedar, the river current lay calm and simple. Waawaashkeshi panted heavily as he paddled toward shore. He swam to the ramp of dirt that led up the bank behind the uprooted clump of the cedar's roots. His front hoof finally found solid ground. It took all of his remaining strength to drag himself onto the riverbank and into the tall pines on the east side of the river.

Waawaashkeshi tried to catch his breath. He had not expected this. He hadn't planned to exert so much energy just to cross the river. Waawaashkeshi had broken his antler tines many times before. He remembered his first season as a young buck, when he'd sprouted two simple antlers, a small fork forming at the end of each. He'd broken one of those antlers clean off while locking horns with another young buck in the group. It had mattered little—by late February each year, the base of each antler weakened on its own, and the antlers fell to the forest floor to decay. A porcupine in the area might even find the antler and gnaw on it all summer. When the February antlers fell off, a new rack immediately began to grow—most years a bit larger, heavier, and perhaps with more tines than the previous year.

Waawaashkeshi shook the water from his fur and stood for a moment, reflecting on the situation. Then he felt a hint of movement on his hip—a weak bite.

"No!" Waawaashkeshi could not believe what he was feeling. "You miserable creature. How am I not rid of you?"

"It takes more than you nearly drowning to get rid of me." Waawaashkeshi felt a stronger bite. "If I knew you couldn't swim, I might have left you at the island. You should have spent more time with your mother. You're lucky I was along to get you out of that mess, and that I am here now to take care of you."

"What! You have never helped anything in your miserable life! Me—not able to swim!" Waawaashkeshi could not believe the little pest would say such a thing. "You arrogant little monster! I'm going to rub you against a tree until you're squashed flat and shredded to pieces!"

"Try it!" Waawaashkeshi felt a strong bite. "You know that won't work."

Bite. Bite. Bite.

"Waawaashkeshi … you're not nearly as handsome with that missing tine."

Waawaashkeshi exhaled in exasperation. What would he do with this flea?

As his heartbeat slowed and the adrenaline subsided, he thought again of the river. How had he ended up in such a situation? He was only following the spirit's pull. Waawaashkeshi knew the spirits always had a purpose behind the obstacles they placed in his path. But sometimes, it was difficult for Waawaashkeshi to figure out what lesson they were trying to teach. Perhaps this time the spirits were simply testing him. Trying to determine if he was worthy for what he would learn at the sacred circle. Not all learning is easy.

For two days, Waawaashkeshi trekked deep into the white pine forest. The canopy blocked the rising sun, leaving only a shadowed hint of daylight.

"This is exciting," he told the flea. "We are getting close." As they neared the journey's end, his nervous excitement turned to a quiet reverence.

The flea tapped his flesh in response.

Waawaashkeshi expected to communicate with the spirit pool at the sacred circle. There were things he wanted to ask. Things he wanted to understand.

Late in the afternoon on the second day, Waawaashkeshi came upon a place where a strikingly different forest grew—the sacred circle.

The flea bit, as if to say, "Listen to that chatter."

He heard a forest symphony. Squirrels chattering and squeaking. Songbirds—chickadees, juncos, goldfinches, cardinals. The beating wings of a hummingbird. Birds that did not play much in the deep pine forest.

Unusual contours on the forest floor certainly set this sacred spot apart, but the trees were a more important difference. The sacred circle's cluster of leafed trees attracted many creatures, for they provided nourishing food that pine trees could not. Oak, maple, hickory, cherry, beech—mighty trees with grand trunks, and as tall as the white pines. All towered over the forest floor, filling a circle a bit wider than the trees were tall.

"I remember my first trip to this place," Waawaashkeshi mused to the flea. "It was in a different age. I took my first trip through the river crossing time portal to visit this place. The spirit pool wanted me to meet the people who cut pine trees from this circle and worked up the earth at its perimeter."

The flea moved on Waawaashkeshi's hip, listening.

"They scraped soil in a deep circular trench from the forest floor and piled it in a mounded ring inside the trench. It was a lot of work. The dirt they removed made a moat and the dirt piled up made a wall about as high as my back. A lot like the beaver dam. But the deep trench exaggerated the height of the circular rise from the outside, and made crossing to the inside more difficult. Do you see the spot where they left an opening in the wall to make it easier to walk in?"

"I see it," the flea bit gently.

Waawaashkeshi remembered that when the aanikoobijiganag cut the trees, the circle became a sunny clearing. Eventually, birds and other animals carried in seeds from outside the pine forest. That happened hundreds of years ago. Now, those trees were part of the mature forest. Waawaashkeshi bent his head to eat several acorns from the forest floor. He loved them—they were his favorite food. Each time he ate them, he felt his strength return. The acorns alone were worth the journey.

Waawaashkeshi stretched his stiff neck again. It still hurt.

"This may take some time to heal," he said to himself, as much as to the flea.

Perhaps the diverse foods in this circle could help. The twigs of the sassafras tree, for instance, should reduce his pain and help restore his strained muscles. Waawaashkeshi could eat many things at this circle that would bring back his strength. Small fruits. Nuts. Leaves.

Waawaashkeshi wondered when, or if, leaves that fell from these trees became part of the spirit pool. They fell to the ground like raindrops into puddles at the tag alder swamp. The trees were still going strong. Healthy. But the leaves they shed were returning to the soil. What about the antlers that fell from his head every spring? Were the fallen antlers already part of the spirit pool, too, even though he was still going strong? Were his antlers like a fallen leaf? Like drops of rain?

"Where does life really begin and end?"

The flea was not listening. Perhaps it was sleeping.

"There is more to this soil than meets the eye." Waawaashkeshi scraped his hoof through to the dark earth.

He saw many small things. Larger than grains of sand but smaller than insects, they had the scent of life.

"This is where you should stay," he said, not really expecting the flea to hear. "At least you would be where there are things smaller than you."

Bite. Bite. "Really. Why would I want that? I want *YOU*. Come on, Waawaashkeshi. Don't you see I am your friend?"

"What is friendship?" Waawaashkeshi sighed.

Waawaashkeshi remained still and unblinking as he had when staring at the cougar. He smelled life in the soil, but he could not see it. He watched the soil he scraped. At first it seemed still. Was the soil waiting, as the Ojibwe had waited, to see who would move first? He needed to be patient. It took a long time. Finally, he saw a tiny, white, hair-like spore shift, ever so slightly. A microscopic blink. Had it moved from one spot to another, or had it simply grown? Waawaashkeshi could not tell. But he decided that it was alive, and that soil must also contribute to the spirit pool.

Where did life really begin and end?

Waawaashkeshi thought about how one kind of living thing was so different from another. A tree. A cougar. An eagle. A flea. Now the soil. But they all became drops of rain in the end. He thought back to his own mother and remembered that she did not live for many winters after he was born. She only gave birth once more, to twins, who quickly became part of the food chain. But they, too, became drops of rain in the spirit pool.

Waawaashkeshi never knew for sure which buck was really his father. They all treated each other the same—the deer were a community. But Waawaashkeshi knew he was different. For some reason, he had been selected by the natural spirits for a special education. He could hear their voices more clearly than the other creatures of the forest, and he was grateful for their guidance.

And here, within the ancient circle, the barrier between the physical world and the spirit pool was thin. He could hear them now, whispering to each other in the wind.

Waawaashkeshi breathed deeply, looked up into the tree foliage, and asked the spirits the question that was weighing on him.

"Was that really necessary? The hungry cougar? The human stalking me? This flea? The problem at the river? I nearly broke my neck. It is still sore."

Waawaashkeshi stretched his neck upward and to the side in a circular motion, lifting his chin. He was speaking to himself. Listening for an answer that would come from within.

"Am I not a chosen deer? Why do you not protect me from such things?"

The spirit's answer seemed to whisper through his mind like wind through the leaves.

"Waawaashkeshi, you know that physically, you are an ordinary deer. You learn from experience as any other living thing learns from experience. You are as big and strong as your kind can be. Your chances of survival are better than other deer because of your strength and the wisdom you've gained from your experiences. Your adversaries are mighty, which will only make you stronger ... if you survive. Your judgment grows, like a river fed by many streams. You would never be able to understand what you must learn if you were not an ordinary deer who faces real suffering. You are not protected from the natural trials of life because trials are a part of life. Do you think you could understand the strength of the river without such a crossing? Do you think you would have found out about the living soil if you had not

crossed the river? Knowing such things is important. Your experiences will guide you in the future. They will help you understand the natural world, the forest, and its inhabitants. They will help you survive. These are your lessons."

The spirit pool did not judge, but it demonstrated judgment based on the sum of its experience. The combination of all its raindrops. The spirit pool helped to remove Waawaashkeshi's opinions. Waawaashkeshi could always see logic in the guidance it provided. By paying attention, Waawaashkeshi honed his ability to listen patiently to the world that the spirit pool placed in his path—to observe, and then to understand. A little more each time. The spirit pool offered wisdom of things that went on in the natural world. Waawaashkeshi was a receptive student. What he received from the spirit pool left him with a stoic feeling of understanding and a curiosity about his purpose. He drew another deep breath and felt a quiet sense of well-being.

Waawaashkeshi wondered when he would know everything he needed to know. When he would know enough. The spirit pool saw everything that had ever happened. It understood everything that it had seen. And it accepted all things for what they were. Understanding in its purest sense. The spirit pool offered a kind of neutral awareness. Wisdom with unconditional acceptance. It often posed deep questions in Waawaashkeshi's mind without providing exact answers.

When Waawaashkeshi had eaten all the acorns and beechnuts that he could manage, he stood for a long minute to breathe the oxygen the sacred circle trees produced. It was pure—cool. It felt restorative. Waawaashkeshi loved the purity of the forest air at this sacred circle. By breathing it he felt he was communicating with the spirit pool.

"Can you feel it?" Waawaashkeshi asked the flea. "The spirit of the trees. The spirit of the soil. The spirit of the ancestors."

He breathed slowly and felt his own spirit drift into the pool. It gave him strength and balance. It made him feel calm. Satisfied. Deep in his soul Waawaashkeshi felt the warmth of fulfillment. He breathed deeply and exhaled slowly. He felt the sacred peace of this place.

"I can," nibbled the flea.

Waawaashkeshi wanted to do one more thing he had not done before; he dropped to his front elbows and touched his nose to the ground. He closed his eyes as the Ojibwe did when surrendering the hunt, and he nodded his broken rack of antlers forward until the tips touched the ground. Respect and gratitude. He suddenly did not want to leave without expressing those things. It was as if he had uncovered a yearning in his heart that, until then, he hadn't known was there. His gratitude added one more measure of wholeness that he did not know he could achieve.

Waawaashkeshi stood and began his walk back toward the river. He felt thankful for the lesson he learned about the soil. Not all deer knew about life in the soil. He felt thankful for worthy adversaries. Waawaashkeshi now knew for sure that despite his special mission, he, like any deer, was destined for a life of danger. How could he possibly survive? The odds were not in his favor. Eventually, something would end his life. And in a remote way that he did not fully understand, he was thankful for his friend—as odd as this flea friend was.

CHAPTER 6
THE RIVER CROSSING PORTAL

AD 1409

It was another week before Waawaashkeshi finally neared the tag alder swamp.

"Can you smell something different in the air?" Waawaashkeshi asked the flea.

"I noticed it yesterday," the flea seemed to bite back. "Maybe it is something from the storm two days ago."

A ferocious storm had whipped through the forest from the east. Spinning winds, crashing thunder, and lightning bolts striking the ground. It caused Waawaashkeshi to take cover under the trunk of a newly fallen tree. The wind continued to drive aggressively from the east, and that often meant trouble. But this seemed worse than normal trouble.

"It smells something like the Ojibwe village, but the village is still further west," Waawaashkeshi breathed deeply again. The air contained a bit more than the clean oxygen he expected.

"It's smoke," the flea bit hard. "Like the village."

As the day went on, Waawaashkeshi gradually felt something inside pulling him. It tugged at him urgently, a tug almost as strong as the river that pulled him toward the fallen cedar. Was it the natural spirits, or was it instinct? For Waawaashkeshi, the two were intertwined.

"We're going to change course a bit," Waawaashkeshi muttered in a deer sort of way. "We've got to move fast. I can feel it. The spirit pull."

Waawaashkeshi knew it was time to run for the *river crossing*—the time portal. The place on the small river near the Ojibwe village.

"Smoke!" The flea bit frantically. "I don't know where you're going, but you better go fast!"

This time the lightning storm must have started something. The fire advanced through the canopy faster than Waawaashkeshi could run. A powerful wind blew flames toward him. Fire leapt from needle to needle in the canopy, a crackling frenzy of igniting sap, consuming the living wood—each twig, each limb, and even the towering, column-like tree trunks. If the wind continued to blow from the east, the fire would move across the land until it ran out of trees, burning most of the white pines. A few lucky ones might survive, but the fire would leave them charred and without needles. In the end they would carry the scar to their graves. Would they live long enough to see offspring rise from the ash-covered forest floor?

Waawaashkeshi ran for his life. And he was not the only creature in a mad dash for safety. He saw the cougar run with long, powerful strides. Not in pursuit of prey. Running to escape. Panic was so thick in the air that Waawaashkeshi could smell it. It mixed with the smell of the smoke racing by.

The trees seemed to scream, **"Run for your life! Save yourself!"**

Forest animals scattered. Inhabitants of the Ojibwe village ran, too, helping each other. They left behind their bark-covered shelters, the ring of rocks where they built their campfires, their stone tools, and a few stray flint arrow tips. As Waawaashkeshi ran for the river, he saw Mikinaak the snapping turtle plunge into the pool where water flowed over the beaver dam. He wondered about the doe and twins he left in the tag alder swamp. They would run. He knew they would run.

As Waawaashkeshi raced toward the river crossing, fire pressed from behind while the spirits pulled from inside. He lunged down the trail as flames jumped from treetop to treetop. Animals of every type scattered. With little thought and a mighty leap, he jumped through a wall of fire on the forest floor. An ancient snag towering in its decay lit up in flames like a giant torch. It spewed sparks high into the sky and exploded. It spread fire in every direction. Waawaashkeshi felt embers bounce off his back.

There are many ways for a deer to die.

Smoke poured into the sky, filling his lungs. Waawaashkeshi could barely breathe. Flames danced in front of him and behind him, threatening to trap him. The fire's heat intensified with each passing moment.

Something else was happening too. Besides the dark haze from the smoky air, daylight disappeared as a circular shadow seemed to take away the sun. On another day, Waawaashkeshi would have stopped for a few seconds to look through an opening in the canopy to watch the shadow move, but he did not have time.

He ran with all his heart until he suddenly drew up at the east bank of the small river—the crossing, the time portal.

The sky, already obscured by smoke, suddenly plunged into an eerie darkness. The eclipse had arrived. Waawaashkeshi stepped into the shallow water and walked quickly toward the opposite bank. As he reached the center of the stream, the sky began to lighten again, and the eclipse shadow passed. The sky was clear and blue with a strong, brisk wind blowing from the north. Waawaashkeshi caught his breath. Pure oxygen. He breathed deeply. Lifesaving cool air whipped across his back. He felt his own temperature descend, and the drum of his beating heart begin to quiet.

Waawaashkeshi walked up the rise where he expected the small river's bank to be. Now he found only a short step up from a shallow gravel trench. The tall, dark forest of white pines that he knew to cover the landscape was missing. There was no evidence anywhere of the raging fire he had escaped. No flames. No charred embers. No lingering smell of smoldering destruction. Behind him, where the river once flowed, there was only the small, clear, cold trickle of a fledgling creek coming off a massive glacier.

What was this place?

Waawaashkeshi looked upon the tundra in wonder.

CHAPTER 7
ARCTIC TUNDRA

8500 BCE

Waawaashkeshi knew at once that he did not belong here. He felt the weight of its vast emptiness. The land here was barren, with only a few lonely black spruce trees growing across the open landscape. He looked at the trickle of water running timidly where the Kayeskikan-ziibi would someday be. It did not flow from one of the glacier's ice fissures but from below the glacier. He could see the undercut ice at the glacier's edge, not unlike where river water of the Muskegon undercut its bank near the sacred circle in the forest.

No sign of life existed where the glacier reached down from the north. It seemed like an endless mountain of ice standing large against a cold, blue sky. Waawaashkeshi saw melted pockets on the glacier's surface, perhaps leading to a network of caves expanding in the ice below.

Cold beauty inhabited this frozen world.

"You still there?" Waawaashkeshi waited for the flea to do something.

A small movement, then a bite.

Waawaashkeshi buried his snout in his hip fur briefly, scratching the flea's spot with his teeth.

"What is this place?" Waawaashkeshi was now happy to have the flea's company.

He felt the power of the spirit pool as he breathed in the cool air, but these were not the same spirits he knew. Something was missing. The spirit pool was notably smaller and simpler, not containing enough raindrops to make it a Great Lake.

Though Waawaashkeshi did not think in these terms, what made the spirit pool incomplete was ten thousand years of missing history. History yet to come. Generations of trees, each moving from birth to death. Generations of human ancestors, plenty that predated the aanikoobijiganag. Generations of insects, birds, turtles, and fungi, all yet to drift with the spirit current. And the soil. How many times would the soil cycle through decay and renewal over the coming millennia, each time contributing to the spirit pool?

Where did life really begin and end?

A strong and steady wind raced down the glacier's slope where it intercepted an eastbound current across the open land. Waawaashkeshi felt sand in the wind. Some of the sand built into a large drift on the opposite side of the trench Waawaashkeshi had emerged from—like loose snow drifts in a winter blizzard.

Someday, this sand drift would form the high riverbank where the Ojibwe people built their village.

If the wind instead came up from the south where the world had already warmed for 4,000 years and where plants already lived and died and decayed, the wind might bring with it rich soil rather than sand. But the wind only occasionally blew from the south.

"This must be the beginning of the forest," Waawaashkeshi blurted out. "Its birthplace. This must be what the spirits want me to see, to understand."

The flea acknowledged him with a tickle. The little flea had been unusually quiet since they crossed the river. Was it awestruck? Scared?

This was Waawaashkeshi's first view of the world like this, back in time so far that even soil did not yet cover the ground. The barren landscape still required millennia to evolve into a real forest. Now, it was as different as an egg is from a flying bird. For a forest to begin, soil first needed to develop where plants could root. Soil could make its start here in a small way. Once something rooted—even something small—and lived its life, it eventually died and decomposed. What it left behind became more soil, deeper soil—better soil. A succession of plant life continued, one round after another, each a bit more robust, each leaving a bit more soil.

As one new kind of plant replaced another, migrating from warmer southern ecosystems, so would insects and animals who helped plants regenerate and survive. Plants helped insects and animals by providing food, surfaces for insects to deposit eggs on, and shelter for animals to raise their young. Animals and insects helped plants with seed placement and pollination. Humans followed other animals. Given time, eventually the forest Waawaashkeshi knew as home would emerge.

Waawaashkeshi took a few cautious steps and looked more

closely at the earthy landscape that began where the glacier left off.

"Actually," he whispered, "this place is not quite as barren as it looks."

Lichen splashed green-gray splotches on rocks that jutted above the earth. Small dwarf shrubs, born from seeds blown in on the wind or carried in the droppings of birds, grew out of the crevices and hollows in the uneven ground. They established themselves in spots where small amounts of windblown soil collected. Their roots could not reach deeper than the very shallow ground above permafrost level, and so only short plants with shallow root systems survived.

Wind also carried in fungi spores that helped plants to thrive and eventually generate rich soil on their own. Mycelium filaments of fungus surrounded roots and existed in a symbiotic relationship benefiting both the fungus and the root. The fungus helped roots to absorb sufficient volumes of nutrient-rich water from the soil, much more than was otherwise possible.

"If I don't find some food," Waawaashkeshi told the flea, "we will both die."

The flea bit once, as if to say, "Okay, let's get going."

Waawaashkeshi needed to eat leaves and twigs from this tundra brush to survive—perhaps even lichen, if he was desperate enough. He was not sure how long he would be in this new place, or whether he would live long enough to get back to his mature forest.

"Where are the other animals?" Perhaps animals could not

survive in this place. "There is not even enough food around to keep a bird alive."

Only the air had a voice here. The wind whistled long, low, strung-out tones in notes that blended up and down as it whipped across the empty land and brought a measure of life to the surrounding world. But the place was eerily devoid of bird songs and pine branches rustling together, sounds Waawaashkeshi remembered so dearly.

Besides the glacier, he saw three things that interested him: scattered lines of the stunted bushes; clumps of black spruce trees that were few and far between; and a low mossy area that seemed oversaturated with water. This place was both tundra and muskeg.

This must be the very beginning of a forest—the moment of its birth.

"We need to rest."

The flea was silent. Already fast asleep.

Waawaashkeshi was exhausted, weak from his race with the burning forest. After seeing this barren place for the first time, with its signs of simple first-growth, he sensed the fire they escaped was not the first time his forest perished. Perhaps this, too, was what the spirits were trying to show him: the forest burned to the ground or perished in other ways many times since its beginning. Each time the forest perished, the soil restored life, and a new version of the forest burst forth. Each time, the forest began anew with soil more fertile than before. And each time, the character of the forest changed.

As soil developed and the black spruce grew to maturity, something would take them out, perhaps a flash population of beetles eating their way through their entire food supply. The beetles would die with the spruce, leaving the landscape barren again. This suicidal behavior of an entire population did not make much sense to Waawaashkeshi. If only they could follow the all-knowing wisdom of the spirits—moderation. But when their eating frenzy finished everything there was to eat, they also would take a place within the spirit pool. They would carve their mark—their story—into the bark of history.

"Remember not to eat your way through your entire food supply," Waawaashkeshi advised, joking with the flea.

Waawaashkeshi felt a painful bite in return.

After the beetles came and went, and with a layer of soil from decomposed trees covering the ground and the glacier receding beyond view, a new type of seed would migrate in to slowly replace the black spruce. With a kind of ecological inertia, hardwood forest would follow the warming climates, filling in the spaces left by dead spruce.

Oak. Elm. Ash. The cell structure of these hardwoods could not tolerate extreme cold as the black spruce could, whose sap flowed in the tissue between its living cells and froze without killing them. Oak, elm, and ash retained sap within their living cells. When temperatures dropped to the coldest arctic extremes, the living cells died—and with them, the trees.

There are many ways for a tree to die.

Centuries later, when fires swept through and wiped out the hardwood forest, eastern white pine moved in, advancing westward a little each year from the eastern side of the Appalachian Mountains. White pines invaded space left open when hardwoods disappeared. At a minimum, they were in the right place at the right time. Their seeds found receptive soil in cool, dry areas opened to the sun. In phase with the trees, a new batch of migrating insects, birds, and mammals arrived.

"We're in the open," Waawaashkeshi commented. "We're exposed. No cover. No protection."

"What does it matter?" The flea bit back. "We're the only ones here."

"You won't live long thinking like that," Waawaashkeshi warned. "We can't just race across the tundra as if we have no enemies. As if we are not part of the food chain."

"And you're sure there is a food chain here?"

"Who knows, I may need to eat you." Waawaashkeshi exhaled with frustration.

"You aren't clever enough to catch me, my friend. But I can drain your blood any time."

Contours of topography provided their only cover. No thicket was there to hide them. Plants were too few and too small. Perhaps a group of black spruce would work, but Waawaashkeshi needed to cover a lot of open ground before reaching the closest group of spruce. Waawaashkeshi's instincts screamed that he was vulnerable.

So, using the contours of the land as his cover, Waawaashkeshi walked downstream, following the small ditch carved out of the earth's surface by water trickling from the glacier. He followed it for several hours, stopping to eat leaves and twigs from scrub bushes when he could reach them. If he found a spot with the ditch close enough to a group of black spruce, he intended to bolt from the ditch and take cover under the spruce.

The spruce were all stand-alone groups of three or four young trees. Young? What did that mean to a tree? Fifty years? These trees were fifty years old. Unlike the shady, mature forest where the sun only reached the canopy and branches with live needles were far beyond Waawaashkeshi's reach, the black spruce had branches with live needles from the ground up. Waawaashkeshi would enjoy munching on the branches he could reach. What a delicacy—the spicy taste of black spruce needles and the crunchy branches that went with them.

An hour later, he found the spot he wanted. He stood and stared at the clump of spruce.

"What do you think, flea. Should we try?"

Just as he was about to jump to the spruce clump, Waawaashkeshi noticed a small movement near the base of one tree.

"Did you see that?" He stood still, watching patiently.

It was the first sign of animal life in this frozen tundra. Another flash of movement. Waawaashkeshi saw the small pile of sand and soil built up in front of a narrow hole in the ground. He did not have to wait long before a chipmunk emerged and raced toward a cone from the spruce. Taking it in its small mouth, the chipmunk darted back down its tunnel.

"A chipmunk." Animal life existed. Waawaashkeshi found it a comforting thing to know.

"Why don't you stay with the chipmunk, flea? This may be your destiny."

But the existence of any animal always had two sides: if there was a chipmunk around, another animal might be close by to eat the chipmunk. Perhaps a fox or wolf. Waawaashkeshi lifted his nose to the air, trying to detect the scent of another creature.

"We need to be careful." He breathed in.

Could a predator here also be a danger to Waawaashkeshi? Waawaashkeshi waited longer, and when he was finally confident that nothing watched, he made two powerful leaps to the group of spruce. Waawaashkeshi's enormous antlers dipped naturally to get under the lowest spruce branches. Once inside, he curled up on a soft bed of needles and fell fast asleep.

Bite. Bite.

The flea woke Waawaashkeshi while darkness still engulfed the land. Cautiously, he stepped from the small spruce group to see a star-filled sky. He stood next to the tree, his dark body blending with the dark trees. A strong wind howled around him, and an eerie glow rose above the glacier. The glow danced in the sky like flames burning beyond the horizon.

"Another fire?" asked the flea. "I wanted to wake you."

Flames shot much higher than Waawaashkeshi remembered the forest fire flames had, even when the snag lit up like a torch and shot fire straight up into the sky. But something in Waawaashkeshi's instinct told him this was not another forest fire.

"I don't think so."

What could burn on the glacier? It was all ice. Thick ice. Flames danced in the atmosphere, lighting the sky to its peak. Perhaps the flames reflected wind or the spirit current. Waawaashkeshi decided it was so. Perhaps wind was also a living thing. Waawaashkeshi already knew the wind was alive with natural spirits.

Hidden in the darkness, Waawaashkeshi walked quietly back to the ditch and continued south, downstream. Now, he knew for sure that he did not belong in this frozen land. That *they* did not belong in this frozen land. Everything was different. The spirits here were different. When he listened to them speak, he heard what seemed like another language. It was difficult to listen to them over the unceasing howl of the wind. He saw only one chipmunk; there was no sign of other animals.

Daybreak arrived slowly. The whole world brightened gradually long before the sun peeked over the eastern horizon. When Waawaashkeshi lifted and turned his head, his eyes scanned east and west across the land, but it was a low view.

Finally, when he came to another group of spruce, Waawaashkeshi jumped out of the ditch and stood next to the trees so his silhouette would not be visible from across the tundra. The new position gave him a better look at the surrounding landscape. Waawaashkeshi could no longer see the edge of the glacier to the north, but he saw the tall icy mountain that was beyond the edge. Without trees to confine his view, the sky seemed impossibly vast—clear, deep, and blue. There was not a cloud to be seen. Scattered spruce groups dotted the landscape.

From his spot next to a spruce, Waawaashkeshi scanned the surrounding world. It seemed like a simple world, one without much variation. He stepped to the other side of the spruce clump to look in another direction.

"Look!" Waawaashkeshi twitched his hip muscle.

"I see it," the flea bit back. "Stay still!"

Waawaashkeshi watched a large, dark shadow emerge from just

beyond the next group of spruce. It was bigger than any animal he had ever encountered. Behind it, another large shadow appeared, and then a smaller version of the same creature. As the creatures stepped from behind the spruce, Waawaashkeshi saw how strange they were; a fifth leg extended between their eyes and mouth. Perhaps it was an arm. A large, straight stick protruded from each side of their mouths. These tusks might be antlers, like the ones growing on Waawaashkeshi's head. But they were much, much longer.

The first creature—the largest—extended its front arm to a spruce trunk. The arm curled around the tree, and with a mighty twist, broke the tree off at midpoint. Then, with an impressive backward jerk, the creature—the *mastodon*—pulled the top half of the tree from its base and turned the broken tree section to its mouth.

"I get it," the flea muttered with a bite. "There are many ways for a tree to die."

The large mastodon stepped aside as the child approached lower branches and tugged at them with its strange front arm. This was a curious sight for Waawaashkeshi. Almost entertaining.

The mid-size creature now caught his attention. It was held back in some way. Slowed down. Not as agile. Perhaps it was injured. When the group of three devoured much of the spruce clump and moved to the next group of trees, Waawaashkeshi saw the large rock moving along the ground, dragged a bit further by the mid-size creature each time its rear leg moved. Waawaashkeshi looked more closely to see a flexible cord wrapped around the mastodon's foot which connected somehow to the rock not far behind. This cord looked like so many things the Ojibwe made—an animal's hide cut into strips.

How had the cord become wrapped around the foot of such a large creature? Waawaashkeshi clearly saw the trail the mastodons followed. It led from one spruce group to the next. His eyes scanned the trail to the third group of trees. He noticed a small movement in these spruce trees. Waawaashkeshi froze.

"Do you see them? There. By the next group of trees. One. Two. Three ... six! I see six! Humans!"

There, hidden inside the third group of trees, Waawaashkeshi picked out the humans trying very hard to blend in with the trees. Waawaashkeshi felt his own heart beat more quickly.

The flea shuddered.

Waawaashkeshi was alert but curious. What was happening here? The humans were not well hidden; they waited. The mastodons moved on. Now, the mastodons ambled between the second and third group of trees. The mid-size creature trailed behind, obviously weary from the weight it dragged.

"What is wrong with these creatures? Don't they have a sense of self-preservation?"

Even Waawaashkeshi smelled the humans on the wind. He knew the leg-restraint must be of humans' doing. He wanted to blurt out his warning—*shhhh ... shhhh*—but he realized it would mean nothing to the mastodons.

"Don't do it," bit the worried flea. "We don't need the trouble."

The mastodons already knew the humans were around. Their keen sense of smell caught everything. One long inhale through nostrils at the end of their swinging arm tickled smelling sensors all the way to their mouth—more smelling sensors than would fit in any other animal. They easily detected the smoky human scent before they left the first group of spruce. But they were not concerned.

Waawaashkeshi saw the large mastodon look up and consider the humans, then continue on. These creatures were far too trusting. They needed to run, but they simply carried on, lumbering toward the third group of spruce. The humans let them come in. First the big one, then the child, and finally the mid-size creature dragging the rock.

Before the tired third mastodon reached the trees that the other two were already ripping apart, the humans cut it off. They circled it with long sticks, longer than the creature's front arm, longer than the tusks extending from the edges of the creature's mouth, and then the humans slowly closed in. The mastodon did not know what to do, and the other two in the group seemed unconcerned. The creature let the humans come closer. It turned its head from one direction to the other to see what was happening. It tugged on its foot. The rock moved like an anchor along the ground.

At the end of each long stick the humans had attached a thin, shiny, pointed rock, much larger than the ones the Ojibwe fastened to the ends of their arrows. The humans moved closer, thrusting their spears in front of them, seeing if the creature would let them get close enough for one to touch the beast with the tip of his spear. The mastodon passively let them approach. The humans crouched as they cautiously shifted their feet along the ground. The mastodon looked from one human to the other. The beast was surrounded. What did the humans want?

"That creature is just too trusting," Waawaashkeshi repeated his thought.

The flea bit gently in agreement.

The humans taunted the mastodon by thrusting their spears in its direction and retreating. Waawaashkeshi thought the humans possessed no courage. They slowed the beast down with their snare, tried to render it nearly defenseless, and now darted in and out with timid, pestering assaults. Why did this mastodon let them close in?

Finally, the human on the creature's right tapped the mastodon on the shoulder with his spear and jumped back a few steps. The mastodon turned as if to acknowledge the contact, lifting its left foot to step around as it turned to look at the human that tapped it. Instantly, the human on the left raced in and thrust his spear deep into a soft spot in the creature's flesh, directly behind the extended front leg. The mastodon let out a deafening cry that blasted from its mouth and its outstretched front arm. It heeled back on its rear legs as the human jumped away, leaving the spear imbedded in the creature's side.

The humans knew they had lit the fuse, but they wanted to get a few more spears into the creature. If they brought it down here, they would not need to chase it halfway across the tundra just to collect the meat.

No sooner did the mastodon rise on its hind legs than, in a well-orchestrated plan, the first human raced back under the beast and lifted his spear high against the exposed chest. As the beast came down from its rear legs, its full weight fell on the spear, impaling its body. The mastodon felt the wind punched from its lungs.

Waawaashkeshi felt its pain. He exhaled and groaned with the creature. His own knees weakened for an instant.

The flea gripped tighter.

The mastodon gasped for air while foamy blood ran from its mouth. When the spear entered its chest, a third human thrust another spear into the back of the leg caught in their snare.

It was already too late, but the mastodon erupted into a fury of moaning bellows and thrashing limbs. It spun on its rear legs, whipping its powerful front arm in a circle around it. With each stomp, the ground shook like thunder under the creature's enormous weight. The young human trying at that very moment to thrust a fourth spear into another rear leg was knocked off his feet by the creature's flexible arm. In one swift motion the mastodon wrapped its front arm around the human's waist and thrashed him to the ground. The human hung limp in the mastodon's arm. Blood gushed from the human's head, spraying the ground as the creature whipped him back and forth.

The other humans stood at the perimeter and watched. They could do nothing for their young brother.

Finally, the mastodon threw the limp figure into the air, letting the body land in front of it and stomped its large front foot on the human's chest, flattening the limp human to the ground. With one final tug, the beast pulled its captured leg forward and the rock moved further along the ground. The exhausted mastodon drooped.

Waawaashkeshi watched with amazement. The remaining

hunters watched, too. Waiting. The other mastodons simply lumbered off in their perpetual search for food. But the dying creature, breathing heavily with blood running from its mouth, chest, and legs, slowly collapsed to its front elbows and rested its huge white tusks upon the ground. It curled its flexible arm back under its head and lowered its whole body to the ground. A large pool of blood began to form. Human and mastodon blood blending together. The hunter and the hunted.

Where did life really begin and end?

The creature lifted its great head and looked with glassy eyes directly at Waawaashkeshi. It nodded its head. Waawaashkeshi dipped his antlers in a respectful bow and watched.

The human hunters waited as the mastodon's spirit slowly evaporated from its body, carried by the wind's current.

Waawaashkeshi watched the mastodon's last, misty breath blend into the cold arctic air, the mastodon's massive front leg draped over the lifeless human body. Raindrops in the pool. Waawaashkeshi turned and soon was far down the ditch, paying attention to his instinct—the spirit current. Waawaashkeshi did not belong in this place.

CHAPTER 8
DIRE WOLVES

8500 BCE

Waawaashkeshi continued his journey south, downstream. Dark clouds crossed the distant horizon. He'd left the glacier's edge six days ago and spent much of the journey looking for food. So far, Waawaashkeshi had survived on the leaves and twigs of dwarf shrubs, along with the lower branches from a group of black spruce. But it wasn't enough.

"I feel weak."

The flea shifted around in his fur. "You're right. Unless you eat something more, we will both die."

The flea knew Waawaashkeshi was slowly starving. Blood did not flow as it had. The flea needed to work hard for its own blood meals.

Waawaashkeshi's skin stretched tightly across his bones. The contour of each rib showed under his fur. His body longed for the long grass of his tag alder swamp, or perhaps the acorns and beechnuts that littered the ground in the sacred circle.

At this moment, Waawaashkeshi thought little about what the natural spirits might be trying to teach him in this unfamiliar age of ice and wind. He thought little about the flea. Waawaashkeshi thought only of survival.

He followed the ditch, looking for food as the water path meandered across the tundra. In spots, other glacial trickles intercepted the ditch with water that combined to make a small creek. He entered a deeply eroded ravine, with ground worn down by the flowing water. Another drift like the one at the edge of the glacier stood on one side of the ravine. There were even places downstream where enough water flowed to form a cliff-like bank of sand.

Waawaashkeshi's thick coat of fur kept him warm in the crisp air. On his back and neck, each brown hair was long and hollow. This kind of fur insulated him well, helping to retain his body heat. It also repelled water and kept him dry. The hair on his belly was different—white and soft. At times, his belly hair became soaked with sweat, and on hot days it helped to cool him.

Waawaashkeshi looked again at the clouds moving up from the horizon.

"Those dark clouds look like trouble."

Dramatic, dark, billowy clouds raced toward him.

The flea bit in acknowledgment. "Rain will start soon. I feel it in my legs."

Even from his distant position, Waawaashkeshi felt uneasy. Wind rushed past him, and flashes of lightning reached down from the clouds to strike the tundra. Each bolt lit the sky with a green glow. Waawaashkeshi knew he should take cover, but there was nowhere to go. Not even a fallen tree to crawl beneath, or a grass-covered hollow to shelter in.

Finally, Waawaashkeshi thought it best to curl up against the side of a ravine where erosion had carved out the stream's bank. He found a spot with steep banks on both sides, the small canyon offering some protection from the wind. He bedded down against the wall to wait out the bad weather. Waawaashkeshi didn't have the energy to acknowledge the flea's small nibble.

The flea knew better than to bother Waawaashkeshi right now.

Waawaashkeshi heard a low rumble of thunder as the clouds approached. They were still distant, but moving fast.

When the storm front hit, it came with force. Rain battered the ground—then hail. The clouds spun low and horizontal as they raced by, roaring with a mighty voice as lightning crashed all around. Out of the storm's direct path, Waawaashkeshi lowered his head and waited for the aggressive weather to pass. This was no small storm; it was ferocious, traveling fast.

After two hours, the storm front reached the glacier, now far to Waawaashkeshi's north. It hammered the glacier with driving rain and hail. Every drop from the sky took with it several drops melted from the glacier's surface until sheets of water poured off the ice. Water rushed into the ditch that, only a few hours earlier, had been a timid trickle. Water in this ditch collected rapidly from the glacier and the surrounding tundra. The farther downstream it traveled, the more force it gathered.

Curled against the canyon wall, Waawaashkeshi heard the rumble of water rushing toward him. He looked up, unsure of what to expect. The water came as a wall down the gully faster than Waawaashkeshi's brain could react, faster than he could process information. Waawaashkeshi stood in the canyon and turned to look upstream when the wall of water hit him broadside, knocking him off his feet.

"Hold tight!" Waawaashkeshi, again caught in a current, felt the flea grip as the powerful water pressed against his body on all sides.

The current swept Waawaashkeshi downstream at breakneck speed. He could only surrender to its rushing flow, watching anxiously as the landscape raced by. He churned his legs, searching for a place to hop out.

The current carried him a long way before the stream's banks lost their steep sides. The water opened into a wider, shallower, slower flow. Waawaashkeshi swam to the edge and stepped out. He shook the water from his back, unsure of where he was—only that he was far downstream.

Bite. Bite. The flea let Waawaashkeshi know it was still around.

Waawaashkeshi felt an urge tugging him back to the glacier, but he knew that to survive the trip, he needed to eat something more nutritious than what he had found so far.

"We're turning back," Waawaashkeshi told the flea. "I need to get back to the river crossing. I feel the pull."

"You'll never make it without something better to eat." The flea was thinking about both their survivals.

Here, in the tundra, the flea needed Waawaashkeshi.

"If I wasn't eating for two it would be a spring walk for me. I could make it, no trouble at all," Waawaashkeshi responded weakly, though he knew what he told the flea was not true.

The flea bit hard, bit twice.

Waawaashkeshi winced, knowing he had struck a nerve with the flea.

"You want me to get off? I'll jump off right now." *Bite. Bite.* "Don't let me get in the way of an important mission for the almighty Waawaashkeshi!"

"No. No." Waawaashkeshi had grown fond of his irreverent flea friend. "Stay where you are. We'll do this together."

Waawaashkeshi began his journey north, upstream, roughly following the gorge. His memory was sharp enough to realize that the storm had changed the stream's path and topography since his downstream journey. Rainwater followed paths of least resistance across the landscape, creating dozens of temporary feeder creeks that quickly drained the tundra into the ditch, knocking down banks and introducing obstructions.

Water pooled in natural basins along the way. It flowed in but not out. Large bogs were filled to the brim with water. Mats of green spikemoss had broken free of their loose moorings and now floated like rafts on the surface.

Waawaashkeshi waded from a pool's edge out to the mossy surface of one muskeg and nibbled on spikemoss. This was just what he needed. As he ate, he noticed several small mice and a shrew wiggling through the moss—imprisoned, or perhaps protected, on a floating island until the surrounding water either evaporated or was absorbed into the ground.

A few sparse willows growing at the muskeg's edge, stunted by the climate and the soil, were firmly rooted in the ground. The muskeg reminded Waawaashkeshi of the tag alder swamp. The saturated ground his hooves sank into felt much the same. While his swamp came to be from a beaver dam, other tag alder swamps not far from his forest could trace their beginnings to ancient muskegs like this.

Leaving the water, Waawaashkeshi noticed tracks and smelled the residual aroma of a predator. The animal had wandered around the water's edge looking for the mice or shrew and eventually left the area. Everything was part of the food chain.

"You see the prints," Waawaashkeshi nodded toward the pugmarks—the footprints. "What do you think?"

"Something big," the flea moved on Waawaashkeshi's hip. "Look at the stride. Maybe a wolf."

Waawaashkeshi looked closer. Yes—most likely some kind of wolf. Its stride was long, but the paw prints were deeper and smaller than those of the wolves he was accustomed to.

Waawaashkeshi trotted back toward the stream they followed. He had to admit, he was worried. There was little cover. Only instinct protected them now. Only the glacial creek and the pull of the spirit current guided them back to the crossing.

By the beginning of the fifth day traveling north, Waawaashkeshi knew they were being followed. He could not see their adversary, but he sensed it. A dangerous creature in the vicinity. Perhaps it intended to trap him—to corner him in a spot where his chances of survival were slim. Or perhaps the predator sensed that Waawaashkeshi was weakening. Maybe the creature intended to chase him into the thick mud of a muskeg where he would become severely bogged down. Once he was exhausted, the predator would move in for the kill.

Waawaashkeshi knew he was being trapped ... like the mastodon.

Late in the afternoon of the sixth day traveling upstream, Waawaashkeshi finally saw it—a shadow moving far off to his right. The wolf kept pace with them. Waawaashkeshi leapt up the embankment to his left and quartered away from the stream. He did not run. He needed to save his energy for a fight if it came to that. Back in his white pine forest, a wolf would not give serious consideration to Waawaashkeshi with easier prey around. This creature must be dangerously hungry to be interested in him.

From a distance, the dark form of this ice age wolf—this dire wolf—looked different. It was about the same size as the wolves he was familiar with, but the head was disproportionately larger, and its chest looked much more powerful. Waawaashkeshi did not like the idea of this big head and powerful chest. A bigger head meant bigger teeth.

Waawaashkeshi looked to the left and saw a second wolf, also keeping pace a safe distance away. Two against one ... but could they outrun him? From their position, Waawaashkeshi knew that they were trying to herd him back into the stream. But why? Waawaashkeshi was not as trusting as the mastodon had been. But for now, while they were a safe distance away, he could not do much more to get away. He needed to reach the glacier and the crossing. He felt the pull—an eclipse was coming—but did not know how far he was from the crossing. Looking at the mountain of ice on the distant horizon, he doubted that the wolves would wait that long.

"We're in trouble," Waawaashkeshi drew in air in a worried way. "Serious trouble."

"I see them," the flea bit lightly.

"This is going to turn into a race. Maybe a fight. You jump off at the first good spot. I mean it—really. I need to focus now. If I don't make it, I will see you again someday in the spirit pool."

"No way!" This time the flea bit hard. "I'm staying with you. We're in this together."

As he stepped back down into the streambed, Waawaashkeshi sensed more predators following, keeping their distance. Waawaashkeshi began an easy trot, hoping to win the long-distance marathon.

The intense storm had changed the contours of the ditch so much that he did not recognize his location. Finally, as he felt the wolves at his sides were closing in, he recognized the spruce trees that the mastodons had torn apart on the tundra to his left.

The wolf on the left suddenly broke stride, pausing to lift its nose first into the air, then to the ground.

Waawaashkeshi knew what was happening. The wolf smelled blood. The mastodon. The human. Even he could smell it. The combination of smells seemed to confuse the wolf. Waawaashkeshi imagined the wolf weighing its competing instincts, deciding whether to explore the mastodon distraction.

Fate is shaped by such decisions, and this one could save Waawaashkeshi's life.

The wolf on the left soon found the mastodon carcass. Much of the meat was gone, but the whole human lay crushed and lifeless on the ground. Raising its snout to the sky, the wolf let out a long, deep-throated howl. In response to the call, the wolf pack split into two groups. Three wolves scavenged the carcasses, but two continued to trail Waawaashkeshi—one closing in from the right and one running up the streambed from behind.

Waawaashkeshi leapt from the streambed and broke into a sprint, quartering away from the wolves that pursued him. His legs moved faster and faster, muscles driving him forward as the spirit pool pulled him. How long could he keep this up? How long before he succumbed to exhaustion?

The tundra vanished behind him as he raced on. He panted hard, desperate for air. With each stride, he reached deeper into his soul, drawing from the last dregs of energy. Suddenly, an unnatural darkness began to sweep across the tundra. The eclipse had begun—but he was still too far from the trickle of water. The glacier's edge loomed ahead, rushing toward him. The two wolves ran together now—and were gaining. Waawaashkeshi made a sharp turn to the right, following the glacier's edge. His hard hooves clicked against the frozen earth. Would he reach the crossing in time? He stretched his stride.

One of the wolves veered right to cut him off while the other raced on from behind. The sky darkened further as a shadow swallowed more than half the sun. He could see the small streambed, but the wolf would intercept him before he reached it. Waawaashkeshi didn't think. Pure instinct made him turn and charge the wolf at his flank. Waawaashkeshi lowered his massive antlers and caught the wolf broadside, sinking his largest tine deep into the wolf's neck. He pulled back and curled his neck to slash open the belly of the wolf.

The wolf let out a pained, deafening death-howl. It struggled to get away, its front legs pulling at the ground as it bucked violently on its side. Foamy blood bubbled from the wolf's mouth and from its neck as it exhaled a final breath, leaving only a few trailing twitches in the leg that had worked so desperately to escape.

The sky was black—the sun gone. Waawaashkeshi was only a few strides away from the closing portal. Ready to cross over, he felt the teeth of the second wolf rip deep into his hip. The powerful jaw—brimming with jagged fangs—clamped down, tearing through Waawaashkeshi's hide and into his flesh as the wolf readied to twist its neck and throw Waawaashkeshi on his side. Waawaashkeshi kicked his back legs so high in the air that he somersaulted before landing on his back. He scrambled on the ground. The hoof from Waawaashkeshi's pumping leg struck the wolf in its temple and laid it flat.

With blood gushing from his hind quarter and flesh ripped away, Waawaashkeshi used his front legs to drag himself into the trickle from the glacier. He was exhausted. His muscles burned from the exertion. Ached from pushing past the physical limits of his strength. His hip throbbed. The leg no longer moved properly. He needed to escape. To cross through the portal.

A thin sliver of the bright orange sun began to reemerge from behind the shadow.

The groggy wolf struggled to regain consciousness and was suddenly on its feet with flesh and hide still hanging from its mouth. It leapt for Waawaashkeshi. Its front legs folded between its back legs, teeth bared to make the final attack just as Waawaashkeshi dragged himself across the trickle and into the river. The shadow of the eclipse disappeared from the sun. The portal closed. Waawaashkeshi was across. He braced himself for the wolf, but the wolf had somehow disappeared. Evaporated into its own ice age.

Waawaashkeshi lay exhausted in the river—completely spent. He bent his neck to lick his injured hip and leg. A patch of hide was torn away, exposing muscle and ripped flesh.

But that was not his first concern.

Where was the flea? He prodded his side, suddenly frantic.

Where was the flea?!

No. ...

Waawaashkeshi wanted to scream in anguish. But after a moment of contemplation, he exhaled sadly, knowing that his steadfast friend clung tightly to the patch of skin now left behind with the dire wolf in the ice age.

It serves the wolf right. Bite hard and bite often, little flea. And when my time comes, I will look for you in the spirit pool.

Waawaashkeshi looked at the sand bank where the Ojibwe village should be, but the village was no longer there. A thin blanket of November snow covered the forest floor.

Something was wrong with the trees.

Waawaashkeshi—now Split Toe—drifted under a leafless willow that reached out over the water. He found a perch where he could rest and buried his mighty antlers among willow branches, keeping most of his body submerged in the river. He needed time to heal. The river's cool current felt good on his injured leg. He might live.

CHAPTER 9
LOGGING

AD 1870

When Split Toe was injured in the past, he'd always tried to lie in the river until he felt well enough to return to his daily life. The healing power of the spirit pool felt strongest in the cool water and fresh air. Water and air gave a new start to everything: a new leaf to the tree, a new flower to the plant, a new sunrise on the morning horizon, a new coat of skin to cover a bloody wound.

Feeling cold stream water washing his raw flesh where the dire wolf had ripped the hide from his hip made Split Toe wonder what became of his tiny friend, the flea.

"*Don't worry, Waawaashkeshi,*" Split Toe could hear the flea's voice in his mind. "*I am waiting for you here in the spirit pool. Ha ... That mangy old dire wolf ... Well, I pestered it for a whole season. Tormented it relentlessly. I bit so many times it finally chewed off its own leg. I thought you might want to know. All is well.*"

The voice calmed Split Toe's mind, but he was still struggling. From birth, Split Toe had learned to never sleep too deeply. He was out of action for now, but his senses remained alert. That night, though the water numbed the pain of his injured leg, he did not rest well in the river. A few heavy logs floating by disturbed him. One came close enough to bump him gently toward the riverbank as it followed the current downstream. Split Toe was only half asleep when he woke to the sound of a loud *whack* just after daybreak—and to the smell of smoke.

Whack. Whack.

Without leaving his position, Split Toe watched through the brush as several humans worked on the opposite side of the river. These humans were different from any he had seen before. They did not look as though they belonged in the forest. Their bright clothing, loud voices, and forced way of movement did not blend in. They walked with loud, heavy steps, their feet wrapped in solid dark covers. Not flexible, soft moccasins. They seemed to do everything the hard way, without simple elegance to their motion. And they had hairy faces. Very hairy faces.

Each man used a long stick with a wide tooth on the end to cut through a mighty white pine. They felled a tree much larger and older than a beaver could have managed. A tree that had defied wind, snow, flood, drought, disease, and decay for 450 years. A tree that harbored countless nests of birds and squirrels as it stood like a permanent tower in the forest, formed by nature into a sentinel for its species. A tree with many generations of offspring, wisdom etched into the patina of its rough bark.

To everything in the forest, trees like this were sacred, having earned respect over many seasons. Split Toe remembered when the Ojibwe boy had bowed to the forest of old white pines as he surrendered the hunt.

The tree the humans were working on was nearly cut through. One of the humans stepped around to the opposite side of the tree.

Whack. Whack. Whack, the axe spoke.

Split Toe heard the tree groan in pain as it leaned toward its deeply cut side and started to fall with an inertia that only the forest floor could stop.

There are many ways for a tree to die.

When the tree groaned, the human who took the final whack at the back of the tree looked up to see the shifting canopy and responded with his own call.

"Timber-r-r!" the human shouted, scattering the others as they scrambled away from the falling tree.

It reminded Split Toe of the mastodon hunt. Six hunters against one. Six loggers against one tree. Not a fair fight.

With a loud crash, the tall tree dropped to the ground, and the forest fell silent. No one bowed. Split Toe felt the tree's spirit drift into the spirit current. Another drop of rain traveling to Lake Michigan.

Split Toe closed his eyes and dipped his antlers toward this grandfather of a tree and felt a small gust of wind drift across his nose. Split Toe looked at the spot on the ground where the tree fell. The stumps of countless old white pines covered the area like a graveyard. In fact, the entire peninsula on the low side of river was cut clear of trees. This tree fell among the remains of its comrades. An entire family of trees, taken down one by one.

The humans leaned on their axes, catching their breath. "That one was a beast," one logger finally proclaimed.

"They're all beasts," his comrade shouted back. "One more down, the whole forest to go!"

"Get 'er into the river. There are more of these bastards we gotta get today. You know how it works," the boss shouted.

They all picked up their axes and headed toward another tree.

Near the base of the peninsula, several animals unlike any Split Toe had seen before were tied together with ropes and guided by a human while they pulled another tree to the river. Each log dug at the forest floor as the animals pulled, taking a little of the forest's rich soil with it into the stream.

The cream-colored beasts were larger than Split Toe, with long pointed horns extending from each side of their heads. Split Toe thought it was curious that these large animals would do the heavy work for the loggers.

"Get them oxen moving," Split Toe heard one of the loggers shout. "Get them logs outa the way! We got more comin' in."

Split Toe looked on in disbelief.

"What is going on here?" Split Toe asked the spirits.

"Split Toe. You know things these humans may never understand. Things their ancestors forgot many years ago. Pay attention to these humans. There are things for you to learn. But do not let their ways confuse you. What you already know is important. Trust your instincts."

Several loggers cut the mighty tree into sections to make transport possible, like the ice age hunters did with the mastodon. They rolled the log sections into the river where the logs floated downstream with the current.

These humans only seemed interested in taking the main trunk of the trees. Each tree's canopy was dragged away and burned in the huge fire at the base of the peninsula. Live needles from the canopies sent thick, white smoke into the air.

Split Toe thought back to his friend Mikinaak, the old snapping turtle, who lived for nearly two centuries in the pool where water ran out of the beaver dam. Mikinaak had finally died of old age, though it was hard to tell if that was the real cause. The turtle eventually lost her mobility. She slowed down. Everything about the turtle was tired. Mikinaak could no longer catch the small fish that swam in the pool. One thing led to another, and she finally surrendered to the spirit current, too slow and famished to live any longer.

Is it possible for a tree to die of old age? Split Toe silently wondered.

A tree is not like a snapping turtle. Each year, regardless of the tree's age, it begins anew with fresh growth. The centuries of life it has lived fold into its interior, while each spring the tree adds a new layer to the exterior. New needles. New bark. New branches. New feeder roots. Certainly, a limb below the canopy might age out and drop off from time to time, particularly when blocked from sunlight, but the tree replaces old branches with new ones that are better positioned to reach the light.

Leaves and needles fall to the forest floor each year, but a fresh batch replaces them in the spring. Like leaves, small feeder roots die each year, replaced by new growth. When a tree reaches its height limit—growing so tall that it can no longer draw water and minerals to support the highest needles, leaves, or seeds—it continues to grow in girth, expanding its trunk a bit more each year with fresh layers of bark.

Split Toe could not remember ever witnessing a tree simply dying of old age. Too many other things were more likely to happen to the tree during its lifespan. It often took so long for a tree to die once the fuse was lit that it might be mistaken for dying of old age, even when it hadn't. The older the tree got, the more it was exposed to danger. Larger trunks with more surface area presented predator insects with a bigger target to latch onto. Bigger trees had more branches ready to break off in ice storms, inviting mold and decay to enter the heart of the tree when weather warmed.

More seasons—a longer life—also introduce more opportunities for things like drought or flood.

Some tree species connect with each other through common roots. Even if the main trunk topples due to decay, the new sucker takes over from the same base and become another mature iteration of the same tree.

After the Ojibwe village burned in the fire, the first trees to appear were shimmering aspens. Split Toe knew that aspen roots extended endlessly, with sucker stems popping up from roots all over the forest floor. Each new shoot above the ground helped to extend the common root system below the ground. When one stem died, it was like a limb falling from a mighty white pine. The tree continued on, renewing itself each spring, missing a part it could live without. Split Toe did not know for sure if the aspen grove was one tree that went on and on or a forest of many trees.

In a way, an aspen grove resembled the spirit pool where many made one.

If a mature tree that lived for centuries just slowed down, like the turtle, perhaps it could no longer produce new growth easily. Perhaps its life-sustaining mechanisms become too inefficient to keep a tree of so many seasons going. Maybe that is how a tree dies of old age. Split Toe could not remember seeing it happen, but that could be because the timescale of life and death for a tree differed so much from his own.

There are many ways for a tree to die. Old age did not seem like one of them.

Late that night, after the humans left the peninsula, Split Toe arose from the stream and stretched his stiff muscles beneath the starry sky. He felt his strength returning and his injury healing. He bent his long neck around to lick the wound on his hindquarters. His own saliva would help his wound to heal. Split Toe jumped up the riverbank to the forest floor opposite the peninsula and stepped once again into a white pine forest, this time with a noticeable limp in his right rear leg. His hooves left large, deep prints in the snow.

Split Toe was traveling in a different age when in the early 1800s the first of these new humans—the first Europeans—came to explore his white pine forest and the river. By then, many white pine trees in the forest were 400 years old.

He was also gone in 1837 when Michigan became a state—something Split Toe would not have understood the purpose of. He missed all the years between 1835 and 1844 when surveyors laid out his part of the state into rectangular segments that divided the state into townships and one-mile square sections.

He was not around in 1856 when new surveyors resurveyed unsettled areas of Michigan, partitioning it into half and quarter sections, which were offered in 1862 as 160-acre parcels to settlers for one dollar and twenty-five cents per acre.

Split Toe's time-travel life skipped over all these times and events.

Split Toe did not understand money or land ownership. He had not noticed the hardwood stakes that a surveyor drove into the ground at the corner of each section, or the "witness trees" with section markings carved into their trunks. Split Toe was gone when the first new human settlers, only a few of them, found small clearings in the forest and made their simple log shelters in the early 1850s.

Split Toe did not see the man who arrived alone in a canoe. A "timber cruiser," who walked with a backpack through his forest looking for the surveyor's stakes driven into the forest floor, taking notes and identifying tracts of old white pine not far from accessible river tributaries. The timber cruiser estimated the lumber that could be produced from the trees. He registered the tracts as claims for the logging company he represented. He lit the fuse.

There are many ways for a forest to die.

For weeks, Split Toe watched these humans—the loggers—chip away at the forest on the west side of the river. They cut a crude trail through the forest—a trail that twisted around large trees they would eventually cut. Their project started at the Clam River. As they cleared trees, they maneuvered them in pieces around the stumps and slid them into the stream.

Snowy ground helped the animals move the logs, but the whole process left a huge mess. They churned up rich soil, sometimes wearing through to sand or gravel below. Seeing this, Split Toe couldn't help but wonder how long it would take for this forest to heal. To start again. Longer than if it burned to the ground in a fire. The problem was that much of the soil also needed to start over. When the river began to freeze, the loggers accumulated large piles of logs on rollways along the riverbank where, after the spring thaw, the logs could easily be rolled into the water one after another to "run the river."

The logging humans lived together in a primitive shanty they'd built for themselves in the forest. It was like a small village all under one roof. Split Toe imagined that when they used up this part of the forest, they would build a similar shanty further down the line, perhaps further from the river. A chimney pipe protruded through the shanty's roof, releasing white smoke that billowed into the forest air. It pumped out smoke day and night.

Every few days, as wet snow fell to the ground, Ol' Split Toe watched a team of horses arrive, pulling a sled down the forest trail. The sled was heaped with piles of supplies stacked high.

"What do you have today?" a logger yelled over the winter wind as he walked toward the sled.

"I've got it all," the driver shouted back, stepping down to tend the horses. "Flour, pork, beans, molasses."

He walked to the sled and looked over the side. "Axe heads, saw blades, ropes, chains, and shackles. Spare harnesses, ammunition, and a few bottles of liquor. I'll be back in a day with marsh hay and the new clothing and boots you put in for."

"Oh, ho," the logger responded with a smile. "We can always depend on you. Shall I pour you some hot tea?"

"Not this time. But thanks, my friend. With the storm comin' in, I gotta get this rig turned around. See you soon." He waved his hand, setting the team in motion.

When snow disappeared for the season, the driver exchanged the sled's runners for wheels and made a wagon. These were the first wheels Split Toe had ever seen. Loggers now fed marsh hay to animals working in the forest. Soon, the loggers began harvesting marsh hay from large, grassy wetlands north of the tag alder swamp. These fellows did not miss a thing when it came to harvesting. But Split Toe thought there was plenty of marsh grass to go around.

Split Toe heard gunfire for the first time when the loggers came to the forest.

Snap-KABOOM. It sounded like thunder. A large turkey dropped in its tracks.

Later that day, it was a squirrel—***Snap-KABOOM***. Split Toe, hidden from view, watched flames flash from the end of the muzzle loader.

So, that is how they hunt?

Like the wolf, or the cougar, or like the Ojibwe for that matter, these humans also needed food. But unlike the Ojibwe, they did not bow respectfully to honor the life they took—to honor the spirit they released into the spirit pool. They displayed no reverence for a drop of rain. Were they not connected to the natural spirits?

A few days passed before Split Toe heard the *snap-KABOOM* again. He later discovered a deer he knew well lying lifeless on the forest floor with its muscular rear legs removed. Split Toe stared at the incomplete carcass.

"*These* humans are not like the Ojibwe." Though he could accept that these humans, like other living things, needed food, he wondered about their wastefulness. "Why would they do this thing? Taking so little of what they destroy. ... They will need more soon."

An owl watching from a nearby branch hooted its thoughts. "Are they leaving part of the animal as a gift for other forest creatures?"

"I don't think so," Split Toe grunted. "They don't seem to pay attention in that way. These humans use too little of everything they take from the forest. They take only the long trunks of the trees. They burn the rest. They take only the back legs of the deer. They leave much on the forest floor."

"Because they waste much, they need more," the owl hooted in agreement.

Split Toe did not think the humans were careful about their place in the food chain. When the Ojibwe took a deer, the entire village ate the meat and organs. Everything that could be eaten, was. The Ojibwe used the hide for many important needs of the village. They crushed the deer's bones for marrow or made them into knives, needles, and other tools. They used the deer's brain to tan the hide. They converted the hard antlers into handles or tools. Scraps that were left for the crows or mice were miniscule. Almost nothing.

Split Toe knew that other wild animals would consume whatever the humans did not. The coyote. The bear. The eagle. Mice. And the forest soil would benefit from any composted remains, nourishing the trees.

"It is a matter of respect," Split Toe exhaled.

"The forest remembers the Ojibwe," the owl hooted, gliding closer to the carcass. "They did not waste their kill. And they killed no more than was necessary for their lives. Yes, respect."

"What is important to these logging humans?" Split Toe wondered.

"They seem to take much without giving anything back," the owl blinked, its eyes surveying the nearby debris. "They remove the trees that all breathing beings need to survive—including themselves. They take over the river for their logs. The logs scrape away fish nesting grounds, making it difficult for my eagle and kingfisher cousins to see fish they depend upon for food. It is an abuse of the food chain." The owl became restless. It wanted now to glide to another part of the forest, perhaps a place farther away from the humans. "Where does this end?" the owl perched in silence for a moment, its question hanging in the air, then flew away.

Split Toe stepped quietly to the river's edge to watch the floating logs. A deeper explanation from the spirits drifted through Split Toe's mind.

"Logs moving in the river bounce off its sides, taking a little from the bank with each bounce. The logs slowly widen the

river, making it shallower with more surface area, and as a result the river becomes warmer. Fish and other creatures that depended on the cool stream for survival need to find a way to cope."

"I would not have thought of that." Split Toe subconsciously thanked the spirits. "Now I understand."

He continued his puzzled thoughts about the loggers. "They hunt down and kill animals that would help to replant the trees. Can't they see where this is going? Have they no instinct? Where is their own sense of self-preservation? Where is their connection with the natural spirits?"

"This forest will need to start over," Split Toe heard the natural spirits telling him. "Do not worry, Mother Nature will make it so."

He thought back to the forest fire. Nearly every tree north and west of the Muskegon River burned, and many of the animals with it—the same animals that could have helped with the forest's regeneration. That happened more than 450 years ago, but the forest recovered, step by step. Perhaps what *these* humans did was no worse than the forest fire. He did not like watching the forest die. Recovery would take a long time, but he knew that the world worked in a kind of action-reaction way.

Once, while eavesdropping close to one of their evening campfires, Split Toe heard the Ojibwe talk about *Mother Nature*. It sounded like Mother Nature managed an all-powerful system of actions and reactions that took place everywhere. Climate warmed. Glaciers melted. Warm weather plants migrated to new warming regions. The plants lived and died and decayed and covered ground that was once barren of soil. The soil sustained more plants. Insects, land animals, and birds followed the plants.

As water trickled from warming glaciers, it cut into the earth, making pathways for bigger rivers. Melting water evaporated, producing more climate change, different wind patterns, and rain. Humans migrated, following the animals they could hunt, water they could drink, and fuel for their fires. When a species of insect ravaged its entire food supply in just a few seasons, not permitting the plant's reproduction to keep up with the eating habits of the insect's own growing population, the insect species died, and the plant that was their food source regenerated. Mother Nature kept things going.

Action. Reaction. Mother Nature.

Split Toe thought he heard the spirits' voice in the wind.

"You are learning well, Split Toe. But there is more you need to know. This part is a hard lesson. Things are changing."

Split Toe exhaled, "Show me. Help me to understand."

"Use what you know, Split Toe. Think about what you see. Understand. Think for yourself. One thing builds on another. Your curiosity will take you far. You were born for this."

Split Toe tried to think the situation through. The logging humans disrupted the forest soil and the river, which the forest fire left mostly untouched. Alternately, while the loggers added smoke to the air, it did not seem like as much smoke as the forest fire created.

"Are these humans simply repeating what Mother Nature has already done many times?" Split Toe wondered.

"And what *are* these humans doing with all the trees?"

The humans seemed too clever to go through all this work for no reason. They spent one day cutting down a tree that took centuries to grow, a tree that beat the odds of disease, weather, animal destruction, and decay.

What did the destruction of the tree provide that the living tree could not? To Split Toe, the cut tree did not seem to add to the food, shelter, or fuel that the logging humans needed for living.

Had Split Toe known about the $26 per month that a lumberjack received, it would have made little difference to him. Split Toe did not think in such abstract terms.

"These humans certainly think differently than the other animals in the forest. And very differently than the Ojibwe thought," Split Toe concluded. "These humans seem disconnected from the spirit pool. They seem to ignore it altogether."

Split Toe knew trees of the forest, forest animal ancestors, Ojibwe ancestors, air, and soil were all part of the living spirit pool. But he was not sure about these humans. Split Toe needed to pay attention to them to find out if they were really part of the natural world. Part of the action-reaction that always happened.

"What goes through these humans' minds?" Split Toe asked again. "They do not seem to care what their actions may cause down the line. Maybe results they can't see or don't notice or simply ignore don't matter to them. Or maybe they just don't understand the timescale of Mother Nature's action-reactions."

Split Toe continued his thought, "After all, Mother Nature's timescale can often be like trying to find a tree dying of old age. They might have to wait for centuries for the results. The reaction often takes more time than what *these* humans can imagine."

Split Toe mulled it over in his mind for a few more minutes. Finally he came to a realization. "Or maybe *these* humans think they can outwit the power of Mother Nature."

Split Toe needed to know more about civilization. More specifically, the civilization of these humans who seemed unconcerned about what they consumed. He must be patient and continue to observe the humans.

Split Toe was born into the wilds and lived in deep harmony with nature's principles. Each living thing competed for its own survival. Rarely did something in nature needlessly disrupt something else. Certainly, animals had disputes. They fought. They defended territory. They battled in mating rituals. Parents protected their young. Sometimes a mother protected her child from the instinctual, lethal aggression of the child's own father.

Split Toe saw a certain harmony in it all. Balance. Life was rarely taken without reason. Being truly part of the wilds meant being integrated with other natural things into the food chain. It was automatic. It was understood. It happened without much reflection. Split Toe could live no other way.

CHAPTER 10
EDRA

AD 1874

Split Toe watched the loggers for several seasons. One by one, they cut the mature white pines south and west of the Clam River. The loggers cleared the land of all trees, beginning with the peninsula, then moving to the low areas bordering the river, and finally to the hills the river meandered beside.

When they were far enough from the flowing water that dragging the large logs along the ground became impractical, the loggers brought in a new tool.

"What 'a you think of this cart?" Split Toe heard one logger ask another.

"A beast. Never seen wheels this tall, but that's what you need if yer gonna lift the log under the belly. Amazing these oxen—or even the team of hosses—can pull it. The thing do get the logs to the river real quick."

This wheeled machine amazed Split Toe. He had to admit, these humans were really clever. Split Toe watched as the wheels cut deep ridges into the soil. Before long, the wheels cut through to sand or gravel.

What a mess, Split Toe could not help but think as he looked over the cleared area.

While most of the treetops went up in flames in a fire that burned day and night, scraps and stray limbs remaining between stumps on the forest floor made it nearly impossible for Split Toe to walk through the debris. His hooves constantly caught on the logs and limbs that littered the ground. The many deer in the area had worn grooves into the logs they crossed regularly.

Some forest animals seemed to thrive in the debris. Perhaps, for now, it was a gift for them. Bobcats were big fans of the entanglement of leftovers, as were many small animals the bobcats hunted. Grouse. Rabbits. Ground squirrels. And the debris was certainly a gift to the ground where it eventually decomposed and developed into soil.

In fact, by the time the third logging winter was underway, aspen saplings already sprouted up in the area where the loggers removed the first white pines. Action-reaction. Mother Nature. When Split Toe slipped across the river at night, he ate the leaves and twigs of these young aspen. They also provided a good bit of cover when he wanted to get by the humans without being seen.

Now logs floating in the river seemed to hang up at every bend. They piled up in groups until one of the humans went to the obstructed spot and broke the logs free, then shepherded them from that group into a single-file line of moving lumber. There were two men who did nothing but keep logs moving. Split Toe secretly watched them carry long poles with iron hooks to help rotate the logs and pry them free. These humans really were clever.

One day, after the loggers had traveled a considerable distance from the river, they shifted operations to the east side of the Clam River. Split Toe had not expected this, but he knew what it meant for his forest—and for him.

Eastside logging work began with the removal of enough large white pines to make room to relocate the loggers' shanty. Breaking the shanty down happened easily, since it used no nails for construction. The loggers took it away log by log, carrying each piece across the river, and then reassembled it at the new spot.

Several days later, as the loggers took down more of the large white pines, something else unexpected happened. When the supply sled arrived, it carried a second person: a woman. She was not like women of the Ojibwe village. Her hair was tucked under a hat, not braided. Her clothing was different.

This woman seemed altogether different. It was her movements. Her purpose. Her authority. She was not part of a village. There was an independence about her. Or perhaps it was confidence. The woman arrived bundled up for the cold, wet snow, as were the logging men, but she wore a heavy ground-length skirt that covered her boots. She stepped down from the sled, gripping its side as she placed her foot in the snow. The logging supervisor, the foreman, met her at the sled.

"Sir, I think you were expecting me."

"Yes ma'am. We figured you'd be here any time now."

"So, can you show me the corner? The northwest corner of the parcel?"

"We'll try, ma'am. But I have to say … to ask, ma'am," the foreman paused. "What are you doing out here? I mean, what are you *really* doing here?"

"Well, sir, I do think you know what I am here for. I appreciate your help finding the corner."

Split Toe watched from a hidden spot along the riverbed. The other loggers tried hard not to make it obvious they were watching the woman.

Together, the woman and the foreman walked along the river until they reached the furthest point where men worked to roll logs into the river. They continued thirty more steps upstream to a shallow gravel bed where they could wade the cold current and avoid logs drifting down the river.

The woman and the foreman made their way downstream again on the east side of the river. They both searched around the forest floor looking for the surveyor's hardwood stake that was driven into the ground years earlier, marking the corner of the section. When they found the stake, the woman looked pleased. She placed her hands on her hips and looked around, assessing the situation on both sides of the river.

"Well, this is it, then. It will do nicely," the woman said.

"Okay, missus," the supervisor replied. "We'll take the lumber. You take the land. Is that our understanding?"

"Yes," the woman nodded, "and please call me Edra."

"Yes ma'am. Thank you, ma'am."

Edra moved a few more steps downstream and looked at the high sandy riverbank where the Ojibwe village once was. Split Toe remembered this spot: this was where sand drifted to form a dune south of the glacier. He watched as the woman climbed the hill, walking through snow between mature white pines. Edra could not suppress her wide smile. She seemed to bounce as she walked, her arms swinging in broad movements as she excitedly gestured to the river and its path through the landscape. Finally, her gaze followed a majestic old tree's trunk up to the canopy. Her smile broadened. Split Toe watched Edra point out twelve individual trees along the river's edge. Split Toe could tell these twelve trees were particularly lovely, well-placed specimens.

She spoke to the foreman. "Save these twelve trees along the river for me. Will you?"

The man nodded respectfully to the woman and walked from tree to tree with his axe, slashing a single gash into the thick bark of each tree. By the time the two returned to the sled, the supplies were offloaded into the snow, and the sled turned around to follow its own tracks on the outbound journey.

Edra spoke again to the foreman. "I like this place. It feels right. It has everything anyone would need to survive."

The foreman returned a puzzled look, then finally responded politely, "Thank you, ma'am. Come see us again. Any time."

With a smile, Edra stepped into the sled and sat on an empty crate.

Edra looked down the snowy trail they would follow back. Two sled tracks, separated by a runway of broken snow packed down by the horses, wound between tree stumps and over rolling terrain.

Edra knew what she wanted. The change from her city life would be extraordinary. She did not look back.

The foreman shook his head and wondered what a woman like this wanted with a piece of land so far from the village. He could not see how it would lead to anything but hardship.

The behavior of the foreman and the woman puzzled Split Toe. What were they planning? He watched the loggers suspend a rope above the river. They transferred supplies from the side where the driver delivered the supplies to the side where the loggers now had their camp, using the suspended rope to make the transfer. Split Toe had to admit they were clever fellows.

He watched curiously for several days as the loggers dropped one old tree at a time to the ground, cut it into sections, and muscled it into the river. This part of the forest seemed larger and deeper to Split Toe than the west side of the river. It would take these humans some time to remove it.

Split Toe retreated into the tag alder swamp. The swamp was peaceful and safe, but Split Toe could still hear the distant *whack, whack* of the cutters and, once or twice each day, the painful moan of another tree followed by a loud crack as the tree crashed to the ground.

At times, Split Toe could feel the muffled thud—a single thump that shook the ground and resonated through his curled-up body like a distant, final heartbeat.

It seemed to notify the surrounding forest, *"I am done."*

Another drop of rain.

One morning, Split Toe again sensed the urge: the spirit current pulling him to the river crossing. He knew what to do. Slowly, Split Toe got to his feet, stretched his legs and neck, and began walking. The limp in his rear leg was slight but still there. Split Toe thought it might be part of his walk for the rest of his life.

Split Toe followed the trail to the edge of the thicket, then walked along the trail that traced the ancient mound constructed by the original beavers at the swamp's edge. He wondered what the natural spirits would show him this time.

When Split Toe reached the edge of the cleared logging area, a shadow began to swallow the sun. As he cautiously waited behind a white pine, he heard the rhythmic chopping of the loggers fall silent. They looked up in awe at the impending darkness. When the shadow covered most of the sun, Split Toe stepped out into the open. He would be exposed for a short distance, but if he waited for the last possible second before moving, Split Toe knew he could dash through the river crossing portal without pursuit—perhaps without even being noticed.

He remained still, waiting. The sun was nearly gone, and the loggers were still distracted by the eclipse. Split Toe began to walk slowly. There were only a few seconds left. With a mighty leap, he made for the crossing.

Split Toe skidded to an abrupt stop at the riverbank and watched his plan suddenly unravel. Shifting logs jammed the river in front of him—there was no clear way across. The sun had disappeared. This was the moment. Split Toe pranced from side to side, searching for a way across. Looking back through the darkness, he saw the loggers watching him in silent, wide-eyed amazement. As the sun began to reappear, its light caught and glimmered on Split Toe's towering antlers.

Split Toe had missed the spirit's call. He turned and looked directly at the loggers, who stood frozen in place. Then, with a respectful dip of his antlers—just as the Ojibwe did when surrendering his hunt—Split Toe leapt toward the forest of tall pines.

As Split Toe sprinted toward the tag alder swamp, the nearest logger laid his axe on the ground and ran to the spot where Split Toe had briefly stood. Another followed. The sun was now fully exposed. The first logger dropped to his knees and placed his large hand over the deep imprint that Split Toe's hoof had left in the snow—the last print from his leap into cover. The logger's hand could not cover it.

"So, this is the one," the logger looked up at his partner. "Did you see the antlers?"

The loggers had seen the prints before—they had stirred gossip around the camp, along with plenty of accusations of exaggeration. But this was the first time they'd seen the deer. Now they knew.

"Look at the print," the second logger answered. "It is huge. See how the front toes of the hoof split wide apart? It is the mark of a very large buck."

And so, the European legend of an extraordinary deer began.

It upset Split Toe that these humans had come between him and the spirit's calling. The spirits always guided him to the right place at the right time, but this time, the humans had blocked the way—and with the corpses of trees no less. He wondered how long their logjam would last. Would it forever block the chance of following the spirits' call to cross the river? Was this the end of the journey the spirits had planned for him?

Perhaps Split Toe needed to learn something from the way things turned out. Perhaps this failure was meant to teach him something.

CHAPTER 11
DYNAMITE

AD 1878

As the humans cleared trees deep into the white pine forest on the east side of the river, shimmering aspens began to grow among the debris and pine stumps on the already-logged west side of the river. The loggers improved the supply trail to their camp, and now it was a straight road bordering two surveyed sections of land.

Split Toe watched loggers dig around many stumps that were in the way. Two loggers specialized in this chore. They dug to the roots and cut them off with their axes. When enough roots were gone, another logger brought in two oxen yoked together and wrapped a logging chain around the stump, hooking the chain on several roots.

"Git on up there, Betsie," the logger shouted as the oxen strained. "Move, Ginny. Git movin', girl." A logger hit the stubborn root a few more times with his axe, and the stump popped out of its hole. The oxen pulled the stump clear of the trail.

Split Toe liked watching the oxen. They looked like twins. They worked hard for the loggers, and were submissive to every command. Obedient. Split Toe wondered how this came to be. Even though the oxen were much larger and more powerful than the humans, the humans seemed to command them. Perhaps the oxen loved the humans and wanted only to please them, surrendering their lives to them. That was how things looked to Split Toe.

When the oxen—try as they might—could not get a particularly bothersome stump from its hole, and when the loggers had enough of digging and pounding with their axes for that particular stump, one logger often walked back to the shanty and returned with several short red sticks similar in thickness to a tag alder stem. They brought other things that looked to Split Toe like rocks and vines—blasting caps and fuse material.

The senior logger stood back and assessed the stump for a few minutes. He removed his wool hat and scratched his head. Thinking.

"Yaa. Here and here." He pointed. "What you think, Marko?"

Marko pointed to approximately the same spots and drilled holes. Split Toe watched with curiosity as the logger with the dynamite pressed a blasting cap into each stick, attached the fuses, and inserted the dynamite gently into each hole. He measured the fuses equally so both sticks would explode at the same time.

Both loggers stepped away to the other end of the fuses. One pulled out his pipe, drew a long drag of tobacco smoke into his lungs, and lit both fuses with the pipe. The loggers walked away and crouched behind a tree. When the dynamite exploded, the stump flew into the air with an entanglement of roots spinning around it. As the stump tumbled to the ground, crashing with a final thud, the whole forest briefly fell into an eerie, echoing silence that seemed to cause even the natural spirits to pause. The explosion's results were instant. Earth around the stump was loose and filled easily into the hole.

A few weeks later, a logger inspected a charge that did not blow. He bent over the stump just as the finicky dynamite stick exploded, sending a large chunk of wood high into the air and the logger into the spirit pool.

"Could have happened to any one of us. Bad luck," Split Toe heard one of the loggers say.

Split Toe watched from a low area filled with limbs and other logging discards as the other loggers dug a deep hole and rolled in the body of their lifeless comrade. Just like they rolled logs into the river. When they buried the body, Split Toe wondered if he had misjudged these humans. Perhaps these humans did know about the spirit world—not because they stood around the hole and bowed to their fallen comrade after rolling him in, but because they placed him in a spot where his body would quickly decompose and return to the soil that gave life to the forest. Split Toe was unsure. He needed to watch much longer to see how these humans behaved.

The loggers left the graveside and continued pulling the killer stump—and the others down the line. When they reached the river, they used the oxen and the horses together to pull long sections of two white pines in single spans across the whole river—bridge logs. The bridge logs were long enough to extend up the sloping bank to higher ground. They needed enough clearance above the river so logs flowing down the river could pass under. It took most of a full-grown white pine to span the distance.

The humans and oxen worked hard.

Later in the week, the supply wagon arrived with a load of flat wood. It was the first flat wood Split Toe had seen, if he did not count the door of the shanty, which the loggers had sawed into a slab from a single log. Split Toe did not know exactly what these boards were or where they came from. Split Toe saw they had the consistency and strength of a tree's branch and seemed natural in that way. But their straight edges and flat surfaces were unusual. He watched with curiosity as two loggers worked together to place the boards along the two long pine trunks spanning the river. Split Toe noticed the boards fit well together.

"Gi'me a handful of those nails from the box," one of the loggers called to the other.

Split Toe looked as closely as he could from behind a pile of canopy branches placed near the river. Curious. These fellows carried a small box of hard, square twigs—nails—which they used to anchor the flat boards in place by hitting them with the back end of a hatchet. Split Toe had never seen nails before. He watched as the second logger scooped up a batch of the sharp, pointed twigs and passed them to the first logger.

Each board the loggers put in place created a longer flat surface from the west side of the bridge. To Split Toe, the surface looked like it could be ordinary ground. At night, when the loggers slept, Split Toe cautiously walked onto the surface to feel this hard, human-made ground for himself. He felt and heard the click of his hooves. Split Toe lowered his nose to the structure.

His nostrils picked up the distinct scent of white pine. Like the aroma of a live limb that broke from a tree in a windstorm. Split Toe sensed the spirit of the white pine trees in the boards.

When all the nails were in, both loggers stood on a board and shifted back and forth, trying to see if the bridge would move.

"Solid like the rock," the first logger proclaimed.

"Those boards'll stay in place good as that stubborn ol' mule over Pierre's place. Need the army ta get that thing ta budge."

"True. But the whistle from Mary and that ol' mule comes right along. Seen it m'own self."

"Well, this bridge's stayin' put, an' that's the fact," the second logger grunted as he picked up the empty box. He wondered why the first logger needed to bring up Mary and moving the immovable. What was the point of that?

Split Toe watched as the humans walked across the river without getting wet. Next, they led a team of oxen across the bridge. Later in the week, when the next supply wagon arrived, it bounced down the relatively straight logging road, *clickity-clack*, and crossed the river over the bridge with an echoing rumble. On the east side of the bridge, the supply wagon followed a simple trail that weaved between the stumps to the shanty.

By this time, Split Toe spent most daylight hours on an island deep inside the tag alder swamp. The thicket was dense. These humans had no reason to wander into such a complicated place. Loggers removed all the white pines up to the edge of the swamp. All the white pines, that is to say, except the twelve majestic trees standing by the river which the logging foreman marked with his axe—the trees the woman saved. The loggers cut all the other trees into sections and wheeled them to the log-filled river. The canopies burned in the continuous fire.

Where were the animals who once inhabited this space?

Some had tried to make a new home in the debris and aspens on the west side of the river, but the aspens' shade did not provide the cool darkness of the mature white pine forest the animals were accustomed to. There was plenty of food around—more than could be found in the dark forest.

The new habitat also exposed small animals to more danger than they had faced in the past. Eagles, hawks, and owls could easily spot a mouse while soaring high above, leaving small creatures with little chance of escape. Animal habits changed, as did the whole food chain. It adapted. Action-reaction. Mother Nature.

Perhaps to Mother Nature, these humans were like any other animal, any other insect. They just affected the food chain in a different way. When these humans acted, a reaction took place.

Loggers crudely shifted their trails with the topography of the area. As curves around large stumps and mud holes straightened out, forest trails changed to rough and often muddy roads, following section borders where possible.

A winter with little snow, followed by spring months with no rain, began a drought year. By late July, water that normally flowed over the beaver rise at the tag alder swamp stopped running. Water puddled inside the swamp rather than flowing into the stream that emptied into the river. The stream from the marshy wetland stopped flowing to the Clam River in August, as did most other small feeder streams down the line. By September, not enough water flowed into the Clam River to float the logs it already contained.

The loggers seemed surprised and puzzled. They stood at the edge of the river with their hats in their hands, scratching their heads, pointing, chattering.

A few weeks later, a wagon larger than any that had come before rattled down the logging road, drawn by a team of six oxen. It crossed the bridge and wiggled into the forest. Loggers continued cutting large white pines and, with the help of other devices, lifted the logs to form a neat pyramid on the wagon's bed. The team of oxen strained, but they made it across the bridge, up the slope away from the river, and out of sight down the logging road.

These humans were so clever that Split Toe did not know what to think of it.

One wagon always waited with the loggers, one empty wagon traveled en route to the logging site from the mill, and one loaded wagon returned to the mill. Loggers unhitched the team from the empty wagon when it arrived and immediately re-hitched a team to the loaded waiting wagon. The devoted oxen seemed to work continuously. While empty and full wagons made their way down the forest roads, loggers filled the wagon that sat idle at the camp.

Fortunately, the mill on the Muskegon River—which seemed much closer by forest road than by winding stream—still had enough water flowing into the pond behind its small dam to operate the mill's waterwheel. Newly cut logs arrived by wagon to the mill, and logs that backed up in rivers along the way, including the Clam River, remained jammed in place.

Split Toe watched twigs and leaves flow slowly around the logs, but the river was now hard to understand. To cross it, Split Toe waited until the middle of the night and walked across the bridge while loggers were sleeping. Or he found a spot to step tentatively over one log, then another, until he slipped through the mess unnoticed. Each day, the loggers removed a few more of the centuries-old white pines.

Just like the water, the forest was disappearing. The land was being altered, perhaps forever.

What were these humans doing with the trees?

CHAPTER 12
PIONEERS

AD 1880

During that dry spring, a pioneering family moved in on the 160-acre parcel bordering the south side of the logging road to a point just east of the river. Their property included the peninsula, now aspen-covered. They purchased the land for one dollar and twenty-five cents per acre, which was more money than the family had. They settled a portion of the transaction in the form of a loan, which they intended to pay off bit by bit on an annual basis.

At the northeast corner was the surveyor's stake that Edra—the woman who came to the forest on the supply wagon—had found among the trees several years earlier. Twelve tall white pines formed a kind of property line along the common border of Edra's property and the parcel belonging to the pioneering family.

Young aspen and the stumps of ancient white pines covered the pioneer family's land. They cleared a small area near a trickle of a creek and used aspen trees they removed to construct a simple shelter and corral.

Occasionally, the pioneer man stopped the logging wagon as it rattled down the road that ran past their shelter. Split Toe watched the pioneer and the wagon driver talk. He could hear them laugh and see their arms wave in emphasis to help the conversation. One day, the logging wagon returned from a nearby settlement with a few boxes of supplies and a milk cow tied to the back. The driver left the cow in the pioneer family's corral.

Later, the logging wagon dropped off a crate holding four live chickens and a rooster. Finally, it left a large pig that became part of the farm.

Split Toe saw that the cow was closely related to the oxen working with the loggers. All these farm animals were new to Split Toe. It surprised him that they were so connected to the pioneer family. The pioneer family seemed to control the farm animals like the loggers controlled the oxen.

Using a single hoe and shovel, the man, Angus, worked up ground around pine stumps and planted food for the family's own use and for their animals. But the milk cow mostly wandered through the aspens, foraging for its own grass to eat. The cow also ate some of the debris as she foraged and added her own contribution to the new soil. The pig, well, that animal ate anything.

The first winter was particularly hard for Angus's family. They cut aspen for firewood while also clearing more land to expand the next year's planting. The firewood burned quickly but warmed their home. For now, their fireplace and chimney were built from wood packed in mud. Often, the chimney smoldered from the fires burning below.

"Next year, we need to replace this with a proper fieldstone fireplace and chimney," Split Toe heard Angus tell the woman. "I hope this wooden one lasts through this winter."

"I'll keep an eye on it," the woman replied. "We have water in the creek if we need to cool things down a bit."

Angus's wife, Grace, carried water—two wooden buckets at a time—from a small pool Angus dug in the creek bed. Until the winter freeze, each day a few buckets of water flowed into the pool. In the winter, Grace scooped snow from a nearby drift and melted it for their needs. During the first winter, Angus and Grace lived close to the land, much like the Ojibwe. Everything they did helped them survive for one more day.

The family had three young children, and another one always seemed to be on the way. They planted a cross made of two aspen branches on a rise not far from their shelter.

Split Toe watched as the family buried a child who had survived only a few days. He watched as they pushed the cross into the ground, then dropped to their knees to cry quietly. Angus placed his arm on Grace's shoulder as she bent over the grave with her face in her hands. He pulled her close when her body fell limp in grief. Angus and Grace seemed to support each other as they stumbled back to their shelter.

Split Toe thought these pioneers might be part of the natural world. They took no more than what they needed from the world around them—food, shelter, fuel—and they faced life and death respectfully, like a forest animal.

There was plenty of snow that winter, and torrential rains in the spring. Creeks and streams again filled with flowing water. Using hooked sticks, the loggers returned to work, breaking free the tightly packed logs that had lain stuck for more than one year in the Clam River. That spring, a particularly intense rain had swelled the river so high that many of the logs floated out of the river's normal boundaries and hung up on aspens now growing in the river flats. The bridge also floated from its perch and broke apart downstream where the river's swift current made a turn.

But Split Toe observed the unrelenting power of determination in these humans. Why did they do these things? How did it help them with their food, shelter, or fuel? *And what were they doing with the trees?*

When the flood subsided, loggers retrieved the pieces of flat bridge lumber and the large logs the original bridge was constructed from. This time, they devoted more effort to building the replacement. They supported the bridge higher off the river's surface and anchored the ends with long vertical logs planted deeply into the riverbank on each corner. Perhaps the improvements would work. Split Toe had to admit, these humans were persistent and clever.

Logging resumed.

The pioneer family's pig had a large litter, which the family knew was a blessing because they could butcher a pig or two before the year was done. Until now, Angus had ventured into the aspens with his muzzle-loading rifle to hunt for meat.

Snap-KABOOM.

Each time he brought home a deer, every part of the animal was put to use—every scrap of meat and hide. What the family could not use from inside the deer, the pigs happily ate. And when a pig was finally butchered, its hide was used much like the deer's hide.

Split Toe did not see whether the pioneer showed similar respect to the life of the deer he killed as the Ojibwe would have. But Split

Toe heard the shot and could still smell gunpowder in the air as he approached the spot. Split Toe watched as Angus dragged the doe through the aspens with one hand gripped on her front leg and the other hand managing the muzzle loading rifle. Her head dangled and caught on every ground level obstruction.

Later in the summer, when loggers still worked hard to sort out the logjam and continued to cut more white pines, the supply wagon stopped at the pioneer family's homestead to speak to Angus.

"We got so much loggin' goin' on back thar in the woods that we ain't got no time ta round up meat fer our ownselfs," Split Toe heard the logger tell Angus. "You got time ta make a trade? If you 'range the hams from two venison fer us, we'll give you one of the oxes. She's done pullin' the big logs, but she still got lota life in 'er."

Angus and Grace thought this trade was a blessing. A gift. The ox would make things around the homestead so much easier on Angus.

"Reckon so," Angus stretched out his arm and gripped the logger's big hand with his own bony hand. Both had a strong grip.

That evening, Angus stepped into the woods one more time.

Snap-KABOOM. A bit later, **Snap-KABOOM**, again.

Angus spent the rest of the evening pulling two dead deer back to his corral and neatly removing, then washing, all of the hindquarters. When the supply wagon drove by the next morning, it left one of the tired logging oxen with the pioneer family and took the deer meat back to camp in the wagon. Angus was happy with the ox and also had plenty of venison trimmings set aside for his family and the pigs. Life was good.

Split Toe wondered about this trade. Was it like the coyote who took down a fawn and left a scrap for the eagle? And then the eagle later left a scrap of a squirrel for the coyote? Split Toe would need to think about it.

Split Toe was always curious about humans. The Ojibwe. The loggers. The pioneers. But Split Toe was more curious about the loggers and pioneers than the Ojibwe. He felt he could better understand the Ojibwe, who lived closer to nature.

Split Toe did not know about things going on in the background with these humans. As pioneers settled sparsely throughout the land—planting homesteads on logging trails and in other spots they could reach—other humans converted the surveyed townships into counties and set up small villages.

Had Split Toe understood this step of civilization, he would have tried to fit it into his natural way of thinking, and would have had trouble doing so.

Where did Mother Nature's action-reaction mesh with this situation? He knew she always took these humans into consideration. But they seemed complicated. They were more organized than a pack of dire wolves.

Split Toe saw and tried to understand the pioneer cutting aspens on the edge of their homestead, like loggers cut the white pines. Angus used the ox he'd nursed back to strength to pull stumps he'd hoed around the previous summer. Where the pioneer worked up the ground, thick grassy wheat grew like marsh grass. Several rows of corn and mounds of potatoes sprouted from the ground. Green squash vines wrapped around tree stumps that the pioneer still needed to remove.

The pioneer worked hard and seemed to treat the soil with respect. Split Toe watched from afar as the pioneer toiled. He believed that if this pioneer was as determined as the loggers, it was likely to be many years before the land west of the river—the land that the pioneer chipped away at—became a mature, natural forest again … or any kind of forest for that matter.

Occasionally, Angus hitched a ride on the logging wagon. Where were they going? Late in September, when the loggers left a little extra room on the wagon, Angus added bags of potatoes he harvested. On the return trip, a young horse trotted along behind the wagon.

Angus set to work building a shelter for the farm animals. First, he constructed an open-ended shed big enough for the ox, the horse, and the milk cow. He sided it with aspen logs split lengthwise. Next to the large-animal shelter, he built a smaller open-ended structure with its own surrounding pen where the pig and piglets could wallow.

Angus dug a well deep into the ground. Split Toe watched as the pioneer followed a lightly held, thin, forked willow branch around the area close to the shelter. It was the first step … finding where to dig. Split Toe was curious.

"This should work," Angus said to Grace.

Grace smiled with cautious confidence that Angus knew how to do this task.

Angus held the branch with his fingertips, sensing a nearly imperceptible force as the stick dipped. Split Toe knew the spirit current pointed the stick toward the ground at the spot where the pioneer dug for water. The pioneer trusted what the spirit current told him. Perhaps some humans tuned in to the spirit pool and others did not.

Using a shovel, Angus dug the well. He made the hole just wide enough to lower himself in so he could fill buckets with earth from the well's floor.

"Hand me down another one, honey," Split Toe heard Angus call to Grace.

Grace lowered empty buckets and pulled them back up full.

"This is hard work," Grace, who was expecting a child, softly whispered.

She wiped her brow and sat when she could. After a week of digging, they brought up buckets of water rather than dirt. And the whole family—parents and children—gathered around the hole to bow in respect.

The chickens already lived in a simple coop. During the day, the chickens roamed free, but they were always easy pickings for coyotes and other wild animals roaming the area. The removal of the forest disrupted the natural hunting ranges and eating habits for many forest animals, who now often needed to find a meal in the debris-filled open area of the young aspen forest—all while avoiding predators themselves.

The family lost one chicken to a coyote before the first batch of chicks hatched from their hens' eggs. Now there were eight chickens that lived in the loosely built coop.

The pioneers' home looked pretty much the same as the chicken coop to Split Toe. It was a simple shelter meant to keep animals out and small children in. The log walls were loosely fitted. They kept out a good percentage of the rain and bugs. Like the chicken shelter, the floor was dirt. But Grace still swept it once a day with a broom that Angus made anew every few months from twigs and marsh grass. Blankets covering the shelter's windows—one in the front and one in the back—often remained open during daylight. The door on leather hinges looked like it could fall apart at any time, but the blanket hanging behind the door provided a second defense against the open air.

Angus and Grace lost another chicken one night to a mink who slipped under the side of the coop.

Angus did not wait for long before leaving again on the logging wagon. He came home with a dog. This was of particular interest to Split Toe. Angus worked with the dog for a few weeks until the dog stayed away from the chickens. But during the night, the dog confronted coyotes or minks or any other creatures that bothered the chickens. When Angus wanted the milk cow to come in from the aspens, he sent the dog out to retrieve the cow, and the dog did the job.

The dog desperately wanted to please Angus and his pioneer family. When Angus called for the dog, the dog would come, then sit patiently at Angus's feet, its tail wagging. If the dog was out further on the hill, Angus whistled, and the dog came running. What extraordinary devotion. They grew to love each other.

The dog knew about Split Toe. Its sense of smell was much better than that of the pioneers. The dog whiffed Split Toe's scent many times when out fetching the milk cow. When the dog detected Split Toe, he sniffed around on the ground to follow the trail for a short distance, then lifted his head and bellowed a bark or two.

There were times when Split Toe thought the dog might channel all its senses into a single sense like the spirits helped Split Toe to do. But the dog was not a wild thing. It seemed half human and was probably incapable of understanding the spirit world in the same way a wild animal naturally would. Split Toe wondered if the pioneer wanted that: an animal with two legs in the human world and two legs in the wilds.

CHAPTER 13
THE RAILROAD

AD 1885

On the east side of the river, when Split Toe stepped out of the tag alder swamp, he now stepped into the grove of young aspen. The humans had progressed well to the south and east, working their way along the river. They'd moved their shanty twice and constructed a new bridge farther downstream. They rarely drove their oxen or wagon along the original trails and roads they had first blazed through the forest.

It seemed a waste to Split Toe: a trail, a bridge, a straightened road, a human life, countless centuries-old trees. Split Toe still could hear the distant *whack, whack* on crisp mornings and the "Timber-r-r!" call followed by a final painful moan as another majestic white pine crashed to the ground.

"What are you learning about these humans?" Split Toe felt the spirits' voice on the wind.

"I am not sure," Split Toe replied honestly in his mind. "I still don't know what is important to them. Why they do what they do."

"Pay attention. It will take a long time to understand all of it."

Occasionally, Split Toe ventured to the logging site to see what he could learn. It was rarely anything redemptive.

During the summer, growing aspens fluttered in the breeze, revealing the silver underside of each leaf. At the forest floor, an understory of plush green ferns now covered the ground, creating its own canopy that hid smaller animals like opossums, skunks, weasels, and even a full-grown fox. Like the aspen grove, these ferns sprouted up as individual stalks from common roots spreading below the ground's surface. Each stem grew to about the height of Split Toe's belly and then branched out horizontally in a circular umbrella, creating a cool, shady world below.

Much went on below the canopy of this understory that Split Toe never saw. In fact, below these ferns was another understory which was visible early in the spring before the ferns grew up. A thick layer of maple, oak, and ash seedlings had sprouted, but they were no taller than his hooves. They mixed in with patches of white pine, hemlock, jack pine, and tamarack seedlings. How many of these new start-ups would survive? The ones that made it would spend their first few summers in the full shade of the fern canopy.

It could take five or six years before a seedling like this poked above the ferns. At that point, the stem would still be twig-thin. It only told its age through the number of annual whorls that popped out from the main stem like clusters of twig branches each year. Growth rings were simply too small to register. In the fall, after the ferns wilted, leafed seedlings changed color like full-grown trees and blended in with leaves falling from the aspens. Below the leaves was another level of activity where mice, moles, crawling insects, grubs, and worms roamed about: the forest's basement.

Other ferns grew in rich muck along the river bottoms—giant plants as tall as Split Toe's neck. Their long, palmy leaves sprouted vertically in a central circular cluster from a single ground-level base. These ferns grew so thickly together that most of the forest animals followed a single, well-formed path to get through them.

When the first railway came to the area around 1885, Split Toe did not know it had arrived. During his life, Split Toe might never see a railroad, for it passed by a long way from the tag alder swamp. But on crisp mornings, he heard the train's whistle and sensed its faint rumbles through the ground. The railway's arrival brought with it a migration of humans who descended on empty homestead parcels throughout the area. It was a slow process, with only a few families arriving at the start.

When Split Toe visited the sacred circle again, slipping past logging areas and swimming the Muskegon River between two groups of floating logs, he passed three separate settler holdings. Each claimed their 160 acres and began proving it up—five years of occupancy, during which they built a home, worked the land, and made improvements. Everyone built forest trails to reach their simple shelters. Some homesteads were in the old forest. Those pioneers took down enough white pines to let sunlight shine through the canopy so crops would grow between the remaining stumps.

Split Toe slipped unseen past the human activity. When returning from the sacred circle, his instinct guided him back through a dark pine forest. He had not walked through this part of the forest before. This route avoided humans for most of the journey home. Loggers steadily ate their way through the old white pines, taking down one tree after another, a good distance now from the tag alder swamp.

As he passed, Split Toe stopped to observe these loggers again for a while. He did not know if he would ever understand the loggers. They all seemed the same, only focused on removing trees. Watching them work, Split Toe was still not able to figure out what motivated their behavior.

Did loggers want the trees, or did they want to make the land treeless so other people could build small shelters and survive like the pioneer family? Split Toe sensed that the loggers did not care about pioneers or homesteading. What made them completely driven to remove a healthy forest so thoroughly at the expense of everything that lived within it—everything that depended on it? How could Mother Nature fix this?

Split Toe knew delicate dependencies linked all things, from the grandest tree to the smallest creature. But the loggers did not seem to make the connection or consider the importance of the forest to all living things. These humans were willing to take the trees and let everything else fend for itself.

Homesteaders tried to make something of what little was left.

Loggers were clever in everything they did. They knew about many things. Did they not know enough to understand that clear-cutting the forest was a bigger issue than just the trees? More was involved. Split Toe knew the spirit current would find a way to explain their behavior to him someday. He needed to be patient, to spend more time watching. Every day he wondered if he misjudged the loggers.

Split Toe remained well-concealed as he watched loggers chip away at a cavity in a tree's base, like beavers gnawing at a tree needed for their dam. Split Toe looked up into the canopy. He saw an eagle's nest hidden within its branches. It looked like a large platform that was much bigger than the pioneer's pig shelter and woven together from branches as thick as Split Toe's hoof. Dark eyes from a large white head peered from the nest's edge into Split Toe's eyes. Split Toe respectfully acknowledged the eagle with a nod of his antlers.

Whack, whack. Why did the eagle not fly from its nest? Even Split Toe felt the vibration of each strike from where he stood.

"Get ready," the logger called. "This one's gonna go."

If Split Toe could have shouted, he would have yelled, "But the eagle!"

Whack, whack. Finally, the tree bent over with its final moan. "Timber-r-r!"

The white pine accelerated in its fall. Not until it nearly crashed into the ground did the eagle finally soar silently to the canopy of a tree nearby, watching as a single newly hatched eaglet bounced from the nest. The eaglet hit the ground hard and briefly lifted its head before collapsing lifeless on the forest floor.

Split Toe wanted to scream, but it was the adult eagle who did so from its perch at the treetops. A long, anguish-filled screech of terror and agony. Split Toe and the eagle both felt the spirit current take away the eaglet's soul. Another raindrop. Split Toe dipped his antlers toward the eagle, who lowered her gaze.

The loggers did not notice the nest nor the eaglet that had been launched onto the ground. What kind of creatures were these humans? They were so unaware. Their ways, their action-reactions, seemed entirely separate from the action-reactions he knew Mother Nature used to keep things going. Split Toe did not understand how this could be, or how this would end.

CHAPTER 14
EDRA'S CABIN

AD 1885

The woman arrived one summer day on the seat of a buckboard drawn by a handsome, high-stepping horse. Another human rode beside her. They crossed the bridge and stopped their horse at the base of the sandy bluff overlooking the Clam River, the place where the last twelve white pines in the whole area stood—her rescued pines. Edra's long wool skirt dusted the forest floor as she walked.

She pointed to the pines when she spoke to the man. "Isn't it lovely, Jake! It's just as I imagined it would be."

Edra pointed toward the river, to a spot on the sand bluff where ferns grew thick among the aspen. The two spoke to each other kindly.

"This will do," Jake agreed.

Split Toe watched as the man drove four stakes into the ground, a little way back from the edge of the bluff.

The woman stood between the stakes with her hands on her hips. She could see the aspen-filled peninsula across the stream. When she gazed south down the tall dune, she saw sunlight sparkling off ripples of water where it flowed swiftly over a shallow stretch of gravelly bottom, though the steep drop of the bluff's edge blocked the view of the stream directly in front of her. She could see the twelfth white pine, the largest of them all—the grandfather pine—standing silently beside the rippling water at the bottom of the dune. Something about this spot felt right to the woman.

"It's the spirit current," Split Toe whispered.

Perhaps this human was connected. After all, she saved the lives of the twelve white pines. As she stood there, Split Toe thought he heard the trees thank her.

Did she hear it too?

Edra and Jake had both been in their teens, living in Chicago, when their mother died of consumption. Within a few months, their father, who worked for a prominent architectural firm, also succumbed to the illness. The parents left a modest inheritance to the children: their home in Chicago and enough cash to see them through a simple life.

Both children used part of the cash to complete a formal education. Edra attended Northwestern University Women's College and did modestly well in a program of General Studies. Jake pursued structural engineering.

When they completed school, they sold the family house and moved into small, rented flats. Edra used some of her cash to buy this section of land bordering the Clam River. She kept the remaining cash in reserve, to be doled out bit by bit for expenses as life went on. If her planning worked out—and if she lived simply—she could make it through life on the money their parents had left.

Edra looked at the forest floor near her feet. On a spot worn bare by animal traffic, she noticed a thin stone that had worked its way to the surface. She reached down and picked up the flint arrow tip. It must have been buried there for centuries. As she rolled it around in her hand, she felt a connection across time with the forest dweller who had made it using only the tools which the forest had to offer. What had happened to that culture? To the Ojibwe people who inhabited all of Michigan when the Europeans arrived? Edra held the flat side of the sharp stone to her heart and felt its warmth.

Edra knew that some Ojibwe had integrated into the European community. Others were pressed into places confined by a European view of land ownership imposed on them to make room for the European pioneers. Some kind of treaty. Relocation. Reservation. Many were pushed far away. What would they think of her living here now? What would they want her to do? Could she hope to care for the land in the same spirit they had?

Edra's arm dropped slowly to her side, and she quietly slipped the arrowhead into the pocket of her skirt. She would try.

On the aspen-covered hillside beyond the peninsula, Edra noticed movement of a black and white milk cow and a yellow dog encouraging it toward home.

"Look at the dog, Jake. I think it's moving that cow back toward home, and not a human close by." Edra voiced her amazement as she stepped next to Jake, who was already sitting on the buckboard with reins in his hands.

Split Toe watched the woman and the man turn their buckboard around and rattle back across the bridge. Later in the week, the same man arrived at the spot again, managing two horses that pulled a larger wagon piled high with an unusual gray kind of dirt and a supply of flat boards. He arrived with two helpers. Together, they set up a white canvas tent, cleared several aspen, and began to dig between the stakes. They piled sand beside the hole they were digging. After a few days, the hole was a bit deeper than the man was tall. Using the boards, they built wooden walls a short distance from the sand walls of the rectangular shaped hole. Then, using a trough that was on the wagon, they mixed buckets of water from the river, sand from the hole, and gray dirt from the wagon. Trough by trough they filled the space between the sand wall and the board wall using the mixture.

At night, the men cooked over a small campfire built in an ancient ring of stones discovered when scraping soil from the forest floor. They sang songs that carried peacefully on the breeze.

> "I've been working on the railroad,
> All the livelong day.
> I've been working on the railroad,
> Just to pass the time away ..."

It reminded Split Toe of nights at the Ojibwe village. He felt the Ojibwe's presence as he eavesdropped on the campfires from his secluded spot.

After three days of mixing, the men emptied the wagon of gray dirt. One of the helpers turned the wagon toward the bridge and scuttled down the road. Split Toe was not aware that with the new railroad, which was a day's wagon ride away, it was possible to order bulk concrete mixture delivered on the train to the station. This was a kind of human action-reaction that was separate from Mother Nature. With the concrete, Jake could install a basement in the forest using technology for concrete walls that was already in use in large cities like Detroit and Chicago.

Of course, Split Toe did not know about Detroit or Chicago, and he did not know what a basement was or how it would help with the human's food, shelter, or fuel. But when the men removed the wooden boards used to form the walls, Split Toe thought of the space on the forest floor below the leaves. *Humans are a clever lot*, he thought.

Within a month, after delivering several loads of flat lumber to the site, Jake and his helpers completed construction of a fine two-story shelter with two glass windows on each level facing the white pines, the river, and the peninsula. Split Toe had not seen anything like this in his life. It was not a large shelter, but it looked practical and well built. The boards fit together much more tightly than an eagle's nest.

Split Toe sensed that flat boards used to make the home were part tree. He could smell it. But they were also part human, like the machine with the large wheels. Split Toe sniffed again, trying harder to know more about these boards. But he could not smell where the tree had grown, or how it had floated down the Clam and Muskegon Rivers where it had stopped at a mill and was sawn into flat lumber. Had Split Toe been able to figure how all of these connected, he would have thought humans very clever indeed.

But all Split Toe could know was what his single sense told him. And that was the thin hint of a tree's spirit radiating from the boards, the spirit of the earth that was in the concrete, and the kind spirit of the woman who was behind it all. Somewhere, this human action-reaction must blend with the action-reaction that Mother Nature was also managing. Split Toe thought it was inevitable that the two would intersect, and he hoped that ultimately, the human action-reaction would not overpower that of Mother Nature.

The men were still cleaning up their project when Split Toe, sleeping in the tag alder thicket, felt the urge pulling again. Split Toe remembered the time he missed the call more than a decade earlier and did not want to fail the spirit current's summons ever again. He got to his feet and began to move along the ancient trail that traced the swamp. Split Toe felt an urgent need to run. He picked up his pace as the shadow began to take away the sun.

Angus felt the eclipse coming too. He sent the dog to fetch the milk cow, who had strayed over the hill and foraged clear down to the river. By the time the dog turned the cow toward home, the sun was half covered.

The dog noticed several humans working across the river and wanted to see if these were the same fellows who pulled up in their wagon to talk to Angus a few days earlier. He saw the humans stop their work to watch the sun disappear behind a shadow. As he trotted along the stream, crossing to the east bank, he picked up a new scent. Perhaps a raccoon or a river otter. He kept his nose to the ground, sniffing around the base of the grandfather tree.

Without warning, and with the sun nearly gone, Split Toe came sprinting around the south end of the bluff, his neck stretched and his massive antlers bouncing with each stride. He ran as hard as he could toward the shallow water overlooked by the grandfather pine at the base of the bluff. Without stopping to assess the stream, Split Toe smoothly vaulted over the water with a series of leaps; one from the nearest bank, another from the water, and a third near the far bank. A final leap landed him on dry ground.

The dog, still standing next to the grandfather pine sniffing the trail, did not think. Instinct drove the dog, and it told him a chase was on. He did not want to hurt the deer, but he loved to run, and he would run the legs off this deer. With a loud bellow, the dog plunged into the river and crossed just as the sun disappeared fully.

The men on top of the bluff watched in awe as this exceptional deer bolted across the river, with Angus's dog in hot pursuit. The men, surprised, walked quickly to the bluff's edge to watch the race through the aspens and across the peninsula. But both animals had disappeared. Only the far-off bellow of Angus's dog carried on the wind like a distant echo.

"Where did those animals disappear to?" Jake quietly asked himself.

CHAPTER 15
THE LAST WHITE PINE

AD 1911

Split Toe did not stop to look at the world around him. He knew he was being chased, and he knew he would have to run. He followed his instinct and ran like the wind across the open field toward a tree line half a mile to the south.

The dog paused briefly when it reached the opposite riverbank. He sensed where he was, but everything was different. It stopped him in his tracks. A smooth green field of alfalfa following the pleasant contour of the earth's rises and dips filled the peninsula in front of him. Not a stump remained, nor a single tree growing in the field. A man worked to smooth out a badger hole near the top of the far hill. The dog did not have time to consider this. His instinct was engaged. He needed to chase this deer. And chase he did. The dog flew through the alfalfa in large strides, his long feathery tail bouncing with each leap. The dog's tongue flopped out the side of his mouth as he ran, panting heavily.

The man stood and watched as the massive deer with its huge antlers raced from one end of the field to the other, a dog pressing the deer from behind. The old pioneer did not know what made him do it, but he whistled once, loudly. The dog threw up his head and saw the man watching. Without breaking its stride, the dog made a wide turn toward the hill. Angus put his hands on his knees while the dog raced to him. When the dog reached the man, panting heavily from the run, the dog sat quickly at Angus's feet, tail thumping the ground and ears back. Angus dropped to his knees, taking the dog's head in his hands. Looking directly into the dog's eyes, he rolled the dog's floppy ears through his fingers. Tears trickled down the man's cheeks. He picked up his shovel, turned toward the farmhouse, and Angus—now thirty years older—and the dog who had not aged a day, walked slowly across the rolling field of alfalfa. What would Grace say?

Split Toe watched from the tree line. When Angus and the dog started across the field, the dog glanced over his shoulder at Split Toe. Split Toe acknowledged with a nod of his mighty antlers, and the dog could not help but return a single happy yelp. Angus did not know what all this meant. He simply accepted the return of the dog as a blessing.

To the loggers and many of those who made up the logging industry, it seemed the supply of white pines covering Michigan was endless. But there came a day when the trees were all gone. Only a few of the old trees that were set aside, like the twelve trees along the Clam River, were left.

When loggers reached the sacred circle, they passed it by,

not out of reverence for the unusual earthworks—they did not even notice—but because the trees were not white pines. So, the sacred circle became like a seed amid a field of stumps. Plenty of growth-promoting sunshine soaked into the surrounding stump field, and the trees in this unusual spot expanded outward around the circle, filling the area with oak, maple, and beech. Mother Nature was looking after things. Every part of the wilds felt the influence of the spirit of the ancestors who built the sacred circle, the spirit of the earth that it consisted of, and the spirit of the trees that were sacrificed all around it.

The pioneer family felt fortunate: when they worked the field on the peninsula, they could see the twelve trees across the river, towering above anything else in the new forest that was growing on the river's east side.

Edra, who lived alone in the house on the bluff, felt lucky because she could see the remaining twelve old pines every day as she sat at her window or walked around her small home. She was glad she rescued these old-timers. They meant the world to her.

Edra was now slowing down, feeling a bit less mobile. She felt age gradually taking over her body. Perhaps it was time to move back to Chicago, close to her kin, where life did not take as much effort. But the daily activity in the forest made her feel alive. Every day she carried water from the river, fed her few chickens—the ones who survived existing so close to the forest food chain—and prepared food from jars that lined a shelf in her basement. She also looked for tree limbs that fell naturally to the ground. Edra cut them up for the fire in her cast iron stove, a stove which she used for heating and for cooking. A two-horse barn stood a few paces down the dune to the south of her house. She kept a handsome horse which she cared for in one stall and a buggy that she took to town from time to time in the other. The town was eight miles away by country road.

Edra often saw Split Toe, and he learned of her admiration for him. The spirits let him know of her affection—that he was safe around her. He deliberately let her see him occasionally. And he intentionally left plenty of signs indicating his presence.

Some mornings, Edra found Split Toe's distinctive print on the forest floor up close to her house, evidence that he had looked in on her from the cover of night. On cool autumn days, if Edra watched just before sunset, she saw Split Toe step out of a thicket on the far side of the peninsula and walk cautiously to the edge of the alfalfa field, bending his long neck and massive antlers to the ground while he nibbled on the sweet alfalfa. Edra noticed Split Toe's limp.

Even though the loggers were long gone, Split Toe realized his questions about them were still unanswered. He might never understand why loggers did what they did. He respected their determination and cleverness. But what did they do with all the trees? Split Toe couldn't help but compare them to industrious insects who ate through their entire food supply.

Something new was already beginning to take the place of what the loggers had taken away. Split Toe guessed that was what Mother Nature thought about. Action-reaction. Perhaps the spirit pool was showing Split Toe where Mother Nature's actions-reactions intersected with actions-reactions humans managed on their own. Split Toe still wondered if humans would overpower the system that Mother Nature kept going.

CHAPTER 16
THE FAMILY FARM

AD 1911

The pioneer family was no longer living precariously from day to day. They were now farmers. Ten years after beginning their first homestead, Angus and Grace expanded with a second 160-acres, land they bought cheap from a new family who had given up after being worn down by frontier life. A country road separated the original homestead from the new parcel. Angus and Grace built a new home across the road from their original simple shelter with the help of a neighbor who owned a start-up farm one mile to the north. They constructed the home using flat boards which the pioneer purchased from the mill.

One of Angus and Grace's children took over the original shelter, though it had been greatly improved by the time their child's family moved in.

Angus and Grace used rocks they'd collected from their fields to build a foundation, a stone fireplace, and a chimney for the new house. But the family relied mostly on a cast iron stove for heat and cooking. A tall barn stood close by and a corncrib stood next to the barn. The entire community, which now included about one family per square mile, helped to erect the barn.

Not far from the house and beside the new animal pen, a tall windmill pumped water continuously from a hole in the ground to fill a trough where farm animals could drink. The trough's overflow ran into a straight ditch that Angus dug with his shovel. The ditch led to the stream that trickled close to their original shelter. He dug several ditches of this sort to drain water from low spots in the fields.

One day, Split Toe heard Grace comment as she walked to the windmill with a small child in tow.

"This windmill is just fine, my dear," Grace smiled affectionately. Her face was putting on weight.

"I like it, Mummy. I can hear it while I sleep. I want to climb to the top."

"What would you do up there at the top of the windmill?" Grace looked down with a simple smile.

"Oh, Mummy. It would be fun. You know it would be fun. I'd talk to the dog from up there."

"Well, I don't know, my dear. I think you'd best keep your feet on the ground for now, and don't put any climbing ideas into that dog's head. He is likely to hurt himself if he follows you up the windmill."

Split Toe could see how the windmill helped Grace with gathering water—both for the home and the animals. Angus and Grace now had more young children, some who were about the same age as the children of their oldest daughter—their grandchildren—living across the country road in the original shelter.

Gray hair flowed in natural waves down to Grace's shoulders, and wrinkles lined the skin below her eyes. But a warm peach glow still colored her cheeks above a smile that befit her name.

When Angus lifted his straw hat, there was very little hair left on top. He, too, was happy for things in life that made the family's farming lifestyle easier. He remembered the days when he worked the ground by hand with a hoe. Things were different now.

It took Split Toe some time to review all these new things and to understand them. What clever creatures humans were.

For several weeks, Split Toe tried to count the animals that Angus's family cared for. He quietly crept up to the fence in the evening as the sun was dropping near the horizon and watched them amble about. Sometimes they looked up from the hay that Angus piled in the corral for them to eat, and Split Toe always dipped his antlers in acknowledgment.

In addition to two oxen and six horses that were kept for working the farm and transportation, the family had many more animals now than when they started: beef and milk cows, pigs, ducks, chickens, rabbits, dogs, cats, and a group of geese. One of the children also started a thriving beehive as a hobby.

The farmers seemed to bring a different animal out of the barn every day. For working the ground, Angus now attached a double-bottom cast iron plow to a team of two brown draft horses with cream-colored tails and manes. The plow was made with self-scouring steel moldboards. It peeled through the dirt in neat rows. Next, Angus pulled a row of discs across the plowed ground followed by a fine, rake-like implement. Angus was aware of tractors with gasoline- or steam-powered engines that covered ground more quickly than his horse, but that was not the kind of farmer he was. He preferred his horses.

As he tilled the ground into smooth fields, Angus picked up rocks that worked their way to the surface each year. Sometimes he joked that his main crop was rocks. He put in large sections of alfalfa, corn, and grass for the animals along with wheat, potatoes, and a full garden for the family. Angus and Grace had a relatively large operation going, with plenty of mouths to feed. Six adult children helped with the farm.

Three more crosses stood on the rise by the original shelter.

Angus's family left a wooded section unfarmed at the rear of the second parcel: the back forty acres. They allowed trees to grow there naturally, which they intended to thin out a bit every year to satisfy their own firewood needs.

Angus's family was in many ways self-sufficient, but they still needed to pay taxes, pay off the bank loan, and purchase a few things they could not make themselves. Split Toe watched, and in his own way, made sense of the human things unfolding before him. The family harvested what they needed to sustain themselves and their animals and brought their excess to town in a wagon, either to trade or to sell. What they sold brought in cash which enabled the family to make a payment on the land loan and to pay the taxes. When things were going well, they could also purchase a few items that were not made in the community, things they could not get with a barter transaction—like new canning jars, crocks, and milk cans. The scale of the whole system amazed Split Toe.

The farming family's operation worked well for Angus, Grace, and all their offspring. They traded goods, bought and sold goods, and frugally used nearly everything that was available to them. When scraps were left over from cooking or eating, they fed them to the pigs, right down to the eggshells. Burnable waste went into the woodstove or a fire behind the house. They carried other things such as broken jars, empty medicine bottles, and used-up grease cans to the back forty acres and left them in hidden spots between the trees.

Of course, people living in the village—people Angus's family depended on for village things—had village-size lots with nowhere to hide their trash. Angus saw no harm if they also left a few broken items between the trees on his back forty acres. There was plenty of room. In fact, Angus became so blind to the debris—his own and others'—that he did not notice it at all when he walked through his wooded section. He just stepped over it as if it was a natural part of the forest.

Even Edra had a hidden place where she dug a hole that she'd dropped a broken earthenware pot into, and later the parts of her first burned-out cast iron stove.

The Ojibwe, on the other hand, used little in life that did not easily decompose in the natural way. By the time the pioneers became real farmers, there was little trace left of the Ojibwe who once lived in the forest. Only the occasional stone arrowhead or axe. Angus's family felt lucky when they found such things.

CHAPTER 17
THE GATHERING

AD 1911

During the first thirty years that Angus and Grace had occupied their land, a simple dirt road was cut along the mile border of nearly every parcel in the county. In some spots, it was impossible to build the road because of the wetlands and rivers that dotted and crossed the land. The road simply stopped on one side of the obstruction and picked up again on the other, perhaps in the hope that someday a clever person would find a solution that would connect the two road ends.

The tag alder swamp was such a place. Roads stopped short of the swamp in both directions, unintentionally ensuring the swamp remained a wild spot where Split Toe could live.

County roads made it easy for humans to get from one parcel to another and for everyone in the community to reach settlements in any direction. These humans, though they lived in open farming spaces, seemed quite fond of gathering. They did it frequently. Children gathered at school. Everyone gathered at church. From time to time, the community gathered for a meeting to talk about how to make their community more efficient or more safe or more organized.

Split Toe remembered eavesdropping on one human gathering. Many people from the community came together at the homestead of Grace and Angus. Some came in horse-drawn buggies. Others walked. Split Toe thought their clothes showed a little more contrast than what he saw them wear in the fields. Simple but clean. Black and white.

A man from the community stood in front of the crowd, addressing them in a loud, clear voice.

"And God blessed them, and God said unto them. ..." The man paused and swept his arms in a wide arch, urging the crowd to listen closely.

Split Toe watched with interest as the crowd fell silent.

"Be fruitful and multiply, and replenish the earth, and subdue it; and have dominion over the fish of the sea and over the birds of the air and over every living thing that moveth upon the earth."

The man paused again and continued in a confident voice that enthralled the group.

Split Toe could see Edra standing near the rear of the crowd. Her face was stern.

"And God said, Behold, I have given you every herb bearing seed, which is upon the face of the earth, and every tree, in which is the fruit of a tree yielding seed; to you it shall be for meat. And to every beast of the earth, and to every fowl of the air, and to everything that creepeth upon the earth, wherein there is life, I have given every green herb for meat: and it was so."

The man lowered his voice. "And God saw everything that he

had made, and behold, it was very good. And the evening and the morning were the sixth day."

The man bowed his head reverently as he concluded in a soft voice. "Thus, sayeth the Lord. Genesis 1:28 through 31."

The people standing in the yard, most with hands clasped respectfully in front of them, all murmured, "Amen." All except Edra.

Split Toe did not know what to make of this. Replenish the earth. Have dominion. Subdue it. How did that work with the balance Mother Nature governed in the world? Split Toe did not know what "God" was, and did not understand why these words inspired so much passion in the man and the people. Split Toe thought the man spoke with a voice that was eloquent. Almost poetic. Like snowflakes falling on the smooth surface of a beaver pond. Most of the humans seemed captivated by the speech.

Split Toe thought back to what the Ojibwe said about Mother Nature and the natural spirits at their sacred fires. "Action-reaction," he remembered. Split Toe was puzzled wondering about how the man's words fit in with what he heard from the Ojibwe. He continued to mull this over while the humans mingled like a group of deer foraging in a clearing.

By the time the speaker finished, Edra had fire in her eyes. She was not buying it. Everyone else in the gathering seemed inspired by the message. Edra was not, and she felt no need to fit in with the crowd. After living for so long with the forest, she questioned words like "replenish" and "have dominion." She was familiar with the passage. In college, she had discussed the passage in class with her instructor, defending her point of view. Then, it was an academic debate. Now, it was personal—and she'd never felt more certain of her position.

Split Toe looked at Edra. He could tell she was upset—this side of her was something he rarely saw.

Edra remained silent, standing alone while the others moved about carrying on social conversations. Split Toe saw her tapping her finger on her leg. A nervous twitch. No one else seemed to notice. Split Toe sensed that each tap was ratcheting up the frustration building within her. Just a tiny bit with each tap. A silent crescendo rising toward an explosion.

Split Toe was sure he heard Edra mutter, "Rubbish."

A few seconds later, he watched her make a beeline for the speaker, weaving through the crowd of people with a look of determination on her face.

"Pastor," she said as she faced him, standing as tall as she could on her tiptoes, her arms straight down with fists clenched and one finger still tapping her leg, "You know that passage is rubbish."

Edra was mad.

"Have dominion! Well, that's a notion. Giving that responsibility to the human race is akin to handing a slab of red meat to a pack of hungry wolves and asking them to care for it until you get back. It may sound possible in the book and in Sunday School, but what do you think will happen when humans believe that they can decide for every other creature? Every other living thing? You know human nature and what humans are capable of. They can barely look after themselves without one kind of a fight or another.

"Replenish! Really, pastor?" Edra sighed, the fire in her eyes beginning to cool. "You mean like fill the earth full-up with humans?" Edra was no longer tapping her leg.

The pastor did not expect this kind of confrontation at a community gathering. Particularly from Edra, who was ordinarily quite congenial. She did not look like she was ready to back down. The pastor had never thought of the passage from Edra's point of view. He was neither prepared nor equipped to handle her assault.

"Now, Edra, you can't just go on questionin' the intentions of God." The pastor was building up to say a bit more, thinking of what to say. "Why, His word is …" but Edra had already turned around calmly the moment he'd argued "Now Edra," and was making her way to her buggy, weaving quickly through the crowd without so much as a "Hello" or a smile. Several people watched in shock as she zipped by.

"Now what's gotten into her?" the pastor muttered as he watched Edra tromp away.

Split Toe thought the speaker—the pastor—seemed to be a good human, as far as humans went. The words he spoke sounded lyrical, like a finch singing on a branch in the morning. But what was one to make of it? Replenish the earth. Have dominion over it. Split Toe did not know what to think.

The crowd spontaneously erupted into a chorus of *Amazing Grace*. Split Toe wandered off, the haunting melody fading into the background as he headed back to the tag alder thicket.

CHAPTER 18
EDRA'S FOREST WORLD

AD 1911

A few days later, while Split Toe stood between two rows of corn not far from Grace and Angus's corral, he heard the *putt-putting* sound of a motorcar coming down the road for the first time. It was still a long distance away. Soon, he noticed that the family had all stopped what they were doing to run to the roadside where they could get a close look as it passed.

The car belonged to Jake, Edra's brother. He'd driven the new network of country roads all the way from Chicago. The trip took a full week. Angus's family members elbowed each other, vying for the closest viewing spot as the motorcar approached. But the closer the eighteen-miles-per-hour machine got, the more its high speed scared them. Finally, when the vehicle was about one hundred yards away, the whole family scattered to a safer distance where the high-speed driving machine could not run them over.

The motorcar followed the road between the original shelter on the east side and the new house with the barn on the west side of the road. The driver tooted a horn at the family as he passed and waved his arm over the windshield. The motorcar soon reached the intersection with the trail road that went east down to the wooden bridge over the Clam River, and up to Edra's home on the sand bluff. Split Toe tried hard to understand this machine and the human who seemed to be guiding it.

These humans … was there no limit to their cleverness?

Edra had waited patiently for several days, not knowing exactly when her brother would arrive. She thought back to when he poured concrete for her basement walls and built the house that she had lived in for thirty years now. For her, it was an idyllic life. But she deeply missed Jake. When she heard the motorcar *putt-putting* over the wooden bridge, she stood up, flattened her wool skirt against her legs, and tucked a few stray strands of gray hair behind her ears.

An aunt and cousin whom Edra had known since childhood were still living in Chicago. They had lost track of her a few years after she moved to the forest. They eventually gave up on her. Edra knew they wondered about her sanity.

She could still hear her aunt saying, "Edra, that is a crazy idea. Give it up. You have a place here. And there are plenty of men in Chicago. Good catches."

"Oh, yes, Barney Mathews is quite a looker," her cousin chimed in. Edra remembered the conversation fading into nothingness as the cousin rambled on.

Edra simply had no interest in city life. They would never understand the beauty of forest living.

Edra did not return to Chicago. Not even for a visit. But she still felt a deep kinship with Jake, who understood what the forest gave to her. He did not judge her for the life of solitude she preferred.

Jake was always there if Edra needed him. But she rarely did.

When Edra purchased the eighty acres, it was half the normal size of parcels typically offered. The General Land Office of the United States Government agreed to sell Edra the reduced parcel because much of her claim was a vast, virtually inaccessible tag alder swamp. No one else wanted it. The tag alder swamp was an exceedingly difficult piece of land. In fact, county roads stopped in both directions when they reached her claim. It was unclear whether the surveyors had ever placed a corner stake deep in the swamp or if they simply indicated that it was "so many feet due east from a known marker and so many feet due north of a known marker."

Edra knew she would not need more than the Land Office agreed to sell her. She was pleased with the simple beauty of the parcel she selected. The river. The old-growth pines. The sand bluff. A place that began where the roads literally ended. She fell in love with the smell of the pines on her first visit, and even now, breathing in the aroma gave her joy. It did not bother her that the loggers removed all but twelve of the old-growth trees from her parcel. She would rather they hadn't, but she knew it was the way of things. She just felt lucky to have the twelve trees that she had saved.

Edra talked to the old trees every day. Living alone in the forest, a person finds themselves talking to trees. They always seemed to encourage her.

"How are we going to get along when the cold weather comes, old timer?"

She spoke as much to hear her own human voice as to communicate with the large white pine in front of her home.

"We'll all do just fine," she could hear the tree reply. And she patted the tree on its bark. It gave her comfort.

The Land Office required her to prove up her piece of land, and she did so with a garden near the house, though she was not really serious about the garden.

"Am I doing this right?" she asked the old trees.

"Just put it in the ground, add a little water, and let Mother Nature do the rest," she seemed to hear in reply. And she patted each old tree on the bark as she walked to the stream with an empty bucket.

She was excited to see what new forest growth Mother Nature brought to her parcel. She knew the new forest would come—she just didn't know what it would be like. What kinds of trees would take root? Edra was determined that it all take place naturally. Action-reaction. Loggers had removed the mature white pines from the forest. What would come next? She hoped she would live long enough to watch the process take hold.

Now, thirty years after coming to the forest, she looked at aspen trees growing straight and tall where white pines had once stood. It was the first round of regrowth. Cedar also grew in clumps along the river flats. Edra watched closely and concluded that aspens were a temporary tree in this climate. They were beautiful trees, but they were not hearty. Good trees, but there were better. Aspens grew fast and rotted quickly. Their thin bark made them a favorite tree for insects and later made them a favorite feeding opportunity for a batch of woodpeckers that fluttered around the area.

The trees grew close together. Occasionally, a particularly fierce storm chose this group of tall aspens to batter about. The first tree dropped into the arms of its neighboring tree, which in turn bent for support from its neighbor. Standing alone with shallow root structures, the wind would easily have ripped each tree from its moorings. But the community of trees saved most of its individuals and the group. The ones that fell enriched the soil for others in the community.

Cedar clumps near the river carried on, but oak, maple, birch, and beech—trees with a longer-term track record—gradually replaced the aspens. The hardwood trees had deeper roots to help them withstand wind, they had stronger branches with more capacity for ice and snow, and they seemed more difficult for insects to burrow into. Now, the hardwoods were about twenty years old and looking more like trees than saplings. What Edra wanted would take time. A lot of time. She knew that and was prepared to let it happen. She wanted to let the forest on her eighty acres restore itself in the natural way without further human interruption. It was an experiment for her—one that she was passionate about. She knew that even if the experiment worked, she would never live long enough to see the results.

"What do you think about this plan?" she asked one of the old trees.

"*It is a noble thing you do,*" she heard the voice of the tree on the wind. "*You are one of us.*"

The woman patted the tree on its bark, feeling a kinship.

At first, this forest lifestyle was a hobby for Edra. But it grew on her, and after several years of forest life, her curiosity only expanded and her passion for the forest took over every aspect of her life. She was inseparable from this new, living world.

As the forest changed, Edra noticed animal behaviors changing as well. Deer were plentiful and following their old trails. Birds of all types that had left the area when loggers took the forest were returning. An eagle now nested in one of the nearby tall pines, observing the river and periodically swooping down to grab a fish. Curious owls visited, perching on the branches of new oaks and maples. Most often they were barred owls, but great horned owls and the occasional snowy owl appeared from time to time. The owls glided from high branches to eye-level landings where they seemed to look directly into Edra's eyes. She stared back and then watched the owl spin its head without moving its shoulders. Edra often wished she could twist like that. Songbirds danced around the tree branches, calling to each other, building nests, and heralding each day with a symphony.

Occasionally, Edra saw a flock of turkeys forage on the ground before flying up to the canopy branches of the grandfather pine, where they roosted all night. At daybreak, she watched them glide down from their roosts, crashing through aspen branches and other trees to land with a thud at an open spot on the forest floor.

It was never a soft landing. Edra wondered how such a big bird could control its flight. To her, it seemed like putting wings on a large sack of flour. When the flock all crashed to the ground, they began their morning debate, chattering back and forth until the lead turkey decided the conversation was over, and the forest once again fell silent to their clamor.

A pileated woodpecker created a large hole in a mature aspen. It was not long before a wood duck hen assumed residence in the hole. Her colorful mate often sat on the limb of a tree nearby. When the hen flew from her nest in the tree, her mate followed, and together they made a low sortie along the river, landing at one of its dark pools.

Each spring, Edra noticed a large snapping turtle climbing the cliff side of the sand bluff which faced the river. The turtle dug a hole in the sand and laid its eggs, each with a soft white shell, then covered the hole with a layer of sand. Perhaps doing so protected the eggs from creatures like mink and opossum.

Edra knew this turtle was very old in human terms, born nearly a century before the logging began. She wondered what stories the turtle might tell if they learned to understand each other. But for now, the turtle stayed silent, and Edra simply watched whenever she saw it. She sensed wisdom in this creature. In the summer, Edra found the empty remains of the soft shells and a trail in the sand where newly born turtles had dug their way out of the nest and instinctively made their way to the river.

Edra's curiosity kept her constantly observant. One day, as she stepped through the door of her home, she saw a blue racer snake slip behind the stone step at her entry.

"What are you doing here?" she wondered aloud, pondering how this creature fit into the forest ecosystem.

Later, when she found it slithering across the floor of her kitchen,

Edra wisped the snake back into the grass with her broom. Had these forest inhabitants accepted her as another one of them?

Occasionally, Grace came by Edra's home with one or two children on the buckboard. One child often carried a loaf of warm bread to Edra, the other perhaps a cured ham. Edra gave each child a hug and a cookie from the jar on her windowsill before the children disappeared into the woods to play while Grace and Edra enjoyed a bit of human conversation. They both seemed hungry for the human connection.

"We ended up with a little extra," Grace said, referring to the loaf of bread and the ham.

But Edra knew it was not true. She knew that everything Grace brought was a sacrifice from what Grace's own family might need. Edra was truly grateful.

"You are such a good neighbor," Edra replied. "What would I do without you so close by?"

Grace always worried a bit about Edra, alone in the forest.

"How are things around the farm?" Edra asked.

"The new house is so much better for us. We're getting along just fine. You must come to see the new calf."

"Let me bring you by a basket of berries next week." Edra was happy she could offer something from the forest in return.

"That would be lovely, my dear," Grace said, genuine in her gratitude. The children were climbing back into the buckboard. They always politely called her the "Forest Woman."

"Goodbye, Forest Woman," they waved as the buckboard rattled down the old road and over the wooden bridge.

Edra waved fondly in return.

From time to time throughout the summer, Edra saw a black bear. She suspected the bear and her two cubs lived in the tag alder swamp. It was a good place for a bear—and for Split Toe. The large bear and her cubs wandered into the open to eat raspberries that seemed to be popping up everywhere.

Thick patches of raspberries and blackberries took hold amongst the ferns. Edra picked raspberries in July and blackberries in August, making several jars of jam that she stored in her basement. Occasionally, Angus or Grace brought her a slab of alder-smoked bacon in exchange for two large jars of raspberry jam.

Edra also found the small, shiny leaves of wintergreen growing close to the ground in thick patches around her house. She chopped the leaves, boiled them for thirty minutes in river water, and drank the soothing tea at breakfast or in the evening when she had a fire burning and a candle or kerosene lamp lit.

"I am so grateful for these gifts," Edra whispered to no one in particular, her gaze searching the open air.

"We see your thankfulness," the wind whispered back. *"Enjoy the bounty of the forest. It is there for you."*

The forest gave much to Edra. Though Grace worried about her, Edra never felt truly lonely.

From his concealed spots, Split Toe watched the woman as she foraged for the many kinds of mushrooms and fungi, each popping up at a different point in the season. From spring until fall she could always add a tasty mushroom to her evening meal.

Blueberries grew in a thick patch near the marshy wetlands. She gathered them when they were in season. While returning home, she often picked a new bouquet of wildflowers for the vase sitting on her kitchen table. She added a turkey feather or two when she found them along the trail.

Edra often harvested a small section of sassafras root to add variety to her tea habit. But she struggled with a dilemma when harvesting the root, not wanting to injure or destroy the tree.

"I mean you no harm," Edra respectfully thanked the tree for the root she harvested, as the Ojibwe would have. And she made good use of what she took.

One February, after a few maple trees added enough girth, Edra thought it might be possible to tap the largest maple tree and collect its sap. Using the brace and auger her brother had left in the basement, she carefully drilled an upward-angled hole at waist height, two inches deep into the south side of the tree. She whittled a small but sturdy stick into the shape of a miniature trough and hammered it into the hole using the back of her hatchet. During the last week of February, a clear liquid began to drip into the bucket she placed on the snow below the trough.

Edra, who kept a fire going day and night in her cast iron stove, poured the liquid into a pan and simply left it on the back of the hot stove's cooking surface as she continued with everything else in her life. She let the liquid boil and evaporate, adding each day's new sap that had dripped into the bucket during the night. As the sap boiled down, it concentrated into a delicately exquisite syrup. When she sat down for tea in the evening, she always scooped a spoonful of the syrup into her cup.

"This is a true wilderness treasure," she would say aloud.

And from somewhere, she imagined a voice on the wind replying, *"It surely is. Enjoy the treat we gladly offer."*

Late in March, when the maple tree began to bud and the sap stopped flowing, Edra finally boiled the syrup down into a thick consistency. She poured most of it into a canning jar and placed it on a shelf in her basement, where she could take a scoop from time to time throughout the year. She reduced the remaining syrup further until it formed coarse crystals on the bottom of the iron pan. She scraped the crystals together, compressed them into small maple sugar cakes, and stored them in the basement.

And during every step of the process, she thanked the maple tree that brought her the sap.

CHAPTER 19
JAKE'S VISIT

AD 1911

Edra loved it when Jake visited, and he loved visiting too—especially for the delicious tea she brewed. He kept a small apartment in Chicago where he worked as an engineer for a bridge-building firm. His office was in the city, but he often found himself on the western frontier, working with a railroad to support track through a canyon or over a river. Edra knew Jake was not impressed with the loggers' bridge over the Clam River, though he said it was "not bad for rural conditions."

Jake did not visit often, but he frequently wrote letters. Three or four years might pass between Jake's trips to see his sister, who lived where the roads ended. In the past, he took a train to the nearby village where he rented a buckboard and horse. He always arrived with a load of supplies he knew his sister could use.

This time was different. Instead of a horse, he drove a nearly new Model T Ford Runabout. He paid nine hundred dollars for the motorcar in 1911, more than nine times what Edra paid for her eighty beautiful acres when she took up life in the forest. Five years later, in 1916, a Model T with the same features cost only three hundred and forty-five dollars, a testament to Henry Ford's determination for mass production … and his clever way of doing things.

Ruts and mud holes covered the roads that Jake traveled from Chicago. They were single-lane pathways used by ox carts, horse-drawn buggies, people and animals walking, the occasional bicycle, and a motorcar or two. The journey was a constant process of lining up behind slow-moving buggies, pulling to a clear spot alongside the road to let others get by, and often backing up to find a clear spot where the bypass could take place. It was a slow-moving shuffle of leapfrog.

But on the road, most people gave way to the motorcar and stared wide-eyed as it overtook them. While the car was theoretically capable of going forty miles per hour under perfect driving conditions, Jake's car never reached those speeds, and he doubted he would try it even if the conditions *were* perfect. Twenty miles per hour felt like flying. Not a day went by without him repairing a tire puncture. It was part of the routine. People who drove these motorcars accepted it.

"I just love seeing this countryside," Jake often proclaimed out loud as he drove by fields and forests.

Jake was curious about what he saw. Farmhouses no longer resembled pioneer outposts: now they were constructed using milled lumber produced from white pines taken from Michigan's forests. Some of the homes were made of stones gathered from the farmer's fields. Barns were substantial and also sided with milled lumber. Shingles for the roofs were produced at sawmills on Michigan's rivers.

Had Split Toe been able to connect the dots, he would understand where all the trees went. He would see that humans used them to build structures and other things across a continent filling with people. But who could really explain such things to a deer?

Jake noticed that the farms had grown larger and now required more mechanized equipment than they had in years past. It interested him. With more mouths to feed, more land was required. Bigger fields. More hay to store. More animals or equipment to work the land. Bigger barns. And, of course, more debris discarded between trees on the back forty acres of every farm. So turned the human world. Action-reaction.

Hopeful people planted a farm of some sort at almost every mile along the road. Humans migrated to this new range as any wild animal would also have done, enticed by the conditions—natural and human. Where a great forest of white pine once stood, the migrants saw a place to survive and grow. A place to build a nest. One hundred sixty acres of their own to make something of themselves.

All the forces of human nature brought them to Michigan: social, economic, psychological, and biological, combined with the natural conditions of livable climate, plenty of water, and rich, tillable soil. Some of the folks were simply escaping another life, and they found an opportunity for a new start here. They imagined freedom, independence, wealth, and perhaps a brighter future for generations of grandchildren and great-grandchildren.

It was obvious which farms were *simply getting by,* and which ones were thriving. Mother Nature had a lot to do with the results. Humans needed her cooperation to succeed.

Jake paused, his mind racing. He tried to look at the world objectively. Perhaps his feeling that humans needed Mother Nature's cooperation was merely humanity's way of looking at the world.

"Hmm ... A human needs the cooperation of Mother Nature?" Something about it did not seem right to Jake. "What a strange way of looking at the world."

Were humans really arrogant enough to believe such a thing? That they were on par with Mother Nature? That they fail when Mother Nature falls out of line? A year without rain or a year with too much rain could prove so disastrous that a farm never recovered financially. Just one bad season could light the fuse of failure. Jake was sure that Mother Nature did not give a whit about finances. Mother Nature. Humans. Who was in charge?

Jake had loaded the Model T with supplies. Though Edra always suspected Jake would bring both useful items and some small pleasures, she never took his generosity for granted. She was always overjoyed to receive his gifts. This time, he brought a bit of wool and cotton cloth from a store in Chicago, along with thread, buttons, hooks, skeins of colorful yarn, and a fur-lined pair of soft leather gloves. He brought large sacks of flour, sugar, cornmeal, oatmeal, salt, and dried beans, along with smaller supplies of coffee, molasses, and cornstarch. He also brought candles, cakes of soap, a can of kerosene, a new length of rope, wooden buckets, several canning jars, a bag of apples, garden seeds, a jar of quinine pills, and a handful of books. It made Jake happy to see his sister's reaction as she went through the things, because he knew all his gifts would be used.

"You really shouldn't have, Jake. Oh, this is just fine," she said as she admired each item, turning it over in her hands.

Edra stored most of these things in the basement, doling them out in small portions to make the supply last. Except for items from Chicago, Jake picked up the supplies in the small village not far from Edra's home. They were things Edra could have picked up herself by taking her buggy into town, but it was a blessing to receive these things as a gift. And to be honest, her cookie jar did not hold enough money to purchase so many items at one time.

Jake knew this and always hid a bit of cash somewhere in the house that Edra was sure to find after he left. It was always just enough to cover her property tax bills and a few other small things until he could visit again.

"Thank you. Thank you. Thank you, Jake," she whispered with deep sincerity.

Some considered Edra poor, and by many standards, she was. But in her own mind, she possessed a kind of natural wealth that money could never buy. Her brother knew this. She loved him—and loved his visits—even without the gifts.

"You are welcome," Jake responded. "Think of me when you use them."

And she always did.

Jake stayed for three weeks. During the first few days, he took his sister for a country drive in his motorcar and made small improvements around the house. He even crawled below the bridge to inspect its support structure.

"Someday, this bridge will need to be upgraded to steel," Jake thought aloud. But for now, the simple construction would do.

Jake worked in the garden. It took him four days to shed the responsibilities of his career and the habits of his busy city lifestyle. On the fifth day, the layers of civilization had fallen away, and he reached the bedrock of his soul. He surrendered himself to the power of the natural world. He relaxed.

Each evening, brother and sister watched the sunset over the peninsula, every sunset a unique work of art painted by Mother Nature. In the morning, Jake was never sure whether it was the light pouring through the window that woke him, or the chorus of crows calling from treetop to treetop—a chorus eventually joined by an ensemble of songbirds that fluttered through tree branches near the house.

Jake sensed that his sister was part of the forest like the other forest inhabitants. She had been accepted by the animals and the trees. He knew it was what she had wanted from the beginning. Her main goal in life now was to protect the eighty acres she was responsible for. Her love for the land shone on her face every day, giving her a natural beauty that reflected the very land she cherished.

It was not until Split Toe stepped from the edge of the thicket one day and looked directly into Jake's eyes that the brother finally felt accepted as a fellow inhabitant of the forest. Jake stood in place, returning the creature's gaze. He remembered seeing a similar deer with a massive body and enormous antlers disappear across the river many years ago while he was building Edra's shelter. But never in life had he been so close to a deer as he was now.

When Split Toe dipped his antlers, Jake knew in his heart that he was being accepted into this natural world. Nothing was said. He simply sensed it. Perhaps it was the spirit current that told him so.

Without speaking out loud, Jake thought, *Thank you, my friend.* And he knew Split Toe understood.

CHAPTER 20
THE SPANISH FLU PANDEMIC

AD 1918

Edra rode to the village in her horse-drawn buggy for a special event. Split Toe watched her go. He remembered seeing it was a happy day in the community, and noticed Edra's excitement. Several of the community's boys had arrived back home from the war in Europe, the war they called the Great War. A crowd met the fellows at the train station. To families in the community, they were all heroes.

"My, aren't you the handsome one in this uniform." Edra quickly stepped up to Angus and Grace's son.

She tugged at the sleeve before giving him a genuine hug and a kiss on the cheek. "Where's the little boy I once knew?"

The soldier smiled back. "Thank you, Edra. You ain't changed a speck. I need one of your cookies."

Edra smiled, "And what's this limp you've picked up? You are beginning to remind me of Ol' Split Toe."

Most of the retuning soldiers wore uniforms. For many, it was all they owned. The whole community welcomed the soldiers back with both happiness and sorrow. Hugs and kisses for all.

Edra returned to her place in the forest with a box of candles and a can of kerosene. She traveled to town so infrequently that she couldn't ignore the opportunity to fetch some supplies.

Around two days after Edra returned, she began to feel a slight cough in her lungs and a growing fever. A rash developed on her chest at about the same time, which she believed was a result of the fever. Her forest lifestyle required constant work, but Edra could tell she needed to take it easy for a few days.

Split Toe quickly sensed something was wrong. The house was quiet, and no smoke came from the chimney. He slipped up to the house and looked into the front window. The woman was resting. She did not look well. She looked pale and frail. Weak.

Through the haze of her illness, movement at the window caught her fading attention. She turned her head slowly; it was all she could manage. She had little strength. The fact was that she could not breathe. Every gasp was hard work. What began with short quick breaths was now shorter and more shallow. She could not fill her lungs with oxygen. She felt fluid invading them. Each breath was small, with minimal benefit. She listened to her lungs rattle as she breathed. At first, the muscles in her back and sides hurt each time she drew in. It was difficult and she was trying hard. Each breath was work. Now all the muscles surrounding her torso hurt continuously. Her lungs felt heavy. They were weighing her down.

Edra was weak, but she looked through the window into Split Toe's eyes as if to say, "It's okay, my dear friend." And she thought to herself, "I don't know how long I can manage this."

Edra pulled a book off her shelf. She remembered it was the

volume Jake secretly left an envelope in containing a bit of cash. It was the second of six volumes from a set: *The Home Medical Library*, written by a doctor, Kenelm Winslow. But the book was written in 1911 and had no specific remedy for the Spanish Flu, the 1918–1919 pandemic that infected one-third of the earth's population and took at least fifty million lives worldwide.

Edra found the general section on Influenza and tried to follow its guidance. It said, "The feeble and aged are those who are apt to succumb." Edra thought back to the beginning of her life in the forest. In 1878, when she saved the majestic white pines, she had been 26 years old. She must be 66 years old now. She could not remember clearly—time did not seem the same in the forest as it did in the city.

"Fatalities usually result from complications or sequels, such as pneumonia or tuberculosis: neurasthenia or insanity may follow." She looked for the treatment. "The medicinal treatment consists at first of combating the toxin of the disease and assuaging pain, and later in promoting strength. Hot lemonade and whisky may be given during the chilly period and a single six- to ten-grain dose of quinine."

Quinine. She thought there might be a bottle of quinine in the basement, among the supplies Jake brought when he visited with his motorcar.

"Pain is combated by phenacetin; three grains repeated every three hours till relieved."

Pain was not her problem—she could deal with the pain. She just could not breathe. And she certainly did not have these medicines sitting around her house.

She drew in a rattling breath. She felt exhausted reading such things.

"At night a most useful medicine to afford comfort when pain and sleeplessness are troublesome, is Dover's Powder, ten grains (or codeine, one grain), with thirty grains of sodium bromide dissolved in water."

It was not that she was sleepless—her body wanted to sleep and to not wake up.

"After the first day it is usually advisable to give a two-grain quinine pill together with a tablet containing one-thirtieth of a grain of strychnine three times a day after meals for a week or two as a tonic (adult). ..."

Oh, Edra felt at a loss. She knew the fuse was lit.

These books were useful to her for other things, but in this case, the advice was not of much help for a weak person living alone in the forest. She had no safety net. No one to help her. And she simply could not do much to help herself. She was not even strong enough to fetch water from the river. How could she think of preparing a meal?

Edra struggled to move from her bed. She crawled to the stairs leading to the basement and lowered herself one step at a time, resting on each step before moving down to the next. When she was three quarters of the way down, she leaned toward the wall to reach the bottle of quinine. Feeling she might fall, she waited. Gasped a breath. Tried again. This time Edra managed to catch the neck of the bottle. She drew it to her, gathered her strength, and then planted a foot firmly on a stair and pushed up to sit on the next step. Another rest. One step at a time to the top. By the time she finally lay on the floor with her legs still hanging down the stairs, Edra blacked out. She could not remember how she managed to get back into her bed.

In a moment of wakefulness, she took the quinine and slept, drifting between deep, healing rest and restless spells of half-awareness, slipping in and out of consciousness. Each time she opened her eyes it was more difficult for her to breathe. In one of her more lucid moments, she realized she was running a high fever—perhaps even hallucinating—and could no longer tell the difference between dreams and reality. She drifted in and out of consciousness until she finally fell into a deep sleep. She dreamed that Ol' Split Toe was staring in the window.

"Was the sunrise orange this morning, my dear friend?" she asked in her dream, "With thin lines of pink and red? What about the turtle on the riverbank? Was she there too? Did she look into your eyes?"

"Jake. Is he coming?" Edra asked as she dreamed. "Did you hear his motorcar? Maybe you could wait on the road for him."

Edra opened her eyes just wide enough to see the window and then closed them again. She wanted to get back into the dream, to catch that dream she had started and pick up where she left off.

"The feeble and aged are those who are apt to succumb." A tree rarely dies of old age.

A drop of rain.

Angus did not see Edra for five days. He grew concerned when she broke her routine of stopping by every few days with her buggy to trade a quart of milk and some cream for something she knew the family could use from the forest. Angus saddled a horse.

When he found Edra lying peacefully under her blanket, one arm drooping to the floor at her bedside, she had already been gone for a day or two. He felt the bottom drop out of his stomach. He needed to contact the brother.

Split Toe watched through the window. As Angus lifted the woman's arm back to her side, a thin arrowhead fell from her hand. The man picked it up from the floor and rolled it between his fingers, his thoughts drifting to some distant time and place. When he moved to set the arrowhead on the windowsill, he stopped, catching sight of Split Toe standing outside. Split Toe bowed his antlers to the ground, then turned and walked to the river at the base of the sand bluff.

Angus pulled the blanket over Edra's face. He put his hand over his own eyes for a moment, catching tears that he could not hold back.

Outside, the sky was beginning to darken. A shadow looked like it was drifting over the sun. Split Toe watched as Angus stepped around the house, looking up at the canopy of the grandfather pine along the river. The man's eyes scanned from one old pine to another. The woman's forest was now forty years old. It was mostly hardwood and showed promise, as Edra had wanted.

The sky continued to darken as Angus walked to the small barn and gathered Edra's horse. He saw Split Toe step out from behind the grandfather pine as the eclipse reached its peak. Split Toe seemed withdrawn. He slowly crossed the river in the brief period of darkness, walking out of 1918 and into 1950.

Split Toe felt the pull of the spirit current, and within it, he was sure he sensed the gentle presence of the woman.

CHAPTER 21
COMMUNITY INFRASTRUCTURE

AD 1950

Split Toe stood at the edge of the concrete basement, one wall broken vertically down its center and pressed inward by a large tree root. It looked as if the tree was slowly pushing the basement to a point of collapse. It was not one of the twelve original white pines doing the work; it was one of their offspring. Growing up from the basement floor, the tops of several other trees already reached ground level of the sand bluff.

Split Toe remembered when the site was abandoned thirty-two years earlier in 1918. Without maintenance, the above ground structure and all its contents had collapsed in on itself. Everything that had belonged to Edra ended up in the basement. It was as if nature was absorbing her life. Her belongings. Her memories. Her spirit. It all was slowly blending with the surrounding natural world. Now, the structure's condition was a forest blight—an overgrown site slowly returning to the wilds—the kind that might eventually be rediscovered by an archaeologist.

Did Mother Nature even return things built by humans back to the soil? Perhaps those creations became part of the spirit pool too.

Split Toe wondered whether the sickness that took Edra had taken many more in the human community, and how it might have changed the new world he'd crossed into. Was this Mother Nature at work? Certainly. Edra's brother—Jake—was too heartbroken to come back to her house on the bluff, but it would not have mattered anyway, because several months later, the Spanish Flu took him as well. Split Toe had no way of knowing this, but he remembered the brother. He remembered looking into his eyes and feeling the connection.

Eventually, in the human system of civilization, property taxes on the eighty acres came due, and no one was left to pay them. Action-reaction. First Mother Nature, then human. A man in the community bought the forest land with its practically useless tag alder swamp. He was the highest bidder.

As he stood at the foundation, Split Toe heard something disturbing. It was the sound of machinery. Much louder than the gentle *putt-putting* of a Model T Ford.

The new owner thought of cutting all the trees off the property again. Some were nearly large enough to harvest. But he came up with a different plan that was more lucrative. He understood how things worked in his community and knew that to improve some of the main roads—to make them two-lanes and able to handle new, high-speed automobiles, trucks, and agricultural equipment—the community needed sand and gravel. He dug around on the back side of the bluff, knowing there was plenty of sand that drifted there thousands of years ago. When he dug deeper, he found traces of gravel, just as Jake had found at the lowest part of the basement.

"John," Split Toe heard the owner talking over the noise of the equipment to a man sitting on a machine, "We're gonna need a road that circles around the back side of this here hill so we can take trucks up from the bottom. We need the trees cut and the stumps pushed out of the way. No need to burn the small stuff, just push it into a pile with the stumps. Move the hardwood logs to the top by the road. We can do something with those."

"That'll take a bit of doin'," John shouted over the machine's noise. "But I'll work it out."

"We'll set up our stuff at the bottom. We need to be able to circle several trucks around, and have room to load 'em," the owner shouted.

Split Toe had not seen such a machine before. These humans were outdoing themselves in cleverness.

While the work on the bluff carried on, the new owner sat down with the village council and presented his proposal to deliver sand and gravel for a few dollars less per ton than they were currently paying. He could do so because he did not have a long distance to haul the material. At the time, sand and gravel were being trucked a fair distance from a quarry in an adjacent county. The township needed the material, and he offered to supply it locally. It was not a difficult sell. It made sense. Humans usually did things that made sense, or at least things that offered the best value.

After the road around the bluff and equipment areas were laid out, the owner brought in a diesel-powered excavator and began digging. First, he removed some of the sand. He dropped each large scoop from the excavator into the back of a heavy dump truck.

"John," Split Toe heard the owner speak. "We gotta get a few more people and a few more trucks. You know anyone lookin' for work who can drive a gravel truck? We need three in all. I'll operate the excavator. You can drive the dozer. If we can find the guys, we'll be goin' full tilt."

"I'll ask around," John replied. "We'll find 'em."

Once the owner had the operation running smoothly, he kept three trucks working, much like the logging wagons: one delivering, one returning, and one being filled. To Split Toe, the workers seemed like the loggers. Why did they remove the dirt? How did it add to their food, shelter, or fuel? Split Toe still did not understand human ways.

While trucks delivered the first loads of sand, the bulldozer pushed other sand aside and pushed the stumps to where tree canopies were piled. The new owner wanted to expose the gravel so he could deliver alternating trucks of gravel and sand. The back side of the sand bluff began to disappear—ten acres of it—forming a deep hole.

The owner set up another machine so the excavator could drop each bucket of gravel into a chute where it would fall onto a wide inclined moving belt. Gravel rolling off the top of the belt fell into a vibrating hopper with a grate that separated big rocks from smaller gravel. The diesel-powered machine shook the ground so violently that every living thing felt and heard it from a mile away.

Rocks and soil trembled at its shaking.

Trees held tightly to their roots, hoping they would not be shaken free from the ground surrounding them.

Split Toe thought it might rattle the antlers right off his head.

As the excavating team worked hard, the township's roads improved. They were widened and straightened, with drainage ditches running along each side. When road builders reached a low spot, they placed a steel tube below the road surface which permitted water to flow from one side to the other. Even during the wet spring, the roads stayed rather dry.

While the original pioneers, Angus and Grace, had passed decades ago, their descendants now had a new motorcar of their own. An automobile. A Buick. They appreciated the condition of the upgraded roads, and they appreciated that the new owner of the land with the twelve old white pine trees provided sand and gravel for the community.

Before long, a series of electric poles lined one side of each improved road in the township, with power lines extending to each farmhouse. A few years later, a telephone cable was added.

Split Toe watched in amazement at how organized these humans were ... and so clever. They all seemed to know what everyone else was doing. Somehow, they found out. Split Toe did not know about the technologies being introduced, and he thought the telephones might be something like the spirit current. A way to know instantly. Had he found out about the radio in each farmhouse, he would have thought the same of that.

Had the humans created a spirit world that was separate from the natural one? Did humans think they could get along without Mother Nature? Perhaps they could. It was hard to see how

Mother Nature fit in to the world they were building. It seemed like the humans were taking over.

But electricity and telephone poles never went down the road that ended at the gravel pit, for there was no longer a home at its end.

It was not only the property with the last twelve big trees that changed ownership by 1950. About half the farmers in the area did not put in place a workable family succession plan for their farms. Many simply sold the farms when they could not work them any longer. Some of the new owners cherished the farmland for the same reasons the original farmers and pioneers had. Others were simply looking for an angle, an investment, a way to take what they could from the land.

A company came through and purchased the rights from landowners to explore for minerals and to extract them from below their ground's surface. They offered cash. This seemed like a real win to the landowners. Farmers pressed the company for the best deal they could, and the company always came to an agreement with the landowners.

For the farmers, the company threw in a free supply of natural gas to the farmhouse for as long as the farmhouse stood. This meant a huge improvement in the farmers' quality of life because it enabled the farmers to phase out all of the work involved with firewood supply. They could install furnaces and cooking stoves operating on free natural gas.

That wasn't the only way in which life had drastically changed. Hot and cold water was available directly at the kitchen sink. Electricity. Natural gas. Automatic heat. Easy cooking. Hot and cold running water at the kitchen sink. What would Grace have thought?

Oil and gas wells popped up quickly throughout the Michigan farmland. Angus's farm now had a grasshopper-like oil well at the top of the alfalfa-covered hill. The family could see the machine from the kitchen window and the ribbon of road running down the middle of the field to get service to it. Though it did not seem to fit in with their green farmland, they eventually ceased to notice it, just like the broken items piled behind trees on the back forty acres.

The natural gas company sunk a well on the back forty acres. They cleared ten acres of hardwood trees for the wellhead and the road to get to it. But the farmer would not need the trees once the company installed free natural gas. And the company's quarterly payments for the well's performance made the difference during a year with too much rain or too little.

Perhaps these humans had created their own system of action-reaction—a way to outfox Mother Nature. Perhaps they did not need her cooperation after all.

Along with its mining of natural gas, the gas company needed an efficient way to transport and store the natural gas they extracted. Everyone in the community agreed. The company needed to install pipelines below the ground's surface, crossing property wherever necessary. The community thought the impact on farms would be small because pipes would be below ground. But workers laying the pipe removed fertile surface soil when digging the trench and filled it back into the trench to bury the pipe. Nobody gave much thought to whether the good soil went on top or below when the trench was refilled. It went back in as a mixture of convenience.

The property that Edra once owned, which was now part sand and gravel pit, was directly in the pipeline's path. And though the path missed the gravel pit, it took out a wide swath of the forest Edra let develop and a corner of the tag alder swamp. The gas company cut the trees and filled in the corner of the tag alder swamp. In fact, the company purchased hundreds of yards of sand and gravel from the man owning the pit to fill in the swamp corner. It was the lowest-cost solution. An easy decision. And the whole community agreed.

Split Toe retreated to his favorite island deep within the swamp, keeping his head low to hide from humans.

CHAPTER 22
THE RUT

AD 1950

When autumn arrived, Split Toe felt an urge to leave the safety of his cover and step into the open, as did other deer. The risk of danger seemed worth a chance to engage with other deer who put their caution aside to be part of this seasonal ritual. Split Toe stood on the east edge of the peninsula's alfalfa field. A stiff autumn wind emptied trees along the river of their leaves. The cold wind bit at Split Toe's back.

The excavators weren't working today, and in the stillness, Split Toe heard approaching movement through crisp leaves that covered the forest floor. An animal was approaching quickly. He watched the dark shadow of a young doe dash down a trail that followed the opposite edge of the river. Two bucks pressed from behind—one racing down the same trail as the doe, the other bolting through the trees along her flank. The buck directly behind her was a large deer with a mature rack. The deer darting between trees alongside the trail and funneling the doe toward the river was an even older deer with antlers that were thick and lined with tines. The necks of both bucks were swollen, geared up for the rut. Both bucks were driven. Ready. They were not going to let this young doe go on her way before they ran her into a sweat and got what they wanted.

The doe was the youngest in a group of seven does and yearlings that stuck close together for protection. As they grazed their way from the alfalfa field to the tag alder swamp, the young doe suddenly noticed that she had fallen behind the group, though not by much.

Both bucks caught the group's scent before the does left the alfalfa. These female deer could not have disguised their musty aroma if they tried—all but the two oldest were in heat. When the west wind brought the does' scent to the male deer, the two bucks were foraging deep amongst the trees across the river. By the time the does crossed, the bucks were already trotting with single-minded determination to intercept them.

The young doe saw that the bucks had singled her out. She decided to make them work for what they were after—to show them that she was not an easy take. She would show them her character. The doe lifted her tail once to let out the scent and then launched into flight. She ran as if her life depended on it. The young doe saw her group scatter in the distance, and she decided to veer back toward the river.

Split Toe realized the doe was done-in when she ran past. Exhausted. Almost ready to give up. She had already circled back twice, dodging trees while looking for another path. Sweat lathered her neck and flanks. She gasped for air with each fast stride. Split Toe watched as she finally plunged into the river, no match for the power of the two bucks who were now so close they could almost bump her. Water splashed in the air as they all leaped in long strides across the stream. When she reached the opposite shore, the larger buck was already in front of her, cutting her off. Running up the far bank was just too much for the doe. Her front legs started to buckle. She had given them a chase to remember. The doe panted heavily when she stopped to catch her breath at the field's edge and finally lifted her tail in submission.

The smaller buck's nose circled the doe's tail and pressed against its base. He could not wait any longer. He sidestepped to align his body when he heard the larger buck's grunt and turned just in time to see the buck's powerful twisted neck with antlers curled for attack charging at him. The lesser buck leaped back to avoid the collision, the larger buck vaulting to knock him away from the doe. The larger buck then spun to face his retreating competitor. The dominant buck instantly lowered his antlers and charged again at the lesser buck, chasing him back across the river.

Now, the large buck turned to the young doe, who shifted her back legs and lifted her tail again, sending a fresh stream of scent into the air. The large buck confidently approached. He caught the hips of the doe between his powerful front legs, then pressed his pelvis against hers. In an instant he was done. Three quick thrusts. He dropped back to the ground, still confident and feeling even more powerful. The small doe nearly collapsed from her own fatigue. Her step faltered as she picked her way gently down the slope back to cover at the water's edge.

The large buck lifted his head to catch the doe's scent one more time. He felt good about himself. At the top of his game. At the top of the herd. It was a spot he had earned and defended over several seasons while Split Toe was away.

He did not expect to hear Split Toe's challenging grunt. The buck did not know what to make of the challenge. Was this one of the other deer in the area trying again to displace him? Or had an ambitious buck from outside crossed into his territory? There was no end to stray bucks wandering into his forest and trying to take his position. The challenging buck would have to learn his place.

The large buck turned in a ball of fury, not taking time to look closely at his target. He simply saw the dark form of another deer step from cover into the open alfalfa field. The large buck's head faced the ground when he made the turn, the muscles of his front shoulders and neck tight with pent-up strength. His front hooves dug into the ground as his rear legs launched him in the direction of his opponent.

The distance was not far. Split Toe watched the charging curl of the buck's neck as white, pointed antler tines bounced with every leap. Split Toe sparred when he had to, but it had been a while. He lowered his head and braced for the crash, his neck tightening for the power of the other buck's charge. A loud clash of antlers echoed through the forest when the two deer collided. The charging buck whipped his head back and forth as the antlers interlocked. Both bucks leaned into each other. Every twist of their necks sent rattling sounds of knocking antlers into the forest. Split Toe stood his ground, letting the other buck twist and turn. Its anger built. To keep his opponent engaged, Split

Toe took a half-step back, giving in a little. There was a point he wanted to make, and he did not want to finish this quite yet.

The buck sensed that he had misjudged his opponent, but it was not in his nature to surrender. He drew back suddenly, pulled loose from Split Toe's antlers, and spun on his heels. Hoping to push Split Toe off his mark, the buck charged again. They crashed, the loud clatter echoing through the forest.

Another buck, hearing the fight, raced to the river's edge to watch the action. The buck could already see more spectators standing across the peninsula—deer gathering to watch the contest.

Split Toe trapped the buck's antlers in his own and put a bit more pressure on his adversary's neck. The opponent pressed and felt like he was gaining as Split Toe, again, let the buck earn some progress.

Surrounding deer watched Split Toe's neck bend closer to the ground.

The buck put all its strength into the fight. A patch of dark sweat puddled on his side. Every muscle bulged. The deer's swollen neck strained against Split Toe's controlled resistance. The deer now knew this would be a long fight, a hard fight, perhaps to the death. But Split Toe's intentional letup also made the buck think he might be able to teach Split Toe a lesson. Chase him back to wherever he came from.

Several groups of deer now surrounded the two massive bucks as they fought, all watching the intense display of strength, agility, and endurance. All anxious to know the outcome. They could hear the two deer snort as their antlers locked. More deer arrived.

Split Toe began to press forward.

The circle of deer stepped back as Split Toe pushed the buck.

The other buck gained a bit, muscling him back to the center of the circle, forcing him to give up one hard-fought step at a time. Split Toe could feel his opponent tiring. He sensed the assault weaken, if only slightly.

The buck pressed and twisted with all its strength.

Gathering itself for a final surge, the buck nearly wrenched Split Toe's powerful neck to the ground.

The crowd of surrounding deer leaned forward, anticipating the end.

Split Toe knew he had given the other buck a good fight—had let him show his character—but now he would finish it. In an unexpected burst of movement, Split Toe unleashed the full strength of his powerful neck and shoulders, locking antlers and twisting his adversary's neck so quickly that the large buck flipped onto its back. As it did so, the entire left antler snapped loose from the buck's head, flying into the crowd. Split Toe, in a movement almost too agile to observe, leaped next to the buck still thrashing with its legs in the air, and pressed a point of his mighty antlers against the fine white fur of the buck's belly. Split Toe applied just enough pressure to let the buck know he was serious.

Split Toe saw breath stream from the buck's mouth in a long exhale. Nothing more was needed. Split Toe lifted his head and looked at the crowd of surrounding deer. He lowered his head in a respectful nod, and every deer in the circle responded with a nod of their own.

The beaten buck's legs kicked in the air as it snorted and turned on its side, then stood. It turned and finally trotted toward the river's edge where the broken-off antler was lying in the alfalfa.

Split Toe lifted his chin high, his mighty antlers almost scraping his back, and let out the same fierce grunt that had begun the fight. The buck turned to face Split Toe, feeling weak and off balance with a missing antler. The buck exhaled deeply and lowered his head in a respectful bow. Split Toe nodded in return.

CHAPTER 23
HUNTING FOR SPORT

AD 1950

While deer hunting in Michigan had technically been regulated since 1859, the regulations did not mean much until people began hunting deer for sport. The first Michigan deer licenses were issued in 1895, costing residents fifty cents each.

Nonresidents, though there were few, paid twenty-five dollars for an opportunity to take a Michigan whitetail buck. But the fact was that if a pioneer or a farmer needed the meat in those days, they simply took a deer that was roaming wild on their property, often feeding on their own crops, and said nothing about the deer they harvested, except perhaps how blessed they were to have it at the dinner table.

By 1950, deer hunting had become a popular sport in Michigan—and a 500-million-dollar industry. Sons and daughters who left the farms for higher education or for a job in the city often returned to the family homestead for opening day, a kind of November 15 holiday when everyone sought out their favorite spot at the edge of a field or a stump in the forest, waiting for an opportunity to drag in a whitetail buck.

Hunting weapons ranged from bolt action .30-06 rifles that were WWI surplus, to lever action Winchester .30-30s, to single-shot or double-barrel 12-gauge shotguns. Most guns had open sights, and many people using them were excellent marksmen. Some were not.

The biggest problem in the forest in 1950 was more an issue of judgment than ability. Seeing a buck during a short season was infrequent for most hunters, many of whom wanted so badly to take their deer that they often overestimated what the open-sight gun could do for them. It was not uncommon for a hunter to take a shot at a running deer far off in a field or one that was moving quickly through the thicket's edge. For every two deer taken, another was wounded. Breakfast table discussions on the second day often included stories of blood trails followed, deer lost, and deer collected that were already carrying a wound.

Split Toe heard hunters talking about a deer that got away, and he could not help but note the indifference in the hunters' voices.

"Well, that's deer hunting," Split Toe heard an older hunter explaining to his younger hunting friend. "It's gonna happen. Get over it. Jus' git out there and try again."

"Least I got some lead in 'im. Knocked 'im down. That's for sure. But he just got up and run off. Why, my daddy told me once he put a slug into a buck running full-out at two hundred yards. One shot with his old single-shot twelve-gauge. Along the old south fence line. 'Knocked 'im right out of the air,' he said. 'Dead as a hammer.' Hell, he told me that when he plugged that deer, after the somersault the deer skidded damn near twenty feet."

"My pappy told me he did the same thing back in '38," the older hunter nodded in agreement. "It sure 'nuff can be done."

"Maybe tomorrow this deer 'll come out again and I'll finish 'im off. Who knows."

Split Toe had his own point of view on the matter. He knew these humans were part of a food chain and were predators of his species. He accepted his place in the natural scheme of things. He also held humans to be extremely clever, in both their actions and the devices they used. The guns they invented were now far superior to the Ojibwe's bow and arrow. It gave these humans a huge advantage. Then, to organize things so the hunters all came to hunt in the forest on the same day made things harder on the deer in the same way a wolf pack was more dangerous than a single wolf.

What these humans figured out were things that any animal might do if their instincts and abilities told them to do so. Split Toe respected that part of what the humans were doing. But laughing about a wounded deer was strange. Why did they not look at life with more respect?

These humans invaded field and forest for a few days each year. Some set up camp for a week in the forest, cutting trees to make way for their tents, trucks, and campfires. Then, twice a day, they fanned out to cover the whole terrain, some shooting with no more than a wish. Split Toe knew he needed to stay put in the tag alder swamp when hunters took to the field. He had lived long enough to know better than to make a mistake and step into the open when predators were hungry for a kill.

How many of these humans were there, anyway? They seemed like a growing crowd.

"*What have you learned?*" Split Toe heard the spirits' voice in the air. "*The world around you is changing. It is an important lesson. Humans have their interconnected ways. There is more change for you to see. Your lessons are going well.*"

CHAPTER 24
HUNTERS BUY THE EIGHTY ACRES

AD 1960

The farmer to the north of Angus's farm had a creative idea. He decided to plant new pine trees on a few cleared acres bordering the tag alder swamp. Red pines. The farmer slipped a small seedling into the ground every few feet in neat rows. The government provided the seedlings. At the time, people were planting red pines all across Michigan.

Split Toe paid attention to these trees as he traveled from one time to another. When the trees began to grow, the farmer was happy. Deer ate many of the seedlings, but many also survived. The trees grew slowly from the point of view of the farmer, but quickly from Split Toe's point of view. Split Toe found these trees interesting. They were certainly trees, but in their long, straight rows, they looked more like crops—and they were. A slow-growing crop. Within fifty years—less than one human lifetime—they would make ideal candidates for finished lumber.

For the farmer, it was a kind of retirement account. He planted the red pines when he was still young, imagining that when he eventually needed to slow down, the red pines would be ready for the loggers. The logging company would pay him for work he performed long ago when he was younger and stronger. Clever.

To Split Toe, this tree crop plan was an effort that had one foot in Mother Nature's system and the other foot in the human agricultural system. The farmer did relatively little work at the beginning and left the heavy lifting for Mother Nature to take care of. She took the red pines from seedlings to log-size trees. Then humans took over again to remove the trees for lumber.

Split Toe was not sure if it was another step in these humans' attempts to control Mother Nature rather than to work with her. In this case, Split Toe gave the farmer who planted the red pines the benefit of the doubt, hoping that the farmer's intention was to treat these trees like a crop so that humans would not need to harvest more wild trees. Perhaps it was a bit like raising a pig to slaughter rather than stepping onto the back forty acres and trying to find a wild deer to take off the land. In the human world, pigs and crop trees had their purpose. Split Toe thought about this for a few days and liked the idea.

It took more than a decade, but eventually the gravel pit owner scratched around at the bottom of his excavation and could not find another scoop of gravel. He took all that the glacier had deposited. There was still plenty of sand, but the money was in gravel. No locals wanted just sand anymore.

Split Toe saw what had happened and thought it was another

case of insects eating through their entire food supply. Even Split Toe did not expect that. He had thought these humans might just go on harvesting gravel forever.

Mother Nature knew better. What would become of the land now? Was there a way to repair it? The damage was done.

"I guess this is it, John. We got it all," the owner, now looking a bit older, said in a restful way.

"Been a good run," John replied as he leaned against the silent bulldozer while pinching tobacco into the cigarette paper he was preparing.

"Hey, can you do one more thing for me? Drive this excavator to Rich's farm up the road. He's buying some of this machinery to make a pond in his pasture—he needs it for the cows. I'll pick you up with the gravel truck, and we can drop that off at the county maintenance yard. They want two of the trucks. One of the boys'll pick us up. Why don't we all grab dinner in town? It'll be a nice way to conclude this enterprise."

"You got it, boss." John started to climb into the seat of the excavator. "See you at Rich's place."

Later in the week, the owner parked the third truck on his own property. He also removed most of the machinery for processing the gravel. But the hopper with the shaker was so worn out that the owner just left it in the gravel pit along with dozens of empty diesel fuel cans, oil cans, and a large half-full bucket of hydraulic fluid. He also left a mess on the gravel pit floor. There were piles of dirt and debris lying around—nothing natural about it. One scoop here. Another there. A pile abandoned haphazardly by the bulldozer and a tall pile of stumps pushed to the side.

A bobcat took up residence in the stump entanglement.

The pleasant contour of the sand drift dropped by the wind at the edge of the glacier many millennia ago was no more.

The owner began looking for a buyer who would take the property off his hands, but in his heart, he wondered what there was left to sell. How could he convince anyone to buy this mess? He had already taken everything from the land that seemed practical to take. Then again, there were always the twelve old-growth pines. Edra would have cried. Even this owner did not have the heart to take them down. Or perhaps they were just too big for him to manage, and there were not enough of them to interest professional loggers. Either way, the trees were lucky.

Split Toe was anxious for a new owner too. He did not like the attitude of this one. He wanted the woman back. She had preserved things well, particularly the twelve old-growth trees. Mother Nature seemed to guide her attitude and every decision. Split Toe could still feel her spirit in the current where everything natural ended up.

When the owner put the word out and finally made a deal to sell, it took quite some time, and it was really Split Toe who sealed the deal—though neither the owner nor Split Toe knew it. It would be a long time before this piece of property had anything to offer that the average person might want.

The person purchasing the land represented a small family

group whose main interest was hunting. They hoped to find a parcel of inexpensive property they could gather at each year for the deer hunting season. Given time, as a distant second objective, they might sell the timber again, lease the mineral rights, and find other ways to make the land pay for itself. The buyer had done this before with other property. The equation worked.

But what caught the buyer's attention most was the large rack of a huge-bodied deer that stepped out of the tag alder swamp onto the gas pipeline just as the buyer stepped onto the pipeline on the opposite side. Split Toe had not expected the human to be around. No one had set foot on the property since the gravel mining stopped. Split Toe stood for a few seconds to assess the human, then dipped his antlers deeply to the ground before leaping back onto the centuries-old trail encircling the tag alder swamp.

The man stood stunned.

This was an exceptional deer. The buyer knew that a deer like this must have fathered much of the deer herd in the area, and the potential to harvest trophy deer could be excellent. The buyer was giddy imagining that spectacular rack on his wall and had already picked out a hunting spot on the pipeline that he would claim in November.

After the deer jumped back into the thicket, the man walked slowly to the spot where the deer had stood. He dropped to one knee and put his hand over the deep hoofprint. His own hand could not stretch to cover it. He remained motionless for a few minutes, thinking.

"Could this be one of the legendary Ol' Split Toes?"

He thought it just might be.

When the eclipse pulled Split Toe across the river the next week, he was not thinking about the human he had met near the tag alder swamp. He did not know if he would ever see the fellow again. Some humans seemed mighty unpredictable.

The man was the second of four brothers who purchased the property together. Through the many years of owning their eighty acres, the man always remembered the day he saw the remarkable deer step out of the tag alder swamp.

People in the local restaurant watched deer with big racks move like shadows along their fence lines, disappearing into thickets, and reappearing in their dreams. Though they rarely said so outright, all the local hunters enjoying morning coffee deduced that Ol' Split Toe was no more than a legend.

"Seen him slip by me just before dark last night. Too dark to shoot. Ol' Split Toe for sure," a plaid-shirted man sipped from a hot cup of coffee as he spoke.

"I know it. He never comes out for me when it's light enough. That Ol' Split Toe is unusually canny."

Occasionally, when one of the men came out of the woods with a Winchester in one hand and dragging a deer of this classification with the other, he was certain that *his* Ol' Split Toe was part of a lineage of large-antlered deer. A unique gene pool. He knew his Ol' Split Toe had already fought off lesser bucks that season and planted his seed in a few does who would give birth to offspring that could continue the legend of Ol' Split Toe for another round.

People in the community *oohed* and *aahed* when Bob finally bagged Ol' Split Toe. But they all knew Ol' Split Toe was just a name—a legend. What else could a deer like that be?

Ol' Split Toe was a standard. A high bar. Nothing more than that. When one fellow called another to say, "I got Ol' Split Toe," the other knew exactly what the caller meant.

The man and his brothers hunted many seasons on the property, and they were often satisfied with large-antlered deer they took from the edge of the swamp. What an excellent piece of hunting property the eighty acres turned out to be.

As the man's memory faded, and he became hazy about other things, he always remembered exactly how big Ol' Split Toe's hoofprint really was and the enormous set of antlers the deer had bowed with. Every time he was in the local coffee shop for breakfast, he found himself yarning with the local farmers about the mythical deer they were all sure roamed the tag alder swamp and low areas along the Clam River.

CHAPTER 25
SPLIT TOE IS SHOT

AD 1974

When the eclipse passed, Split Toe stepped from the river crossing onto the peninsula. A bit of cover that grew up along the river's edge still concealed him. He was not sure what to expect. Split Toe had made the crossing many times and never knew what age he would walk into, what the new world would be like, or what lesson the spirits would teach him. The morning air was crisp and the ground was dusted with a bit of fresh snow.

What happened next was something he surely did not expect.

As he took his first step into the open, he did not know that three nearby hunters had already picked up on his movement. One was in an old hunting blind that stood two hundred yards south along the riverbank. While that hunter's main focus was on the field farther to his south, he kept one eye on the edge of the peninsula to his north. He knew there were several heavily traveled deer trails that cut through the neighbor's property across the river.

The second hunter was atop the sand bluff on the east side of the river—Edra's side of the river—his eyes scanning the forested area between the river and the gravel pit. The bluff hunter stood secluded against one of the twelve old-growth white pines. While the peninsula across the river was on his neighbor's property, he knew the neighbor would not mind if he shot at a deer that was within range there. So, he kept one eye on the riverbank along the peninsula's east side where the deer with the large rack was standing.

The third hunter was at the southwest corner of the peninsula in a new blind he'd put up that summer. It was a good spot.

Split Toe was completely unaware of these hunters. He certainly did not know it was the morning of November 15, opening day of firearm deer season. For some reason, the spirit stream had placed him here at this time. But why?

All three hunters scanned their fields of vision, looking for an early opening-day buck. None of them were sure about what to think of the oddly timed eclipse that was forecast for that morning. On opening day? How strange. These fellows all believed that eighty percent of the hunting season was over by noon on opening day.

They all saw the deer step into the open at the same time. The size of the deer and the enormous rack, which each could see with the naked eye, caught all of them off guard. None took time to inspect what they saw. They each knew this was *their* deer. They did not want to let it get away.

The man up on the bluff had dreamed of such a deer most of the night before. He struggled to get it into his scope because he was shaking uncontrollably. He put the wobbling crosshairs on the deer's front shoulder, aiming down from the top of the bluff.

It was not a difficult shot, and he expected the deer to drop. But it did not.

Perhaps it was that Split Toe turned his head to look south just at that instant. Or perhaps it was just a clean miss because the hunter was too excited. Or maybe it was the other shots that went off all around him at the same time. But miss he did. And he was too surprised at the results to rack a second bullet into the gun's chamber.

The hunter along the river to the south had a broadside opportunity, but it was a long shot—a longer shot than he had ever taken. He saw the enormous rack and was fooled by the distance. The hunter rested the barrel of his .30-30 on the sill of the blind's window, put the crosshairs of his scope onto the heart of the deer, exhaled slowly like he had done so many times, and gently pulled the trigger. The rifle kicked back against his shoulder, and he saw a small puff of dust leap from the snow thirty yards short of the deer. He heard the other two shots and cocked the rifle, chambering another round for a second shot.

It was the hunter sitting across the peninsula whose shot hit Split Toe.

Split Toe was facing him. The hunter did not like a front-on shot because the target did not generally leave much room for error. But this deer was enormous and offered plenty of mass at which to shoot. Even so, when Split Toe turned his head to the south, the bullet missed its intended target and went clean through a meaty spot near the neck's edge. It narrowly missed the spine, a major artery, and the windpipe—all of which would have killed Split Toe quickly.

Split Toe instantly ducked and dashed back across the river. He broke into a full sprint through the trees, crossed the gravel pit and the pipeline, and crashed into the tag alder swamp. His neck hurt, but he knew he would live.

The instinct to escape—the adrenaline—masked the pain as he ran. He needed to lie in the cold water near the edge of one of the islands for a few days to let the water manage the ache and forest oxygen heal the wound. He needed to be careful not to open the wound again.

Rest and hiding—those were the most important things.

The three hunters each came out of their spots and wandered carefully to where Split Toe came up from the river. None really knew what had happened. There were a few drops of blood in the snow, a small patch of hair, and some distinctive hoofprints, larger than any prints they had seen in their lives.

The fellow who was positioned at the top of the bluff could see where Split Toe had run back across the river on the east side. They found another drop of blood in the snow. They each searched the ground around them, pointing, scratching their heads in astonishment, wondering how they could have missed. They made their own tracks all around those of Split Toe.

"He certainly is a wise old deer," the man who fired from two hundred yards to the south said quietly.

"You rarely see 'em like that one," said the one whose shot penetrated Split Toe's neck.

The third man simply remained silent, not wanting to admit how nervous he'd been with the deer of his dreams in his sights.

The fellow to the south walked back to his blind, while the man whose shot had actually hit Split Toe crossed the river and began to follow the trail along with the bluff hunter. It was not such a difficult trail to follow. There was no mistaking the distinctive tracks. While they found only a few more drops of blood, they could see that the deer was racing along an ancient trail.

When they reached the edge of the tag alder swamp, they knew their chances of recovering the deer had dropped significantly. The thicket seemed nearly impenetrable, but they were prepared to go in after this deer.

The problem with the swamp was the foot of water and the deep muck beneath the surface. No tracks were visible here. The peninsula hunter stepped into the thicket and felt water run into his boot on the first step.

He continued for about twenty feet and realized he had no clue about which way to proceed. He did not want to frighten all the deer in the thicket and destroy the rest of the day's hunt. He simply backed out and explained to the younger hunter standing at the edge that the deer was gone.

"Amazing what a deer can go through."

"This one's probably in the next county by now. I've followed wounded deer for miles. If you don't get 'em right off, they'll run like hell. Jus' go on like they never been hit."

They followed their own tracks back to the river. Talking. Pointing to the spots of blood in the snow. Pausing in places to look at the evidence one more time. Marveling at the size of the print. The older hunter reached down to rub a twig where a drop of blood seemed to have landed. Bringing his hand close to his glasses, he looked at the smear of red on his fingertips, then rubbed them clean in the snow.

"Do you think this one will live to see another day?" the young hunter asked.

"I presume so. Don't you be worryin' about that deer none. He's good. I tell you what," the older hunter continued, "you worry real hard for ten minutes. Then you get back up to the top of that bluff and keep huntin' for your buck."

The following morning, the incident of the wise old deer with enormous antlers, the three hunters shooting at once, the drops of blood, the distinctive print, and the sprint to the tag alder swamp were the topics of three separate breakfast-table discussions.

CHAPTER 26
THE BOY

AD 1974

1974 was the year that Split Toe first saw the boy. It was the last day of November—the last day of the deer hunting season—and two weeks after his injury. Split Toe watched from the tree line as a man carrying an old bolt-action .30-06 rifle—a WWI surplus Springfield—slipped through a barbed wire fence and walked cautiously across the field with an eight-year-old boy in tow. The boy wore a corduroy winter coat, cotton mittens, and an orange cap.

The man rarely found time to hunt with his brothers on opening day, but he tried to work in a day or two late in the season. He liked to walk slowly as he hunted. Looking. But his brothers along with their children liked to hunt while sitting still. Waiting. It was least disruptive for the man to hunt at the end of the season when his relatives were already done for the year. After nearly two weeks of intense hunting pressure, the deer had learned to hole up and wait out the danger.

A clear plastic envelope hung from the back of the man's red-plaid hunting jacket displaying his hunting license. The envelope was fat with three years' of old licenses—the man had not taken a deer for any of those seasons. He and his brothers owned the gravel pit acreage, and this was the first time he'd brought his son with him to hunt deer. They slowly wandered the area, spotting tracks in the snow left by deer and other animals.

The boy was cold. Very cold. He curled his fingers in his mittens and curled his toes in his socks, which were inside canvas gym shoes stuffed into black pull-over, buckle-up boots. Walking seemed to help. Despite the conditions, there was nowhere else on earth the boy would rather be. When they walked along the edge of the tag alder swamp, the man noticed a heavily traveled trail following its perimeter. The tracks were clearly fresh. He bent down, spoke softly to the boy, and pointed at the trail.

"I'll stand in this open area," the man whispered and swept his arm to the edge of the clearing. "You follow that trail in for a bit. Let's see what pops out."

The boy began a slow walk as his father had trained him to do. A few steps. Wait. Look. A few more steps. He already knew how to walk quietly. The boy made his way down the trail, stepping over fallen alder stems and into puddles that nearly reached his boot tops. He went on for several minutes and nearly jumped out of his boots when he heard the loud shot from his father's rifle.

KaaBAM.

The boy turned quickly to retreat out of the swamp. As he did so, he scanned deep into the swamp, and saw the face of a deer whose antlers were so large that they looked like the tag alder branches through which the deer was staring back at him. The boy stopped and watched, silent. The two studied each other, and the boy imprinted the deer's image in his mind. The boy slowly lifted his mitten and cupped his hand as if to say, "Hello." The deer bowed deeply, his antlers now separating from the thicket which disguised them.

The deer and the boy both filed the images into their memories.

Split Toe knew immediately that the spirit current had pulled him into this age to meet the boy.

Both turned quietly and walked in opposite directions: the boy to the clearing where his father stood over a buck that was lying lifeless on the ground, and Split Toe heading deeper into the swamp.

When the boy reached his father, he smiled widely. The deer his father took had antlers that extended up and out to about the width of its ears. A fork branched out at the end of each antler. Though the deer was full-grown, the boy thought it was rather small because the other deer he saw in the thicket—the first deer he had ever seen—was much larger in comparison.

The man bent over the deer with his hunting knife. "Give me a hand here, son. Reach in that packet on my back and pull out the 1974 license."

The boy took off his mittens. For some reason, his fingers and toes did not feel cold any longer. He fiddled with the clear envelope on his father's back until the deer tag he was looking for came out. He handed it to his father.

The father and the boy each took hold of one antler and began to drag the deer to their vehicle. The boy tried his best, and he felt like he was contributing to the pull. Actually, he made things more difficult for his father, who was doing the heavy lifting. But the father did not ask the boy to stop.

"You're doing a fine job there, son. Keep pulling and you'll have this deer to the car in no time."

"You go on ahead, Dad. I'll bring this beast to you." The boy smiled and looked up to see the look of mock astonishment on his father's face. "Too bad it wasn't a bear. I'd take care of a bear for you, too."

"Really? Now, that would be something." The father stopped to catch his breath. He looked at his son, raised his eyebrows, and imagined a bear rather than a deer. That *would* be something.

This was a perfect day for the boy. He loved helping his father. He loved the swamp. He loved the snow on the ground. He loved breathing in the cold, winter air. He remembered raising his mitten and cupping his hand to the other deer, and how the deer seemed to return a nod. The boy and his father talked about their hunt all the way to the car. But the boy never told his father about the other deer.

CHAPTER 27
PBB

AD 1974

For the family whose ancestors were pioneer farmers—Angus's family—1974 was not a good year. During the preceding two decades, the farm progressively shifted to a dairy specialization. The family built up a herd of 130 Holstein dairy cows and three beef steers. The steers they fattened to butcher for their own table.

They first noticed the problem late in 1973 when a calf was born without hair. What the local veterinarian saw puzzled him. It was not only the calf, but all the cattle seemed gaunt and lethargic. He took blood samples and sent them to the lab at Michigan State University.

Before the results returned, the calf and two additional cattle died. The dairy farmer rolled the carcasses into the bucket of his tractor and brought them to the back forty acres, where he buried them.

It was not long before the health department came to test the milk. Nothing seemed obviously out of place, but the farmer and the veterinarian both knew there was a serious problem brewing. The veterinarian began seeing similar symptoms on other farms in the area—mostly dairy farms. He suspected poisoning but could not identify the culprit. He continued testing.

Finally, in April of 1974, a small team of people discovered that a chemical manufacturer had accidentally mislabeled between ten and twenty fifty-pound bags of fire retardant, polybrominated biphenyl (PBB), as feed supplement. The granules, which looked similar to each other, were put in the wrong bags. The fire retardant was then mistakenly mixed with other feed nutrients and fed to farm animals—mostly dairy cattle. Action-reaction. Human. The fuse was lit.

In early May, Michigan's health services pulled into the farmyard with three large semi-trucks as the farmer was about to begin the day's milking. They drove down the now-paved road between the old cabin and the main farmhouse. The health services immediately quarantined the entire farm. Everyone worked together to coax the cattle into the trucks. Three cattle died on the ramp. It took five hours.

The oldest-generation human on the farm, the grandfather—Angus and Grace's grandson—cried as the cattle he loved, the herd he had built, were taken, several of the cattle dying from the exertion. He was so focused on his own despair he entirely missed the spirits of the cattle merging with the spirit current. Each cow a drop of rain.

Before the day was through, an entire rainstorm of drops was swimming toward the big lake, all blended into a single spirit stream, visible only to those who understood how such things worked.

Perhaps the grandfather also cried because he understood what this meant to the future of his family and the community. Thirty thousand contaminated cattle from all around were buried in large trenches dug between trees in a Kalkaska forest, and then in a similar forest near Mio, as well as more than 1.5 million chickens and nearly eight thousand other farm animals.

Some farmers were relieved when the State took their cattle because they saw what was happening to their animals and recognized it was already over.

From farmer to zero in five hours.

One of the same trucks later came to empty the farm's freezer of beef they butchered. They removed the remaining feed from the bins and milk from the processing tanks. All the contaminated material was buried in the trenches. Finally, government workers helped the farmer steam-clean the stalls, the barnyard, and the barn so that the place could pass a final inspection.

1974 was not a good year. The farm was left with no cattle—no animals at all—and an empty freezer. It was like when fire had burned all the trees in the forest. Everything needed to start over. It would be a long process.

At least the farming family had free natural gas to run their furnace, stove, and water heater.

The family arranged for a loan from the dairy company. It was their only lifeline. Six months later they began to look for a new herd of cattle.

The human PBB problem spread in an insidious way throughout the continent with the food supply that was already in the pipeline. There was no way to stop it. The fuse was lit. Action-reaction. Human.

Unfortunately, there were things about this catastrophe that were too small to attract much attention. Perhaps people just turned a blind eye to them. Rats, mice, bats, and birds disappeared. Well, they did not actually disappear; they went into the wild food chain and into the soil. They simultaneously became part of the humans' growing problems and the natural spirit pool.

And what about the cattle the farmer buried on his back forty acres?

Fortunately, for every action, Mother Nature always provides a reaction, and the slow process of covering up the human problem of contamination was already underway. It would just take time. Perhaps thousands of years. The traces of PBB would not necessarily go away, but sometime in the distant future, PBB would no longer be considered a contaminant.

It would just be considered part of the natural order. Everything would adapt. Living things would die. Other living things capable of tolerating the new conditions would replace them. For a human, such a path was unthinkable. If humans paid close attention to the insect world, however, they would see how that worked.

The problem was getting humans to realize that they were not so different from an insect in the grand scheme of things.

CHAPTER 28
THE BOY BUYS THE EIGHTY ACRES

AD 1986

Split Toe liked the boy. Something about him reminded Split Toe of Edra. Perhaps he sensed his respect. He remembered the tiny mitten cupping its hand—an innocent friendliness filled with compassion.

As the boy grew older, he learned to recognize Split Toe's massive hoofprint. From time to time, Split Toe showed himself to the boy.

Every time they saw each other, the boy always raised his hand gently and cupped his fingers in a disarming wave, and Split Toe lowered his wide antlers to the ground in an affectionate and respectful bow.

Oh, sure ... the boy hunted. His father taught him to do so. The boy viewed it as part of the natural order of things. But, like the Ojibwe, the boy seemed respectful of the deer and of the forest and of all that was natural. He always took an ordinary deer, perfectly average in every way.

The boy felt the spirit current, and he sensed the presence of Split Toe.

Split Toe trusted the boy. He knew that even if he showed himself to the boy during the middle of hunting season, the boy would pass on the opportunity, raise his hand, and cup his fingers to say, "I see you. Thank you for letting me know you are still here."

And when the boy walked around on the eighty acres, he always looked for Split Toe's distinctives hoofprints.

It did not take long for the boy to find the twelve white pines along the river's edge. He did not know their significance, but he sensed their spirit, and he wondered about the crumbling basement located at the top of the sand bluff.

How could anyone let a shelter in such a beautiful spot collapse? the boy wondered.

When the boy walked to the river's edge, he listened for the whisper of wind drifting through the branches of the largest tree—the grandfather tree. When he closed his eyes, the boy thought he heard the old tree speaking to him.

"You are here in the forest," the tree spoke, *"the natural world. Take some time to absorb it. To feel it. Do not fight Mother Nature, my young friend. She can bring you peace."*

The boy always listened to the tree's wisdom. In time, the boy found he could go to this old tree for sage advice. As the boy grew, he sat by the river from time to time, closed his eyes, and listened as the grandfather tree helped him to think through what was troubling him.

It was when the boy was away at college that the four brothers met and accepted a logging broker's proposal to take most of the hardwood trees from the forest areas of the property. At this point, only twenty-five acres of forest were left. The trees here were over a hundred years old, a mixture of different species that Edra had watched grow from nothing. Ten of the original eighty acres had been converted into a gravel quarry. At least ten acres more were clear-cut for the gas pipeline right-of-way. Maybe thirty-five acres were tag alder swamp.

But loggers still showed interest in the lumber that was available. The trees were mature and healthy. The modern timber cruisers were looking for lumber like that. The loggers agreed to leave the white pines, twelve old-growth trees, and other white pines that grew up with the hardwoods. They also agreed to leave several mature oaks and maples that might help to restart the forest after this logging was complete. "Selective logging," the modern logger called it.

What is this? Split Toe thought as he watched men unload logging machinery from the trailer. *Not again. ...*

Split Toe had never seen logging equipment like this before. There was an articulating tractor with a blade on the front, an excavator with a hydraulic claw where the scoop could attach, and a long trailer set up to accept full-length logs. The logging team consisted of three humans operating large chain saws, a human driving the articulating tractor, and a human using the excavator to load logs onto the long trailer.

When loggers began cutting trees, Split Toe felt bad for the boy. He knew how the boy loved the natural parts of these eighty acres, especially the hundred-year-old trees that covered parts of it. The boy would be heartbroken when he found out what was happening.

The large, knobby tires of the articulating tractor churned in four-wheel drive as the machine dragged one massive log after another across the forest floor. Where it could, the tractor used its front blade to push stumps out of the way and make a smooth road back to the excavator and trailer. The fertile soil was all still there somewhere, but it was no longer anchored to the sandy surface below it. It was displaced in piles, rows, and clumps.

Four main logging trails now crossed the property. One large loop circled from the end of the road and back around. The trailer for loading logs could loop around this trail coming in and going out. From the loop, the loggers built three road arteries. One led to the pipeline and the tag alder swamp on the northeast corner. Another led to a ridge on the southeast corner. The third led below the ridge to where the river crossed the south border of the property.

The loggers were organized. From the forest-covered sectors they cut logs and dragged them to one of the roads and then dragged them to the truck. They cut the logs, removed the branches, and made way for the next tree to fall. The chain they used to drag the logs was not unlike the chain used a century before when it was attached to an ox team or a horse. But now they shackled the chain to the back of the tractor.

As the team removed the logs, a logger assessed major limbs to determine their usefulness. They took some. Most they pushed aside. The loggers left the ground scattered with other broken mid-size branches. The whole process took three weeks. When they were done, the loggers loaded the equipment back onto the trailer and dispassionately moved on to another parcel that could be cleared. The efficiency amazed Split Toe. These humans were more clever than ever ... and noisy.

When all was said and done, the property was a mess. Most of the trees had been removed. What remained could hardly be called a forest. The gravel pit sat there like a missing tooth and the pipeline cut across the countryside in a straight line. What had once been natural was now designed, constructed, harvested, and left in human turmoil. Old deer trails that had at one time crossed from the river to the tag alder swamp were no longer visible. Branches crisscrossing the ground now blocked places where the animal trails once were. It was not pretty, but the mess would eventually break down and start a new batch of soil. Split Toe knew the recovery would take longer than the last time because the big machinery was a lot tougher on the forest floor than horses were. The original logging trails had not been as disruptive as these new scars on the land.

The spirits again whispered on the wind that blew across Split Toe's back.

"What have you learned, Split Toe? It is all connected."

Split Toe knew the question was rhetorical. No answer expected. He must continue to pay attention.

Thankfully, the original twelve white pines and the tag alder swamp still stood. The swamp was truly the only natural area left on the eighty acres—thirty-five pristine acres of thicket.

No one told the boy. It was only when he arrived for a brief walk in the forest on his way home from college for the Easter holiday weekend that he stood at the end of the road and looked at the destruction. Most of the trees were gone. The soil had been churned up by the tractor, in many places scraped bare to make logging roads which provided access to the trees. Several lonely live trees stood as sentinels in the middle of fields of debris. He noticed the twelve old pines still standing. The grandfather pine at the base of the bluff was still there but somehow seemed silent.

The boy stood with his hands buried deep in his pockets. His shoulders drooped. He breathed in slowly to calm his mind. He looked up at clouds crossing the blue sky, and then back down to the destruction at ground level. How did this happen? What would happen next? He was shocked and heartbroken. He could not believe that no one had told him about this. Warned him about this. Asked him about this. But why should they? He had no say in the matter. He had grown to love land that was not really his.

There are many ways for a forest to die.

The boy worked his way to the edge of the tag alder swamp. His breath caught in his throat. At least the swamp was untouched. As he walked along its edge, quietly giving thanks it hadn't been destroyed, he noticed an old, well-used trail—an ancient trail that traced the swamp's perimeter.

His strange connection to Split Toe—one he didn't fully understand—told him that his old friend was there now. In this moment, they shared each other's pain. The machines had stolen something from both of them.

What the boy could not know was that Split Toe looked at the situation differently. After the initial shock of the logger's return, Split Toe saw the destruction with a kind of quiet neutrality. This was not the first time the forest had seen this kind of destruction. Split Toe had witnessed the forest wiped out by fire, by European loggers, and now this newest round of logging. But Split Toe understood how the boy felt. Split Toe remembered his own feelings when fire first destroyed the forest. The spirit pool helped him get through that experience—helped him understand and put it into context. It was all part of Split Toe's education.

Split Toe stepped from the thicket. They recognized each other immediately. The boy raised his hand and sadly cupped his fingers; Split Toe bowed deeply and touched his fresh antler starts to the ground. He saw a single tear sliding down the boy's cheek. Split Toe took two steps forward toward the boy. It was no longer a boy that faced him: it was a full-grown man. Split Toe, however, would always think of him as *the boy*.

Split Toe stared into the boy's eyes one more time and nodded his head. He wanted to gently nuzzle the boy, to let the boy know he understood. To heal his injury. But he was a wild animal, so instead Split Toe lowered his head again, and turned back into the swamp, the only cover around.

The boy exhaled slowly, feeling the deep ache of a broken heart. He wanted to drop to his knees and claw at the ground, to lean his forehead against the earth and wait for something redemptive to happen. Instead, he breathed in deeply, turned around, and made his way back along the logging trail to his small truck.

When the boy started his truck, the radio picked up at the midpoint of his favorite song. The boy simply turned off the radio. He wanted silence to think through what might happen next with the eighty acres—and if there was anything he could do to about it.

When the boy walked through the door, his father immediately knew something was wrong. His son looked at the ground, walking around his father without greeting his mother. His face was distant and blank, and his shoulders slumped in a way that was completely unlike him. Perhaps the semester was not going well. Maybe he broke up with a girlfriend. That must be it. Just give the boy some space. He would eventually be ready to talk about it.

Finally, the boy spoke. "I visited the eighty acres. You could have told me."

The father had given it thought, but telling his son would not have changed the outcome. The brothers were determined.

The father produced a false smile. "The trees were ready to go."

The boy simply returned a sad glance.

"That is why we bought that parcel. You knew this would eventually happen."

The boy knew it was true. He should not have expected anything different. For his father and uncles, it was all about the hunting and the investment.

"Are you done now? Did you get what you wanted?" the boy asked.

The father paused, then nodded. "I think so. Let me talk to the others."

"Then I want to buy the land," the boy said softly.

The father did not show his disbelief. He knew there was not much left for that eighty acres to offer. But the father could see in his son's eyes that he was serious.

"I graduate in twelve months. If you can wait until then to finalize the financial part of the transaction, I would like to take responsibility for the property now."

The father admired what his son was saying. It made the father proud to know that his son was standing up for something he believed in. Something he was passionate about. It had been a long time since the father had last felt that kind of passion. He thought his son was lucky to have discovered a calling so important to him.

"Let me talk to the others."

"I will pay what you paid for the land plus twenty percent. You already have money from the trees. I don't think you will find another offer like this. Not anymore."

The father knew it was true. He knew his son's offer was more generous than it needed to be, and his brothers—the boy's uncles—would recognize that. They would understand the boy's motivation. His son thought things out clearly. In his head and in his heart. Because of that, he knew his son would get what was important to him.

"I will work it out," the father finally said. And he did.

The boy spent every free moment during the next year picking up discarded diesel cans, broken hydraulic hoses, bottles, cans, empty steel drums, and tires of every sort. He loaded them into his truck, brought the metal to a reclaimer, and took the remaining debris to the county dump.

When it came to the abandoned vibrating gravel hopper, the boy spoke to the farmer who owned the peninsula—the great-grandson of Angus. Together, they scooped the machine into the bucket of the farmer's large tractor and put it behind the barn where scrap metal accumulated for a reclaimer to buy once each year.

Each time the boy came to work, Split Toe stepped out of the swamp to let the boy know he was still around. The boy would stand quietly for a minute and watch, then raise a hand with cupped fingers.

Split Toe, who always looked directly into the boy's eyes, dipped his antlers to the ground in an affectionate bow and stepped back into the tag alder swamp. Split Toe was glad the spirits had introduced him to the boy. The boy was connected to the natural world.

By the time the boy graduated in the spring, much of the debris had already been cleared from the eighty acres, and a fresh round of aspen saplings sprouted where the trees once were. The boy had faith in Mother Nature. He knew she would return this land to the wilds if humans did not get in her way. It was the way Mother Nature worked. Action-reaction. The boy believed that Mother Nature would always prevail.

CHAPTER 29
SO MANY DEER

AD 2020

As the sun recovered from the eclipse, Split Toe cautiously stepped up from the riverbed onto the peninsula. A slight limp from the dire wolf attack that took place at this very spot in another age still bothered his leg. He no longer thought about the bullet that had winged him several decades ago on this same peninsula. His neck had healed within two weeks of the injury, and all that remained was an old telltale scar hidden below his fur.

When Split Toe felt the pull—the call of the spirit stream—he always answered. He knew the spirits wanted to show him something important, and was always curious to find out what it was. Split Toe crossed the river and stepped up onto the peninsula. He saw the grandfather tree towering behind him on the river's edge, as well as a thirty-five-year-old natural forest filling in around it. The boy did well to let Mother Nature bring the forest back naturally. The area logged under the direction of the boy's father and uncles now promised to become a mature, natural forest again. Split Toe was happy.

It was late afternoon on a June day, and a fresh carpet of alfalfa covered the rolling terrain west of the river. Split Toe stepped out from the cover of the forest into the open field. Four deer—two does and two fawns—were nibbling on alfalfa on the opposite side of the peninsula. Looking a long way off to the southeast corner of the field, he could see a group of sixty deer grazing peacefully. Many of the deer were likely his offspring.

Split Toe stepped back across the river and began to walk through the thick cover on the river flats toward the group of grazing deer. The plush, green undergrowth that had grown in after the last round of logging provided good cover for fawns and other young animals.

Split Toe skirted the gravel pit, which was also returning to natural habitat. It would never be the sand dune it once was, but nature had begun rewilding it in a new way. The process would take time. First, the soil needed to develop. That could take decades, perhaps centuries. A flat meadow now made up the pit's floor at an elevation slightly higher than the river flats. At its center, a small, deep pond fed by cool underground springs rippled in the breeze.

Finding an old deer trail that was still in use, Split Toe made his way to the corner of the alfalfa field to join the large group of deer.

Two children played with a dog on sand cliffs that defined three sides of the gravel pit's horseshoe shape.

The eighty acres were now filled with trees of many types:

several kinds of pine and spruce, varieties of oak and maple, birch, cherry, beech, and, of course, tag alders. There were also a multitude of other plants: raspberry, blackberry, huckleberry, elderberry, grapes, ferns, cattails, native grasses, and many kinds of wildflowers. All the local wild animal species thrived in this diverse ecosystem—more species than the boy knew the names of. Occasionally, a turtle, snake, or insect that he had not seen before would wander out of the thicket. The habitat provided food, warmth, shelter from severe weather, and protection from predators—predators who used the same features for their own well-being. The alfalfa field was an additional benefit. Grass eaters never lacked a sweet meal.

Over time, the logging roads became part of the forest sanctuary until it was hard to imagine they had ever been scars from an old wound. The boy kept the roads trimmed so humans could easily walk through the property without disturbing the soil and natural plant life regenerating on either side of the trails.

At the furthest point on the last artery of a trail, the boy constructed a small, two-hundred-square-foot shelter. Its amenities were simple: a single room with a bed, a counter, a table, and a woodstove. It had no electricity and used only antique oil lamps. A cuckoo clock in the corner measured out the shelter's heartbeat. Edra would have liked this shelter.

For water, the boy drove a two-inch well thirty feet into the forest floor with his own hands and inserted a hand pump into the pipe. He placed an outhouse toilet eighty yards back up the trail, nestled amongst the trees. The shelter was simple, blending into the forest, but it had everything a human needed to survive.

SO MANY DEER • AD 2020

When the boy stayed in the shelter, he was just another animal in the wilds, as were his children and grandchildren. They all behaved with respect for the world around them, and the forest seemed to accept them.

From his kitchen window half a mile west of the spot where the large herd of deer were grazing, a descendant of Angus and Grace sat in the farmhouse with a pair of field glasses, counting the deer as they popped into the field.

"Thirty-four. Thirty-five. Thirty-six. ... Boy, that's a big one. Hannah, come and look at this big buck." He saw Split Toe take his place in the group.

The farmer could see the buck's antlers with his naked eyes at half a mile. That was indeed a big deer.

"Hannah! You gotta see this." The farmer would have to walk into the field the next day and have a look at the tracks.

"Forty-eight. Forty-nine ..."

"Fifty-six. Fifty-seven. Fifty-eight," the farmer tried to count them all. "Fifty-nine. Sixty. Sixty-one. Hannah, there are sixty-one deer in that south field right now," he shouted across the house. "They're gonna eat everything we have!"

From a human's point of view, the land was just too good. The conditions were perfect for all types of wildlife to thrive and multiply. Humans did not often pay attention to the fact that Mother Nature took care of things in her own way. She kept the wild population in check through food supply, weather, fertility rates, disease, injury, and predators. She even considered the hunting and farming habits of humans. It was all a balancing act that happened automatically under the supervision of Mother Nature.

Humans wanted to believe they were the ones regulating the population of animals they hunted, and perhaps there was some truth to that. From time to time, humans demonstrated they could hunt an animal to extinction, or close to it. Humans could burn through an entire resource they depended on. But Mother Nature then brought in something else to take the place of the extinct species, whether plant or animal. Everything was constantly reaching for balance and equilibrium within Mother Nature's equation of action and reaction.

Disease was a choice remedy for overpopulation, though humans did not like to think of it that way. They did not want the wild animals they hunted to die from disease. Many humans looked at animal disease with disdain, and animals themselves with something between indifference and compassion, but rarely with any consideration for natural population control.

A few hundred miles to the south, where the deer population was even greater than in this alfalfa field, chronic wasting disease reduced the size of the deer population significantly in only one or two years. The disease seemed to pass through saliva of deer feeding on the same food. More deer concentrated in a common feeding area meant more opportunity for the disease to spread.

When the diseased population reached a kind of adaptation and equilibrium with other factors in the environment, a healthy deer population would likely emerge again. Humans never wanted to wait while Mother Nature performed her magic. It could take a long time—too long for a single human generation to see the results. But was the problem overpopulation, or disease?

Either way, Mother Nature would work things out.

CHAPTER 30
CORPORATE FARMING

AD 2020

The pioneer's descendants still living in the farmhouse were about ninety years old. Their son, living in the original cabin, was nearly sixty years old now. They were recognized by the community to be some of the last true family-farm holdouts in the area. Other families that dabbled in farming now treated it as a hobby, a side business. Angus and Grace's descendants hung on with a sixty-cow milking operation until they simply wore themselves out. They were *just getting by* for a long time, surviving by the skin of their teeth. They kept the operation in play exactly long enough to convert their final feed inventory into milk. Then they found a new home for the cattle, auctioned off all their farm machinery, and worked hard at trying not to farm every day.

They loved their farming lifestyle, but they did not have much of a safety net in place. In fact, this *non-farming* situation worked out better for them. They leased the agricultural rights for their fields to a large-scale dairy corporation ten miles away, a corporation with more than three thousand dairy cows. It was an ideal retirement for the pioneer's descendants. They actually had more cash to use and less debt than when they were milking the cattle and working the fields themselves seven days a week. Leasing out their fields required a lot less responsibility and risk.

For operations like the one that leased their land, everything was a matter of scale and efficiency. They needed to maximize the number of milk-producing cattle without increasing the number of workers and administrators. More cattle required more feed; more fields took care of that. Leased fields.

The pioneer's descendants saw that the dairy corporation did not work the fields themselves. This was something that worked well for the corporation but would have been a bridge too far for the pioneer's descendants. They were not those kinds of farmers. The corporation hired another company—a subcontractor—who plowed the ground, planted, fertilized, and harvested the crops. The subcontractor then delivered everything to and from storage areas at the dairy farm.

What amazed the pioneer's descendants—and Split Toe when he observed—was the speed at which everything took place. These humans ... oh, they were so clever. On a day when the weather was good, the harvesting equipment arrived early in the morning. The descendants set out their lawn chairs with a good view of the fields and watched for the whole day.

The old man picked up his glass of water and simply said, "Amazing."

His wife patted his knee and smiled. "They sure seem to know what they're doing."

Watching the work being done made the retired farmers feel as if they were still farming. They were the proud landowners who made everything possible. Equipment streamed into the field, every aspect perfectly coordinated, as if the drivers were talking to each other. And indeed, they were, with radios or cell phones. They cut all the original fields and raked the cuttings into windrows. Then they came through with high-capacity choppers that funneled the rows of piled alfalfa into the front of the machine and shot it out the back as silage, depositing it directly into a series of large open-top semi-trailers that drove next to the chopper in a perfectly synchronized ballet.

Streams of semi-trailers drove quickly between the dairy and the field, so the chopper always had a bin to fill. The chopper was more expensive than most people could imagine, but if it kept chopping all day, every day, the subcontractor said the machine would pay for itself.

On a good day, when the chopping on this property was complete and the machine was already in another leased field a few miles away, a stream of large tractors pulling fertilizer trailers drove into the freshly cut fields. The tractors spread a liquid slurry mostly made from the cattle's manure across the ground. Farming had shifted from a rural lifestyle to a different kind of operation. Part science, part logistics, and part business management.

The corporation owners often did much better than *just getting by*.

Angus and Grace's descendants compared the time it took for them to do the same work. They needed to work for more than six weeks to complete the same scope using their own large John Deere tractor and the implements it pulled.

The farmer thought of his father, who'd worked the farm until the day he died. Family-farm work just wore a farmer out. The father was a bit like the old truck that they drove around the property until the wheels finally fell off.

When that happened, the farmer fondly patted the truck on its hood and said, "Well done, my friend. It's time."

He used the John Deere tractor to drag the old truck to the scrap metal pile behind the barn. The family farm wore everything out to its last nut and bolt. And people to their last breath.

The day they found the farmer's father, he was in the barn, draped over the bucket of the same John Deere tractor, with a wrench he had dropped lying in the bucket. His final expression was strained. But his son saw it as satisfaction. Farming happiness.

"Done for today," the son whispered when he found his father.

He placed his large farming hand on the old shirt covering his father's chest and back. He could feel the ribs and imagined his heart still beating inside. He picked up the wrench and sat down on the bucket to spend a few moments in the barn with his dad before walking to the house to gently inform the family.

A drop of rain.

If Mother Nature cooperated, the subcontractor could take three or four alfalfa cuttings off each field in a single season. If Mother Nature cooperated. At least, that's how humans would put it. But maybe these humans were too clever for their own good.

Split Toe could not know that these humans, in their own way, had tried to bring Mother Nature under the control of their own human system. When too much or too little rain destroyed the year's crops, a farmer could process an insurance claim that gave them cash to replace part of the value of their lost crop, enough cash to help them survive until the next season.

Cash. That was something that Split Toe would never understand. He'd long stopped wondering how their disconnected activities gave food, or shelter, or fuel to their communities. It just did not matter to Split Toe anymore. He saw the results. Somehow, humans managed to stay alive, even when the work they did had little to do with their own survival.

"You are learning the ways of humans, Split Toe," the spirits whispered to their student during a spring rain.

Mother Nature never paid a speck of attention to human cash.

CHAPTER 31
THE GRANDFATHER TREE'S WISDOM

AD 2020

People no longer talked about PBB. Everyone assumed that Mother Nature would take care of it. They took for granted that she would. And she was certainly in the process of doing so, though human expectation regarding the format of Mother Nature's problem-solving, and the time she would take to do the job, rarely matched Mother Nature's real-life action-reaction process. A human generation played out the health tragedy, leaving the next generation to start over. Action-reaction, like the forest.

In some ways, Split Toe observed the humans the same way the pioneer descendant thought about the sixty-one deer standing in the back corner of his alfalfa field. The conditions were just too good for them. Humans thrived and multiplied in their environment. Split Toe wondered where all these people were coming from.

In 1800, there were only about 4,800 settlers in all of Michigan, and perhaps 14,000 Indigenous people. In 1870, there were a bit less than 1.2 million humans in Michigan. In 2020, the number of Michigan people had grown to about 10 million. Split Toe had experienced that population explosion. Had Split Toe been able to understand human populations in a global context, he would have considered that the whole world had about 1.0 billion human inhabitants in 1800, about 1.3 billion humans in 1870, and nearly 8.0 billion in 2020, with it rapidly rising north of 11.0 billion.

Where would it level off? Could it level off? What would cause it to level off? But without even understanding what the planet faced and how it might relate to his own forest, Split Toe trusted in Mother Nature to take care of things in her own way and in her own time.

The boy, now fifty-four years old, sat in his forest shelter, knowing his grandchildren were playing on a sandy cliff in the gravel pit. Cathy, his life partner, left the shelter to walk the shady forest trail to the sunshine of the gravel pit. What made that place so fascinating to children? It was so unusual, with its sugary sand cliffs to climb and a proper forest floor at the top. Children loved to run between the trees and sail through the air off the edge, landing halfway down the steep slope where their legs buried knee-deep in the sand as they skidded to a stop. There was freedom for them at the gravel pit. Cathy liked it too. She could watch clouds blow across the sky and find fossils on the ground. Occasionally, a deer or other animal wandered through.

The boy—the man—stayed in the shelter for a few minutes. He needed time alone to think. He was again pondering a topic of discussion at the forefront of so many people's minds: global warming. He had thought about this subject many times. In his mind, individual humans were capable of withstanding change more readily than almost any other animal species on earth. They planned, individually and in small groups, far more intelligently than most other species.

But with so many competing desires, large groups of humans seemed unable to organize their behaviors to ensure the survival of their own species. Their group instincts often missed basic problems until the consequences were unavoidable. Sure, many people knew about the issues already facing the species. The fuse had been burning for a long time. People now trying to find a solution were not necessarily the ones who lit the fuse in the first place.

Today, people who were serious about the survival of their children, grandchildren, and great-grandchildren also accepted part of the responsibility. They looked for small ways to slow down the consequences of their lifestyles on the world, hoping that Mother Nature might soften the landing for future generations. Many people understood enough of the action-reaction process to realize that everyone was part of the problem—and could be part of the solution.

The boy thought humans as a group deserved the change they would need to endure. Perhaps they also deserved the future condition they would need to conform to. Humans are experts at resisting change. It is in their nature. Uncertainties frighten them. They can adapt, but only when they have no other choice. Often it is too late.

Whatever happened, the boy was confident that the spirit pool, made up of all things past and present, would remain steadfast, continuing through all that happened, through ice age or global warming. This gave him some comfort. The spirit pool was pure—a great coexistence of souls that equalized all conflicts and differences seeming important in the physical realm. No food chain existed in the spirit pool.

The boy was sure that Mother Nature would manage actions and reactions in the way she always had. Insects consuming their entire food supply, leaving nothing left for the survival of their offspring; the deer population overtaking the resources of the forest where they lived … it was all self-regulating. It was automatic. Action-reaction. But the spirit pool would go on without judgment, accepting each new soul, each new drop of rain swimming toward Lake Michigan, continuing to nourish things as the planet changed.

Split Toe watched as the boy walked past the gravel pit to the edge of the river where he could sit under the arms of the grandfather tree. The boy often talked to this tree and felt that he received soft answers. Today, Split Toe listened as the tree asked the boy a question.

"My friend, what is the real problem? The issue that Mother Nature will address to set things right? Is it the temperature of the planet? What is the reaction you expect she will use if she believes it needs correcting? Perhaps you humans should think about your own population. It affects everything. Don't outeat your food supply, my friend. What will the human species do for food, shelter, fuel?"

The tree continued.

"The planet is warming. It has done so before. Perhaps this time humans play a bigger part and are making it warm more quickly. Making the planet hotter for longer than it would have been without them. But humans are living things too. Like any other living thing, they have a place on this planet. It is where they belong. All things are part of the equation. Land will flood. The climate will change. Ice may melt, making larger oceans and less dry ground. Soil will change. Land-dwelling creatures may need to find new ways to exist—to coexist with the world they inhabit—and new places to live. Some may become extinct. More people. Less space. You humans, you are clever. You will discover ways that you cannot even imagine now."

The tree paused and shook its branches in the breeze.

"My friend, I have watched humans for five hundred years. I have seen their cleverness as they try to restore the natural equilibrium that they disrupt. They fix symptoms and cause other problems by doing so. They work within their human system of laws, economics, politics, nationalism, and religion. Each human has a place in the world as does any other thing—living or not. Humans also are part of nature. But today's humans disproportionately impact everything, and in their shortsighted sense of self-preservation, they destroy many things in their path. Few humans today understand the spirit pool that crosses all boundaries. Why do they do everything the hard way? Perhaps they should be like a tree, respecting the ways of Mother Nature rather than trying to assert their own power, their own superiority. Someday they may find such things are misguided.

"My dear friend, I know what is in your heart. You understand that only Mother Nature will determine the outcome. I wish the whole human species would also understand such things before they disappoint themselves. It would be good for them to know. But do not worry. Mother Nature is in charge. Furthermore, all raindrops will get swept up in the eternal spirit pool. All things in the wilds know this. They accept it. It is important to understand."

The boy—the man—did not know how to respond. He simply bowed deeply to the wise old tree and placed his forehead gently against the tree's bark. He felt its energy run through him.

He turned and walked to the gravel pit to hug his grandchildren. Right now, they were too young to understand the grandfather tree's knowledge, but he would explain it to them someday. It was important for them to know.

Split Toe watched as the boy left the grandfather tree. He watched and listened to the whole conversation from his concealed place across the river. He could tell the conversation bothered the boy, that it forced him to think deeply.

The boy walked back to his shelter where Cathy was waiting.

"I remember when my father brought me here for the first time to hunt," the boy said to Cathy.

"Do you miss him?" Cathy asked softly. "I do."

"I feel his spirit out here. The land here was different then." The boy thought of all he saw and thought about in his fifty-four years. "I would like to have seen this place from the beginning," he mused. "I mean, beginning with the glaciers that brought in the sand and gravel with the ice that melted to form the river.

Can you imagine what it was like for the Ojibwe? I often wonder if one of their villages might have been at the top of the bluff, next to the river."

"It would have been a perfect spot," Cathy imagined too.

"I wonder about how many forest fires tore through this place. How many times has the forest had to start over? Oh, the stories my grandfather told me about how the first loggers leveled the mature forest to the ground. Some trees so big three people could not reach around them."

"I'm sure glad the big trees by the river are still with us," Cathy said. "I wish we knew why the first loggers left them alone. I really think it must have something to do with the old foundation at the top of the bluff."

The boy agreed as his thoughts drifted to the twelve old-growth trees.

He thought of his friend and mentor, the grandfather tree.

"I wonder what this place was like before the gravel pit took so much of the hillside away," the boy said. "There are still a few people living who saw it before it was changed. Can you imagine what it was like for the animals?"

Though the boy had bought the land from his father's generation, he never felt that he owned it. Such an idea did not seem right to him. He simply had purchased the privilege to care for these eighty acres, and to care for all living things that depended on the space. It was a blessing and a responsibility.

Had Split Toe understood human ideas of land ownership, he would have thought the boy's perspective aligned with the way Mother Nature behaved. But right now, Split Toe knew that what bothered the boy was not Mother Nature: it was his fellow humans.

How have humans come to where they are now? The boy wondered to himself. *Is it human nature—human instinct—that drives their self-absorbed attitudes about the world they inhabit? Their need to put their own stamp on Mother Nature's action-reaction processes? Why do humans behave the way they do with each other and so often treat other things that occupy the same planet with so little respect?*

The grandfather tree had taught him that humans might be missing the point. Where was it all heading?

Later that year, one of the large old-growth white pines came down in a storm. It broke off twenty feet above the ground. When the boy looked closely, he saw where the heartwood of the tree had decayed. He did not see the decay while the tree was standing. Insects ate and weakened the tree from the inside.

There are many ways for a tree to die.

The boy looked at the other mature pines. They showed no visible signs of trouble, but he wondered if something similar might be hiding inside these majestic creations. He saw generations of offspring from the fallen tree growing close by. The boy left the skeleton where it lay on the ground so that Mother Nature could do her job without his interruption. Another drop of rain.

THE GRANDFATHER TREE'S WISDOM • AD 2020

During the next two years, the boy received what seemed like an endless stream of proposals to lumber off or lease the mineral rights on the eighty acres. These people did not understand the boy. He ignored them all. Now that the land was thoroughly clean of human debris and blessed by thirty-five years of natural growth, many people who saw its beauty were covetous of it. But the boy was not interested. What he now protected was a sanctuary for Mother Nature—a simple eighty acres that he intended to leave alone. He and his children and grandchildren would blend into the background to ensure that Mother Nature could produce a mature, natural forest. They would do so by keeping their human hands off it.

Many people thought relaxing human control of the property was risky, but not because the family wanted Mother Nature to take over. People wondered how the boy would recover his investment. When they saw what the boy was doing, they thought he was simply not paying attention, that he was missing every opportunity. That he was naive.

It was easy to let trees live and die according to the natural order. Trees fell where they fell and decayed where they lay. They grew where they sprang up, whatever species of new trees that naturally started on their own. Seeds blew in on the wind. Forest animals planted them. The results were remarkable. What had recently been a human mess was now a diverse healthy forest with diverse habitat where wildlife and trees helped each other. People wondered when the boy would cash in on this place.

People did not understand that the moment the boy purchased the property, he put no monetary value on it in his own head. To the boy, it was as if he gave the money away. The cash. Gave it all to Mother Nature. It was the responsibility he wanted, not a return on the money he spent. Now that everything of financial value was gone from the land in the boy's mind, he was determined to keep it that way.

The *mature forest* part of the idea was tricky because a single tree—let alone an entire forest—takes more than one human generation to reach full maturity. Generation after generation needed to see value in preserving the natural forest and keeping the idea alive. These values would need to be passed down. The boy knew he would eventually lose control of this goal. Would others see the boy's mission as important?

Split Toe again heard the spirits whisper, **"What have you learned, Split Toe? Understand the things you hear and see. The lesson is important."**

Split Toe did not know what to think. He did not know if he should answer.

"I have seen many kinds of humans." His thoughts reached for the spirits. "They have their own system. There are also a few who would follow the natural way. But most humans seem to exist with eyes only for the human system, which tries every day to find a new way around Mother Nature's way of doing things. Humans are eating their way through one resource after another. What will be left for those in the future?"

"You learn well, Split Toe. Your lessons become more difficult. But you have been prepared for every lesson. You think well. You miss little. You have survived ... so far. Learning never ends, but there are still a few more new experiences you must face. The most important lesson will come soon. After that, it will be up to you to do something important with that lesson. You will know what to do."

One day, the boy began to receive a puzzling new kind of proposal from various companies. He was given offers to lease the acreage of live trees as "carbon offsets." It was a scheme in which a company producing carbon dioxide in their industrial process could pay to keep trees alive so that the trees could convert an equal amount of carbon dioxide from the atmosphere into oxygen through photosynthesis. And why not? Receiving free cash when you plan to preserve the trees anyway seemed like an easy decision. But that was exactly what did not make sense to him: he planned to preserve the trees anyway. His mind brought him back to a question the grandfather tree asked him to consider.

He could hear the grandfather tree now, *"What is the problem that needs solving? What does this do to produce food, shelter, and fuel for the people leasing the trees?"*

The boy considered these questions again for a few weeks. If he planned to save the trees anyway, what good did it do for the environment if he accepted the lease? On the surface, the company could claim that it was adding enough genuine carbon offsets to make up for its carbon dioxide emissions. But in reality, their lease would do absolutely zero to create actual *new* carbon offsets that did not already exist and that *added* real benefit to the environment.

Something seemed disingenuous about the lease proposal. It permitted the company to project an image of carbon neutrality while pretending that they had indeed achieved something worthwhile. The lease satisfied their conscience. It was an angle; a money solution to a problem that had nothing to do with money. The boy thought it best to stay out of this game. Hopefully the companies would spend their money on carbon offsets which actually added value to the planet.

Humans—how did they learn to be so clever? What had become of their connection to the spirit pool? The boy—the man—was happy with his decision.

CHAPTER 32
WINTER CROSSING

AD 2020

Heavy snows had drifted into piles so high they reached Split Toe's belly. Each step was a struggle, his legs plunging into holes that swallowed them to his belly. This was slow going—he was unsure if he could make it to the river crossing before the eclipse began. Regardless, he felt the pull. The spirit current wanted to show him something, but the journey through the snow was wearing him down.

It had taken more than one storm for this sea of snow to cover the landscape. This winter had been relentless, with one blizzard after another always around the corner. And it was not just the snow, but the biting cold, too. Often extreme cold and snow do not mix, but it was the way of things this winter. Six weeks of it so far. Split Toe had not eaten anything of value in more than ten days. He was weak. Very weak. He knew he was starving, but he had no solution. He was only grateful that he no longer felt hunger.

After wild animals consumed everything within reach that would fit in their mouths—branches, twigs, pine needles—they began gnawing at live tree bark. Particularly trees that were young enough to still have smooth green bark: poplar, maple, cherry, and beech that were more than saplings but less than adult trees. Fifteen-year start-ups. Many animals had already died: some from starvation, others freezing to death in their sleep and exhaustion, others falling prey to lucky predators. It was every animal for itself.

Split Toe saw one tall drift where three deer had gotten stuck and froze to death. A coyote that hoped to satisfy its hunger pangs tried to reach the deer. It also became stuck, exhausted, and died. A frozen drop of rain melting into the spirit current.

A group of five mature bald eagles benefited from the carcasses. They hopped like vultures from deer to deer and to the coyote, pecking at the lifeless coats of fur until their strong beaks broke through to the frozen flesh inside. What they really wanted were the entrails. But that would take time and determination.

Another coyote hunched in the snow close by, eyeing the eagles. Whether it was his judgment or instinct—or perhaps the spirit current that told him not to do it—the coyote listened.

It was a good year to be a hibernating animal. The black bear slept contentedly in its den, totally ignorant of the perils outside. A squirrel nested in the hollow opening of a tree somewhere with its winter supply of acorns packed in nearby. Even fish that swam below the surface of the pond remained oblivious to the extreme danger above ground, content to wait until the ice thawed in the spring.

A considerable number of small animals also existed safely below the snow. Mice created networks of snow tunnels just above the soil, their world hidden away from the worst of the weather. They could find food, mate, and deliver and care for their young, all below the snow. It might be their favorite time of year.

The deer's best bet was to huddle together and share body warmth. During a normal snowfall, their torsos left melted impressions clean down to the forest floor. But with snow this deep, it simply did not work like that. Split Toe found a shallow spot in the cover of an upturned cedar root. For a few weeks, this spot worked, but then two feet of snow fell straight down. It even covered areas protected from the wind; areas protected from the first snows. But the straight-down snowfall covered every surface and filled every hole. It closed up Split Toe's secret spot.

This snow was tough. Fallen trees blocked his way. Only his pure determination to answer the spirit's call kept him going. He reached deep into his soul for each step, each jump. One step at a time. The shadow began to take away the sun as he left the gravel pit along the low edge of the bluff. He heard the grandfather tree one hundred yards away encouraging him.

"Harder, Split Toe. You can make it. Come on, old boy."

This was like the home stretch of a marathon, and Split Toe had nothing left to give. The shadow moved quickly across the sun. Now all eleven of the old-growth pines seemed to be pulling for him.

"Do it, Split Toe. Do it! You've done harder things before. Come on, old boy."

Split Toe was panting hard. Each time he lifted his front legs, he put them forward a few inches. Then a few inches more. When they were far enough in front, he bent his neck and leaped with his back legs, then began again with his front legs. His large antlers weighed heavily on his head. He was still a few yards away when the shadow took out the sun completely. He heard a strange cadence blowing on the wind. Perhaps it was only in his mind.

It started out softly as he stretched with all his heart.

"Split Toe. Split Toe. Split Toe …"

It was all the old-growth trees chanting.

He reached the edge of the river and fell neck-deep into a tall drift.

"Split Toe. Split Toe. Split Toe …"

Several eagles sitting on their branches joined in.

Deep in the snow holes enclosing his rear legs, Split Toe could feel ice below his hooves. A frozen river. His hooves slid along the ice as he tried to push forward. He braced his legs against the snow to help push himself forward. His front legs clawed at the drift in front of him.

"SPLIT TOE. SPLIT TOE. SPLIT TOE …"

A chorus of fish, watching from below the surface of the ice, were cheering him onward.

His hoof went over the center of the river as a sliver of sunlight began to appear.

"SPLIT TOE. SPLIT TOE. SPLIT TOE …"

He heard the Ojibwe, and the ancestors, and the mastodon, and the cougar, and the flea, and an entire pack of dire wolves, and his old friend the snapping turtle, and the owl, and the sand bluff, and the river, and the forest woman, and Jake, and the pioneer, and the pioneer's wife, and the dog …

"SPLIT TOE. SPLIT TOE. SPLIT TOE …"

And then he was there. The snow was gone. The sky was bright. The world was green. Split Toe collapsed, nearly lifeless, into the water. In the far-off distance, he heard a muffled echo, **"Split Toe ... Split Toe ... Split Toe. ..."** He was completely spent. He could not remember ever feeling more grateful for the spirit current.

CHAPTER 33
SPLIT TOE UNDERSTANDS

AD 2080

Overtaken by exhaustion, Split Toe dragged himself to the west riverbank and burrowed into a shallow hole where the water undercut the bank. He slid under a root entanglement exposed by the stream's erosion. He needed a bit of time to regain his strength. Split Toe felt the spirit current all around him, and it was comforting. He closed his eyes and simply listened. What he heard soothed him: a chorus of songbirds. He thought they must be fluttering about in the brush that reached over the bank. Cardinals. Finches. Chickadees. Phoebes. Split Toe opened his eyes. He saw the grandfather pine towering over the east bank. He saw small groups of warblers, buntings, juncos, and bluebirds dashing from twig to twig. A robin foraged on the ground below the grandfather pine.

Split Toe lifted his head just as an iridescent hummingbird zipped by. Then, as if the hummingbird noticed something unexpected, it zipped back and quickly circled Split Toe's large antlers. Split Toe liked the attention. He held his head upright and let the tiny bird inspect his mighty rack. The hummingbird stopped in front of Split Toe's eyes. It could have landed on the leathery black end of Split Toe's nose, but instead it hovered in place, with wings moving so fast they hummed. The tiny bird stared directly into Split Toe's eyes, searching deep within, trying to find a path to Split Toe's soul. Split Toe returned the gaze with equal intensity. The tiny bird finally surprised him with two simple questions.

"Who are you? What are you doing here?"

It seemed that the smallest bird of the forest was now its guarding sentinel. After a moment of thought, Split Toe realized he could not answer the question directly. He did not know himself. Who was he, really? He felt like he was part of the spirit current, that many spirits contributed to who he was, and that he had lived through many ages. In that sense, he was not your average deer. Why was he here? Split Toe was not sure. Finally, after his long pause, he answered as simply as he was asked.

"You can call me Split Toe. The spirit current brought me here."

Satisfied, the hummingbird tipped its wings in respect. Split Toe nodded his antlers and watched his new friend zip downstream along the riverbank.

The hummingbird's greeting made Split Toe feel welcomed to the morning. He slowly stood, stretching his legs and neck, shaking the water from his fur before he leapt onto the peninsula. What he saw surprised him. He expected a lovely green alfalfa field rolling across the terrain, but the peninsula and the field to the south were covered by a diverse forest of oak, maple, ash, cherry, basswood, beech, hickory, and birch. Red and white pine, hemlock, spruce, and tamarack grew in patches within the hardwoods. The forest was painted with many colors and textures.

Along the riverbed, Split Toe could see cedars folding over the water from the bank and the twig-like branches of willows drooping from the weight of their tiny leaves. Tall grasses and ferns grew between trees along the riverbank, and raspberries thrived in the sunny spots.

Split Toe was surprised. He stared directly into the peninsula forest and asked of the trees, "Who are you? Why are you here?"

The trees knew it was not a real question. Split Toe did not expect an answer. The trees' leaves simply shimmered in the breeze.

Split Toe skirted the edge of the peninsula, following a trail that was centuries old, and walked toward the hill that was once covered in alfalfa.

What happened here? Where are the farmers?

He continued through the new forest, cautiously arriving at the location where the pioneer's original cabin once stood. There was no sign of the structure. In fact, there was no sign of humans whatsoever. The first hint of the past was a hidden impression of the straight road that once stretched through the countryside and passed directly between the two houses of the pioneer's descendants. Where the houses, barns, and corrals once stood, a forest now grew.

The partially exposed asphalt pavement of the road was cracked and decayed, blistered and crumbling. No longer did a yellow line run down its center. Surface fissures made way for grasses, Queen Anne's lace, and milkweed. Virginia creeper vines, crawling their way across the crumbling surface, buried the road in a patchwork of green. Nature worked steadily to take apart the asphalt bit by bit, hiding it beneath natural cover and a thin soil buildup formed from plant decay.

The forest's understory was clean of debris. Guided by curiosity, Split Toe wandered to the back forty acres, where all the human debris was gone. Two hundred years of human activity, erased from the natural world. A new forest of young trees had replaced the mature hardwoods that once stood there.

Split Toe turned back toward the east until he reached the crumbling road again. He walked north down its center, watching monarch butterflies alight on milkweeds, white cabbage butterflies fluttering around the Virginia creeper, and American Lady butterflies landing on the flowering heads of the Queen Anne's lace. Peaceful tranquility permeated everything. He had arrived into a world of butterflies, songbirds, and plush vegetation. Peaceful, natural tranquility—all the things the boy liked most about the eighty acres.

The dead-end dirt road that originally led east back to the bridge and the sand bluff overlooking the river was much the same as Split Toe remembered it, though a new tree or two now grew in its center. As he crossed the concrete bridge, he noticed the edges crumbling into the water. Split Toe saw fresh vehicle tracks in the mud on the east side. He knew he must be cautious. He stepped from the road and followed a trail through the brush. Animal trails, still in use, had changed little throughout the centuries because they followed the topography of the land. Split Toe knew these trails well.

Split Toe walked up the forest-covered sand bluff. Something seemed out of place, but he did not know what it was. He looked closely. More evidence of human life from the past lay before him. It was the pit where the forest woman's basement once was. Its concrete walls had completely collapsed into the hole, perhaps pushed by growing roots of trees that now surrounded the basement.

Split Toe thought back to when the woman's brother had dug the hole and brought in concrete on a horse-drawn wagon. Split Toe remembered the brother mixing the concrete by hand, using buckets of water from the river. Now, the sides of the hole sloped naturally to the bottom, erosion and time doing most of the work.

Suddenly, Split Toe remembered something else. He spun around quickly and looked toward the river. The tall white pines were gone. All but one. The old grandfather pine still stood next to the river at the base of the bluff. A bit battered, but standing. The other trees, which were nearly five hundred years old when he last saw them, were all missing.

He remembered the trees calling his name, **"Split Toe, Split Toe, Split Toe ..."**

At that moment, he felt a breeze flow through the new trees and heard a soft voice whisper to him, **"Do not worry, Split Toe. We are here."**

Split Toe paused for a moment, then bowed his giant antlers respectfully to the ground where the trees once stood. Of course. He knew their spirits were still here. He walked to the sand cliff leading down to the river and saw a large snapping turtle laying her eggs in the bank. He bowed his antlers again before moving on.

Split Toe needed to see the tag alder swamp. As he walked the ancient trail, he saw prints of deer and many other animals. There was little sign of the logging roads that had become part of the forest when the boy took responsibility for the land. Forest seamlessly covered the ground across every contour.

When Split Toe reached the place where the tag alder swamp had been for thousands of years, it was gone. There was only a small lake with cool dark water rippling on its surface. A vee of Canada geese circled once and landed near another group of geese across the lake. Split Toe could see a black bear and her two cubs foraging for berries along the lake's perimeter.

A magnificent bald eagle soared in wide, slow circles near a milk-colored cloud. Another eagle, perhaps its mate, perched patiently in the branches of a tree at the shore, its white head reflecting the sunlight. The eagle looked intently into the water, and when the time was exactly right, it swooped down, breaking the water's surface with its talons. The eagle returned to the sky carrying a good-sized fish.

Split Toe watched a breeze sweep across the water's surface and felt the spirit of the tag alder swamp that once occupied this spot. What had become of it?

Split Toe had always wondered about the humans' sense of self-preservation. Though he tried his best not to judge them, he frequently wondered about the intent behind their actions and where it would all lead. Split Toe looked at the world in natural terms. He had no feel for many of the factors making up human civilization. He knew nothing about international politics and the brutality with which humans would fight against each other. For what? Food? Shelter? Fuel?

The spirit pool knew. It understood everything. The spirit pool broke things into their simplest components and often disregarded the drama of human interaction. The spirit pool paid attention to actions and reactions. It wanted to tell Split Toe what had happened, but it could not. There was too much human drama involved. The spirit pool could only provide the lesson by showing Split Toe the results.

Split Toe's understanding of human technology was incomplete. He understood human cultural interaction in only the simplest ways. He most often gave humans the benefit of his doubt, as he did any creature. Most importantly, Split Toe did not understand human behavior on a worldwide scale. He could not begin to understand the capacity of humans to fight for peace. Kill to save lives? Destroy to restore? He did not think in those terms. Not even close. Split Toe would have thought it a hard way to get things done. Something about it would not seem right.

That is why the spirit pool knew Split Toe could never imagine or understand the volley of nuclear intercontinental ballistic missiles (ICBMs) launched thirty-five years earlier. Split Toe did not even understand the concept of nationalism or international borders. He looked at things in a natural way. These were not things created by Mother Nature.

Boundaries had to do with range for Split Toe. How far was it practical for him to move from his home location. From the tag alder swamp. Natural geological features had something to do with it. Water obstructions. Places with little food. Split Toe imposed his own boundary limits. Some areas simply were too complicated to travel beyond.

Other animals were the same.

The spirit pool looked back.

The missile exchange did not last long before opposing nations worked things out through discussion. But the missiles seemed necessary to let each side know the other was serious.

Military strategists determined ahead of time that several small nuclear warheads might be more effective than a single large one.

So, when three ICBMs launched into motion against Camp Grayling, the USA's largest National Guard training facility located in mid-Michigan, damage to the military facility was expected to be conclusive. Simultaneously, missiles were launched against other strategic sites across North America. Before the missiles reached their targets, the USA responded in kind.

Split Toe would certainly have wondered, "What was with these humans? Where was their sense of self-preservation?"

The spirit pool continued to look back.

One of the missiles aimed at Camp Grayling hit its target. Partial destruction. Air defense artillery took out the second missile. It detonated high in the sky. Little ground effect. When the third missile came in, no one knew if the person who armed its coordinates made a small error in latitude, or if the missile malfunctioned on its own, or if air defense artillery trying to take it out pushed it off course. In any case, the third nuclear warhead detonated one hundred feet above ground, thirty-five miles south of its intended target, with ground zero exactly where the tag alder swamp once was.

The force blew apart the swamp and the ground below it, launching debris high into the air. Fragments of the gas pipeline melted, leaving only a lake-size crater on the earth's surface.

Not a living thing in the community or forest expected the explosion. In an instant, it incinerated everything within a two-mile radius not hidden by the topography. Here one second, gone the next. From a thriving ecosystem to zero in a millisecond. Action-reaction. Humans.

The whole forest in that circle, including the forest that the boy protected for fifty-five years, suddenly evaporated, as did everything on the forest floor.

There are many ways for a forest to die.

The explosion took out the pioneer's original shelter, the new farmhouse, the barn, every scrap of fence, and all the debris that was ever left on the forest floor, natural or human. In a flash, the explosion cleaned up the back forty acres and the neighbor's woods and everything within the two-mile radius circle except the grandfather pine. The sand bluff itself miraculously protected the grandfather pine from the concussion and the nuclear flash. The dune was a kind of shield for that one old tree and for a few offspring growing beneath the tree's arms.

The siblings of the grandfather tree did not go up in smoke. They instantly turned to dust.

The only remaining evidence of the boy's shelter was the steel well pipe imbedded thirty feet below ground. The hand pump which was connected to the well above ground instantly melted into nothing. Except for a few small creatures who made their home in imperfections of the grandfather pine's trunk, the explosion sent all living things within the radius to the spirit pool in a single instant. Things outside of the explosion radius still had the nuclear radiation to contend with. Many did not make it. Plants, animals, fungi, dead.

Forest soil was immediately exposed. Some of it burned with the explosion. Some blew away with the wind. Some remained but would need a new generation of living fungi to help trees start again.

Split Toe moved through the lush vegetation to check in on the place where the boy's shelter had once stood. He saw a white truck parked in the woods. It must be the truck whose tracks he had seen on the road. He walked further, cautious, and curious. Two humans in fully enclosed white suits worked on their knees inside a large mesh pen. The pen was an enclosed cage constructed from fine metal screens. Natural vegetation could migrate into and out of the enclosure, but animals inside could not get out, and animals outside could not get in.

Had the boy—the man—been alive to see this change, this destruction, Split Toe imagined he would have been crushed. Perhaps it was a kindness that the boy joined the spirit pool years before the incident.

A tree rarely dies of old age.

As Split Toe wandered through the plush vegetation now, thirty-five years after the nuclear catastrophe, he sensed that his concern was no longer important. The boy was part of the spirit pool. Split Toe felt him there.

"Do not worry, Split Toe." The voice came on the wind. "Mother Nature is taking care of this. The spirit pool does not judge. It is simply part of nature.

"Look at this forest sanctuary now." Split Toe was sure it was the boy—the man—who spoke for the spirits. "Two centuries of human debris left at the edges of fields, in ditches, and hidden on the forest floor, debris that no one was taking responsibility to remove. Humans just did not see it any longer. But it was there and cleaned up in an instant. The forest has now started afresh. Even the spirit pool did not expect it would be cleaned so quickly, so thoroughly. We will give it a chance. The alfalfa field is again a growing forest, and humans will stay away for a while.

"This is the way nature works. Everything has its time. Mother Nature gives everything its chance. It is up to natural things to make what they can out of their opportunity. But Mother Nature will always sort things out. Action-reaction. It does not end."

In Split Toe's mind, he could see the boy holding up a mittened hand and cupping his fingers, an innocent sense of wonder on his face.

"Ol' Split Toe, my dear friend. One more thing. This spirit pool ... it is a great place. Go well, my friend."

Split Toe watched the humans work. They were scientists. They handled mice. Counting, inspecting, taking samples. Because mice reproduced so frequently, the scientists could monitor the mice to understand the effects of radiation from one generation to the next. They looked for changes that radiation made to DNA, and how new generations of animals adapted to the new conditions.

They noticed some things in the first generations. Cataracts grew in almost every mouse's eyes. This did not seem to be a genetic factor; it was most likely a simple effect of the radiation. Later, they noticed a difference in the quality of the mouse's skin. Mice with thicker and rougher skin seemed to live longer. Because of that, the thick-skin mice bred more times in their life and quickly passed on radiation-tolerant skin to the mouse population. These scientists paid attention to mutation and evolution. In this case, radiation caused the changes. Action-reaction. Mother Nature.

These scientists knew that their counterparts in Russia had observed a progressive genetic adaptation in wild dogs after the 1986 nuclear power plant disaster at Chernobyl. At that time, the Russian government set aside a large area surrounding the disaster spot. Besides the scientists, all humans were excluded from this area for safety reasons. Dogs remained, perhaps unintentionally, and produced offspring. By 2020, scientists found new generations of thriving dogs, already developing radiation-tolerant adaptations.

Plant life also grew plush and wild again in the exclusion area, perhaps due to a decades-long lack of human footprints on the landscape.

To be sure, the radiation was a danger to life, especially to newly exposed life. But soon a new natural forest grew while humans stayed away, a forest adapting to the new conditions.

Because the scientists' study in Michigan had a specific focus, and because the environmental conditions were so extreme, and because the mice reproduced so frequently, Michigan scientists could see many more multigenerational effects than Russian scientists noticed with dogs during a similar time period.

With mice, a single human study team could observe all this change over the course of only one human lifespan. If scientists had instead selected the snapping turtle as their subject, the study would have been akin to watching a tree grow to maturity. It would have taken many human generations before the results became apparent. Radiated mice were a gift to human understanding.

The spirit pool continued to reminisce about the human approach to the disaster.

After the misdirected explosion occurred and tempers cooled, humans from the government looked at the explosion's results using satellite photos. They compared before-and-after photos and saw that the nuclear warhead had detonated above a tag alder swamp. A veritable wasteland.

"Lucky," the humans thought, and they laughed a bit.

An expensive bomb, millions of dollars, hitting squarely in the center of a swampy wasteland where the roads ended on all sides. What bad luck for the attackers. They laughed again. Of course, none of the humans who laughed had ever before been in a tag alder swamp, and they did not know how old the swamp really was. They thought of all things in human terms. They knew nothing about the spirit current that the tag alder swamp had been a part of for more generations than they could count in their own heritage.

With senior people working on the high-profile Camp Grayling location, the government assigned two young men with little experience to this minor and relatively unimportant swamp detonation. They looked at satellite photos to inspect the affected radius. Eighteen homes and farm buildings completely disappeared. Flattened. Vaporized. This was an area encircling the bull's-eye—the first band of the impact area. Outside of that, there was the transition area—the second band. The area where things burned or blew down but were not totally destroyed. Radiation burns. The men tried to figure out where to begin the quarantine area.

They needed to create an "exclusion zone" well beyond the transition zone, far enough out that animals in the transition zone would not mix with animals, humans, or crops in the safe world. They laid it all out—the bull's-eye where the tag alder swamp once was, the zone of complete destruction (a two-mile radius around the bull's-eye, 12.56 square miles, a bit more than 8,000 acres), and the transition zone (two miles beyond the destruction zone, an additional 37.38 square miles, 24,115 more acres).

"How big should the exclusion zone be?" one man asked the other.

They chuckled because neither really knew what to do. Neither of them had much experience with the migration or movement of animals from contaminated areas to clean areas. Perhaps they could take data from Chernobyl or Hiroshima, but they found little useful information or guidance there. Many things about Chernobyl and Hiroshima were different from the Michigan problem. The Russian government set Chernobyl's exclusion radius at about 18.5 miles.

"One more mile. What do you say we make it one mile? I really don't think the kinds of animals in Michigan travel more than a mile." They laughed again. It seemed practical. To them, it seemed like a long distance.

"We can't just pick one mile." The man chuckled. Then, with a serious look, "We'd lose our jobs."

So, they looked up the typical movement range of wild animals living in Michigan.

- Rabbit — 6 acres in search of suitable habitat
- Squirrel — 25 acres depending on food
- Turkey — 5 square miles
- Coyote — 12 square miles
- Raccoon (Adult male) — 20 square miles
- Bobcat (Adult male) — 30 square miles
- Whitetail deer — Typically 1 square mile, but can roam up to 23 miles based on forest cover
- Black bear — 15 square miles, but adult males often roam up to 15 linear miles depending on food supply

The distances seemed larger than they first imagined, so they picked a round number of two miles beyond the transition zone for the exclusion zone—six miles from ground zero. It added up to an additional 62.8 square miles. In total, the entire six-mile exclusion radius was about 113 square miles made up entirely of farms, agricultural land, and wilderness. Of course, they needed to have radiation testing done beyond the perimeter to make a final recommendation.

The exclusion zone displaced about 600 people, roughly 200 homes. Everything inside the exclusion zone became off-limits to humans except those with scientific permits. And certainly, no animal migration was allowed. The two young men took their final decision seriously. They did their best. They kept their jobs.

But they never understood that their decision made little difference, because Mother Nature was managing the situation.

Water flowed down the Clam River, taking its radioactivity into the Muskegon River and eventually into Lake Michigan. Fish, turtles, kingfishers, eagles, otters, and raccoons living downstream ate irradiated fish that swam wherever the river flowed.

Vees of geese landed in the ground-zero lake on their way to and from their summer destinations. Some laid eggs in nests built using cattails at the lake's edge. Some geese stayed the entire spring, summer, and fall seasons. Squadrons of ducks of many varieties joined the geese. Swans flew in. Egrets and herons hung out in trees surrounding the lake.

Monarch butterflies flew up from their winter roosts in Mexico's Sierra Madre mountains on their annual multigenerational journey, laying eggs on radioactive milkweed within the exclusion zone. Their offspring returned to Mexico to roost for the winter. Other insects blew through the contamination area on the wind.

Many of the living things that spent time in the radioactivity carried with them slight changes in DNA. Most of the affected animals died prematurely, but their offspring bred and produced children with small DNA changes more tolerant to the radiation. Their own offspring lived well within the new conditions. The ones that did not slowly vanished.

What really helped the plants and animals to recover, and what encouraged all the wild things to stay within the exclusion area, was that humans stayed away. It was a gift from the two men to the plants and animals, though the men were only conscious about the safety of their fellow humans.

Many species that over centuries became conditioned to the danger of humans—species who learned from one generation to the next to be wary of humans—now found a place of wild refuge within the exclusion zone. It was a sanctuary. Their own Garden of Eden. New generations of wild animals grew without needing to fear humans or even needing to coexist with humans. There was no need to make allowances for human civilization.

Wild animals only needed to coexist with each other. All were part of a natural food chain they knew and accepted. Now, after thirty-five years with only themselves confined to this exclusion area, they had relearned what life was like without humans.

Seeds blew in on the wind or were carried by birds or were taken from the transition zone a little further into the destruction area by squirrels and other forest animals each season. Renewal did not take long. Trees grew where they did and fell where they fell and decayed, making new soil that became richer and deeper each year. Each fall, leaves coated the forest floor, enriching the soil.

All the new vegetation performed its photosynthesis magic, removing carbon dioxide from the atmosphere and replacing it with oxygen for the animals to breathe. Plants all captured carbon in their structures and eventually stored it again in the earth.

As new trees crept into the destruction area, fungi followed the roots, restoring the vast interconnected network of roots, fungi, and soil. The root network once again enabled the trees to share resources, to nurture their offspring, and to communicate as trees do in their fight to resist disease and repel destructive insects.

Birds nested in branches of the new trees, and the whole forest closed in on its center like a giant sacred circle.

"See how quickly plants and animals adapt," Split Toe heard a voice from the spirits in his mind. "Radiation affects them. True. You might not have noticed, new monarchs are ten percent larger than their parent butterflies."

Interesting, Split Toe thought to himself. *I missed that.*

"There are many other things, too. They all need time to reproduce and find balance for their kind. Humans also. Humans look at the world around them from their own point of view. Their own lifespan. They consider time in terms of human generations.

"Think of a flea. Fleas produce generations more frequently

than humans. How do fleas gauge time in a changing world? And think of trees that live for hundreds of seasons. What is their point of view?" The spirit challenged Split Toe to think.

"Mother Nature also looks at time differently. Small change like this happens quickly from Mother Nature's point of view."

The spirits continued.

"Humans have stepped away from this place for a while. They will not see the small, day-to-day changes. Someday they may be amazed by the results. In this place without humans, plants and animals find their own new equilibrium in a different way."

Split Toe saw that this was both simple and complicated. While humans thought permitting radiation to degrade to levels safe for themselves would take decades—perhaps centuries—plants and animals continued to adapt in their own time. But they needed several generations to adjust. Mother Nature was already taking care of the situation. The time to complete the change would only be a speck in the timeline Mother Nature was used to.

Split Toe was beginning to understand. The spirit current brought him here to show him more about human nature and the human point of view, to help him understand. The spirit current could only do so by ignoring the human blow-by-blow and focusing on the results.

Despite their clever ways—their human systems of civilization, their creativity, their destruction, their mistakes, and their repair attempts—humans' intentions are never a match for the power of Mother Nature. Mother Nature will always take care of things.

Her results will not be what humans hope for. Humans want

things *their* way. Humans, while impatient, seem inherently resistant to change. They need some nudging. Mother Nature is constantly in the business of change—action-reaction—in her own way and in her own time.

Split Toe felt good about what he learned, what the spirit current brought him here to learn. It gave him a sense of relief.

"You have learned well, Split Toe," the spirit voice again drifted through his mind. **"You know much about what is important. Distill what you know into one simple lesson. What you know will help others. The student becomes the teacher. All things are connected."**

He felt the spirit current's pull again, and he wanted to run. He wanted to run simply for the joy of running, to bolt down a forest trail and feel ferns brushing against his legs, to watch trees disappear in his back trail. He wanted to pant hard while breathing pure forest oxygen deeply into his lungs.

He began at a trot on a trail which skirted the edge of the lake. He picked up speed with each stride. His front legs stretched far while his back legs pushed him through the air. He felt his body bank to the left and to the right as he took each turn. His white tail bounced with each leap. His massive hooves kicked up the soil as he went. The largest antlers in the forest tipped up and down on Split Toe's head with every reach of his neck, with each long leap.

Trees and animals watched him fly by. His joy was infectious.

The wind sang in a chorus, **"There goes Ol' Split Toe ... look at him run!"**

The plants and animals joined the song as he raced by.

Split Toe ran like the wind through the forest. With a giant leap, he cleared the east edge of the gravel pit, gliding down its steep sand cliff. He rounded the bottom of the sand bluff making the home stretch for the river crossing. A shadow began to take away the sun. He saw the river only a few long strides away. He still had plenty of time. He wanted to complete the race while running full out. Only ten more jumps. He pushed hard.

The sun still showed behind a partial shadow. The river was there. He had a few seconds. Split Toe put both front feet out and skidded to a stop at the river's edge. He stood up tall, panting heavily in a joyous way. He spun to his left, directly facing the old grandfather pine. He looked at its base and raised his gaze along the trunk to the tree's canopy, regrown around a charred upper trunk. The limbs of the grandfather tree were larger in diameter than the full trunks of other trees surrounding it. He took a step forward and tenderly nuzzled the base of the large tree with his mighty antlers. He stepped back. The sun was nearly covered. Clear water rippled across the river bottom in front of him.

A breeze drifted by, and he heard the grandfather tree whisper, **"Go on, old boy ... *cross the river.*"**

Split Toe stepped gently into the ankle-deep stream, taking in the cool, soothing feel of each step. He breathed deeply, filled his lungs, and with a final short leap was up on the bank on the river's west side.

There was snow on the ground.

EPILOGUE
SPLIT TOE RETURNS — FORTY YEARS BACK IN TIME
THE OLD MAN'S DREAM

AD 2040

Two sets of large, flat tracks made a path through the snow to the shelter of the boy—now a seventy-four-year-old man. There was another set of tracks left by a small supply toboggan the old man pulled behind them on the trail meandering for nearly half a mile through the forest. The walk in was mostly downhill. As they walked, the old man thought about what a mission it would be when they returned in ten days. Uphill in the snow. He and Cathy liked their forest visits best in the winter. It made them feel alive. They stopped to catch their breath when they were only a hundred yards from the gate.

The snow was deep: eighteen inches. They were grateful a descendant of Angus and Grace used a large tractor to clear the simple dirt road leading across the river to the road's termination, where they could park. The road was still not of enough importance for the county to maintain during winter. In conditions like this, the old man always left their small car at the gate. He did not like the thought of being stuck in the snow deeper in the forest.

The man took two more steps and gave the toboggan's rope a

firm pull to bring it along. Each breath formed a cloud of mist as he exhaled into the crisp air. He looked back at Cathy, who was trailing by a few paces. She was aging too, but not as quickly as he was.

"Do you think we're getting too old for this?" he asked.

Cathy chuckled. "Would it matter?"

"It's just breaking the trail that's killing me. It's a mission." The man walked a few more steps, looking at the white blanket of pure, uninterrupted snow on the trail in front of him. To the side, he could see a tree blown over during the last storm. He recognized its scaly bark. A mature cherry tree. The trees it had fallen against still held it off the ground. Thick snow layered its top like a pall draping the casket of a fallen soldier.

There are many ways for a tree to die.

Beneath the tree, the man could see a continuous wide trail left by an animal early in the morning. The man knew this kind of track from other winters. It was an otter's shortcut from the river to the creek flowing out of the tag alder swamp. The temperature was −10°F. Bitterly cold. Ice covered both the river and the creek. The man wondered how the otter would get in and out of the water. Not many other animals moved in this January freeze.

As the old man and Cathy progressed down the trail, only one other set of tracks showed up: the long stride and deep tracks of a massive deer. The old man reached into one of the holes made by the deer's step. He brushed away the snow and looked closely at the impression of two front points and then the rear features of the hoof. He stood up and leaned back a bit on his snowshoes.

Leaning back felt good on his spine. He pointed to the cleaned-off print.

"Ol' Split Toe," he said reverently. "Maybe thirty minutes ago."

Cathy nodded, steam flowing from her nostrils.

"He's on his way to the swamp."

So, Split Toe was here. Of course. The old man already knew that. He felt it. He could always feel when Ol' Split Toe was around. The two shared a connection that he couldn't put into words.

They continued down the trail. Many of the trees were now fifty-five years old and towering above the two of them. It was a beautiful forest. The old man planned to walk to the old-growth pines later in the week. There were still eleven, and they always inspired him—especially the grandfather pine. He felt their ancient spirits, and he often listened to what they had to say.

The old man and Cathy knew their shelter would be frozen when they arrived. Each fall, the man stacked five face-cords of firewood close by for use during the winter. The man always liked to have two years of firewood on hand: a stack by the shelter ready to burn and another year's supply neatly stacked close to the gate. Late in the spring, when a fire in the woodstove was no longer necessary, the man moved the stack near the gate down to the shelter and began making a new gate stack. Preparing for winter was a never-ending cycle. It was best to plan for the season in advance.

Committed to letting Mother Nature manage this forest, the old man often faced a firewood dilemma. He understood the importance of fallen trees in the development of forest soil and as home to some of the forest animals. The trees needed to stay on the ground and decay. The forest needed the soil, and the soil needed the contribution from fallen trees. The man also knew that he did not want to bring in firewood from an outside place. There was always a risk that firewood imported to the eighty acres from a distant county might bring predator insects which the trees were not yet prepared to defend against.

So, each year, he first took trees that fell naturally onto his forest trails. He then searched for a few dead limbs, preferably oak, to trim from live trees, cut into firewood, and split for easy burning. Each time he harvested a limb, the man, like the Ojibwe, thanked the tree for the limb it gave up and thanked the soil for the limb he prematurely snatched away. The old man found that each year the forest on the eighty acres gifted him enough firewood to get by for another season.

Managing firewood was plenty of work, and the seventy-four-year-old felt himself aging out. Each year it took a little more effort. He'd earned the wrinkles on his face from years in the wilds. His skin was both weathered and seasoned.

When people in the community would see him, they would often ask, "Do you feel safe out there all alone? With no electricity, and only firewood for heat?"

The man had honestly stopped noticing he was without electricity several decades ago. It did not take long. He also understood how to manage with only woodstove heat. He kept the interior of the shelter at a comfortable 70°F continuously.

"I manage," the man would reply with a smile that reflected his experience.

True, he was often back in the woods so far that even explaining where to find him would be problematic if an emergency were to arise. But he and Cathy had lived most of their lives without much of a safety net and felt comfortable with those conditions. They realized their forest home was more than a century out of date. But it was a lifestyle they had loved from the beginning. It was an escape from the nightly news of the civilized world, from a cell phone tether, and from human background noises.

Many people would see their lifestyle as burdened by unnecessary physical work. After all, hot water was not available on demand. Water needed to be pumped first and heated second. A thermostat did not turn on a furnace during a cold night. And when natural light faded, an oil lamp needed lighting. Even the box of wooden matches used to light the woodstove and lamps seemed like an antique. Though off-grid forest life was more physical, and lacked the instant results that come with modern conveniences, it was also less intense and always satisfying. What the old man and Cathy got from it was a deep sense of natural peace.

Cathy sat in her parka close to the woodstove, feeling the fire's heat, as the shelter came up to temperature. The man stood outside next to the woodpile watching heat waves escape the chimney top. It would be a frigid night, perhaps −20°F. Maybe colder. The air, in its stillness, had an eerie power and depth about it. There was intensity to the quiet. Winter stillness. A sub-zero silence. Not a whisper of a sound. Not an insect. Silence that seemed even more pure, more silent than silence elsewhere. The man loved the power of this extreme cold.

He listened. The only sounds were a stray breeze suddenly

whipping through the trees, and the single crack of a limb shattering from the frigid cold. They were individual sounds that fell on a foundation of utter silence. The clear, crisp crack echoed through the forest without the interruption of leaves or the distraction of ambient noise. It sounded like gunfire, but it was not. The frozen branch snapped; brittle from ice filling its veins. The sound was a sharp "*Ouch!*" shouted from the tree, rather than the slow breaking groan that branches made when they gave way in the summer. When their bones were more flexible.

If the air remained crisp, every few days they might hear the distant whistle from a freight train passing through the village eight miles away. The only other hint that another world existed beyond the gate was a single jet trail crossing the cloudless sky.

The man brought in an armful of wood that should last the night. Setting the logs next to the woodstove to dry their winter moisture, he watched a groggy tick slip from the log onto his sleeve. The man walked to the door and brushed the tick into the snow.

The tick made him think of the first year he saw a tick in this forest. He'd worked and played in the forest since 1974 and hadn't seen a tick until 2018. In that year he saw several. The following year there were more, and they continued with a kind of cyclical population intensity since then. Ticks followed Michigan's warming temperatures, migrating or hitchhiking on the backs of animals from southern forests a little farther each year to receptive habitats. The animals followed migrating insects and plants—their food sources. All moving north bit by bit. Ticks laid eggs on surfaces of plants creeping into warming landscapes. Or they found moist dark surfaces on a whole new batch of decaying limbs and hidden hollows. Their offspring continued the migration in the same way. A little further north each year, each tick generation launching more generations in new regions. All following factors related to warming temperatures.

The fact that a small temperature increase made Michigan so favorable to ticks amazed the old man. It increased only a few degrees in average temperature. On a day-to-day basis, the change was imperceptible.

Ticks were clever. They knew what they liked and were ready to populate new areas as they became attractive. Their species needed room to grow. The man wondered if ticks would eventually overuse their Michigan habitat, outeat their food supply. Did they have a sense of self-preservation? Perhaps a few cold years would nudge the tick population back into their southern ranges. But would that reduce their overall population, or just concentrate all the ticks into less space?

The problem seemed to be that an individual tick was concerned almost entirely about itself and did not see an overall threat to the species until the threat became a direct threat to the individual. How would Mother Nature, with her action-reactions, manage the ticks?

The man wondered about the southern plants that also inched northward because of temperature changes imperceptible to humans in their day-to-day lives. The old man liked the way forest trees worked cooperatively with root systems sharing resources below the ground and branches supporting each other at the canopy. They cooperated for self-preservation. Perhaps humans were somewhere between ticks and trees—or at least had the potential to be.

The man had slipped a newspaper from the local village into his duffle bag before loading the duffle onto the toboggan. He always kept a few newspapers on hand to start fires in the woodstove. Sitting across from Cathy at the table, he opened the paper and noticed a headline: "Local Landowner Rediscovers Hopewell Indian Earthworks."

"Huh ... Imagine that," he said, pointing to the headline. "This gentleman owned the property for three decades and never realized that the circle was prehistoric. He only found out after showing it to his new daughter-in-law. Evidently, the circle was written about before. More than one hundred fifty years ago, after the logging era. Forgotten somewhere between then and now."

Cathy smiled. She knew how much this kind of thing interested her husband. She reached to the windowsill and picked up an arrowhead she'd found several years ago on the sand bluff above the river by the old-growth trees. The earthworks and the arrowhead were clearly from two different eras, hundreds of years apart.

"Evidently, there are several more of these in this part of Michigan, some that are tall mounds and others that are ringed embankments like the one that was rediscovered. They look to me a bit like the remains of a beaver dam. The article says Hopewell Indians had populations from Mississippi to Ontario from 100 BC to AD 400. Why would a civilization like that disappear? Did the entire population vanish, or did their culture drop out for a while and return as another tribe?"

The old man wondered what would become of the current way

of life, humans who were part of today's global culture. He always remembered the advice the grandfather tree gave him.

"*Perhaps you humans should think about your own population. Don't outeat your food supply, my friend. I know what is in your heart. You understand that only Mother Nature will determine the outcome. I wish the whole human species would also understand such things before they disappoint themselves. ... Do not worry. Mother Nature is in charge. Furthermore, all raindrops will get swept up in the eternal spirit pool.*"

The old man thought about how much he enjoyed the forest; how much energy he received from it. He admired the trees' way of life the most. There was a certain wisdom in it.

That he had not interfered with nature on these eighty acres made the man happy. He had not permitted human civilization to invade it, to further use up its natural resources and its inherent natural beauty. He prevented the ways of humans from taking away its intrinsic wonder.

The man came to realize that humans were also part of the natural equation. They occupied a place on the natural planet as did every other living thing. But humans often forgot that they shared the planet with other living things; that they, as humans, were subject to the same action-reactions faced by other living things. In that sense, all living things were in it together. Certainly, they were all in the spirit pool together.

That night, after he banked the fire, blew out the oil lamp, and pulled the quilts up to his shoulders, the old man slept. He slept deeply.

Split Toe knew the seventy-four-year-old man was nearby. He sensed the man's energy and wanted to visit his old friend. With a clear sky and a full moon, Split Toe walked quietly from the tag alder swamp, crossed the gas pipeline, and stepped into the trees.

The moon projected long shadows behind each tree and walked the shadows slowly across the forest floor as the moon followed its arch across the sky. When a breeze zipped through the trees, the shadows danced together in a waltz. When the air was still, they simply held hands.

Split Toe approached the shelter. He smelled smoke from its fire. Split Toe thought the chimney's smoke smell was comforting because, when it was burning, he knew the old man was there.

The old man was a caretaker. He always made Split Toe feel as though the world was okay. That the forest was in good hands. Split Toe saw where the man had cleared a path in the snow between the woodpile and the door. He stepped up to the window and peered into the darkness. A subdued orange sliver of light glowed below the cast iron door of the woodstove. It provided a faint illumination within the shelter.

The man sensed Split Toe was near, and in a hazy state of awareness somewhere between sleep and dream, he leaned up on one elbow and looked at Split Toe peering in the window. The man closed his eyes and opened them again to remove the haze. There was his old friend. Split Toe nodded his antlers just enough to tap the window.

Cathy sensed the noise and rolled over.

The man lifted his hand and cupped his fingers.

"Rest well, my friend," Split Toe said, and he turned back to the tag alder swamp.

The man closed his eyes with images of Split Toe circling in his mind. His dream drifted to the sand bluff beside the river. He stood there, hidden in the shadow of one of the old-growth trees. The forest was full of these trees. Every tree in the forest was a giant white pine. He glanced across the river to the peninsula. Giant white pines covered it entirely. On the bluff several people in buckskin clothing—men, women, children—focused on a campfire, which was the center of a ring of dome-shaped bark huts. They sat in a circle at the fire's perimeter. Hidden from the campfire, the man eavesdropped. The old man noticed Split Toe standing between two huts.

"Waawaashkeshi!" One of the children excitedly jumped to her feet.

The deer dipped his antlers reverently.

The Ojibwe father stood and placed his hand on his daughter's shoulder. He then bowed deeply to the deer.

"How have you been, my old friend?" Mukwoh asked.

Waawaashkeshi scraped his hoof on the ground and lowered

himself to a curled position at the child's feet. He could look into the child's eyes.

"I have been well, my friend. A few difficulties, but they are minor. The spirit current is strong."

"Mother Nature always looks after things." Mukwoh knew Waawaashkeshi would understand.

"Your daughter is growing. You must be proud."

Mukwoh squeezed his daughter's shoulder affectionately.

"I met a human from the future," Waawaashkeshi went on. "He follows your path. He lives simply and cares for the earth. He will take responsibility for this place. I think you would be pleased with him. He understands the spirit current and is constantly trying to understand how Mother Nature works. Would you please leave an arrowhead for him to find? It will help to show him the way."

Mukwoh picked up his quiver and removed two arrows. With a quick slice of his bone knife, he sliced through the leather threads that fastened the stone points to their shafts. Taking the points, he walked toward the river's edge.

"I will leave two. One for the man, and one for his kin."

He placed the points on the forest floor at the base of two great white pines. He did not see the old man standing in the shadows only a few trees away.

"There is one more place I must go tonight," Waawaashkeshi said. "I will go to the sacred circle on the other side of the big river. Would you like to come?"

Mukwoh knew he could not go with Waawaashkeshi this time. Waawaashkeshi had a purpose he should manage alone.

"Thank you, my friend. You must go without me this time to the place of the aanikoobijiganag—the place of the ancestors. I feel the spirit current telling me so. Go well, my friend."

"Stay well," Split Toe whispered as he got to his feet.

He dipped his antlers to the Ojibwe and then to the daughter and then to the circle of those at the fire.

"Teach your children well," he added.

As he turned to walk away, Waawaashkeshi looked directly into the eyes of the seventy-four-year-old man standing in the shadows. Split Toe bowed deeply again. The seventy-four-year-old man raised his hand, cupped his fingers for a moment, and followed.

Soon, the man found himself standing next to Split Toe at the edge of an earthworks circle: the sacred circle.

"This is a powerful place," Split Toe said gently. "I brought you here to see it, to feel its power, and to help you understand that all of nature is connected like a circle. Like this." He swirled his antlers in a sweeping figure-eight.

Split Toe dropped to his front knees and touched his antlers to the ground. The seventy-four-year-old man also dropped to his knees.

"The sun rises and the sun sets. The moon follows its cycle in the sky. The seasons go and they return. A seed grows and becomes a tree, which casts its own seeds to the wind. The tree dies in its time, returning all that it has become to the soil from whence it came. In doing so, it nourishes the seeds of its own offspring. A tree rarely dies of old age, but it dies in its time and according to the conditions. Mother Nature ensures all of this."

Split Toe rose to his feet. The seventy-four-year-old man followed Split Toe's lead.

"This sacred circle left by the ancestors reminds me of how life works," Split Toe continued.

"Everything is temporary, and everything is eternal. It is the temporary we cling to and the eternal we become. Everything becomes part of the spirit pool. It is neither good nor bad. It does not judge. It simply exists as something providing the energy Mother Nature uses for her action-reaction. The spirit pool nourishes the offspring of everything. It supports the next round as the world continuously changes. It provides opportunity for every new beginning. Many living things destroy themselves. They overeat their food supply. It is one of the ways of nature. But the spirit pool ensures it is not the end of the story, because each raindrop swimming into the spirit pool enriches it in some way.

"The forest is the best example, my friend. You have been a good steward. The forest you care for is pure. It is natural. But like other forests, it will fall and be born again. I have seen this. Each rebirth is an opportunity for improvement. But everything is temporary and then eternal.

"You have worked hard to understand how the forest works. That is a noble effort. You have taught your children and grandchildren as well. You are like the grandfather tree, my friend, and there will be those who love you for that. Particularly the trees, but also the animals. Anything that breathes oxygen returned to the air by the trees. You have given more than you have taken. Not all will have eyes to see such things, but your raindrop will deeply enrich the spirit pool."

The seventy-four-year-old man stirred from his dream. He reached over and put his hand on Cathy's back. He felt her breathing. What an extraordinary dream. He wanted to tell her about it. Instead, he slid from under the covers, opened the door of the woodstove, raked an iron through the coals, and added two more log splits.

He walked quietly to the east-facing window, the one that looked toward the tag alder swamp. A line of orange peeked out below a thin, gray cloud on the horizon. The forest sunrise would be beautiful this morning. Looking at the snow, he saw deep tracks leading to the window and perhaps the smudge of a nose left on the outside pane.

Ol' Split Toe, he thought, and raised his hand, knowing that the legendary deer, a real deer, was out there in the tag alder swamp. Perhaps sleeping. He felt it.

"Thank you for the dream, my friend." He cupped his hand, then touched it to his heart before lowering it to his side.

The sun painted the thin cloud orange and the sky behind it red. The old man watched the sunrise form, knowing a sunrise is a moving picture, always changing and then suddenly gone. At that instant he realized that all of nature is like a sunrise. The spirit stream had tried for a long time to show him this. Nature is changing. Always changing. Evaporating in front of your own eyes and then waiting for another morning. Lowering his gaze to the windowsill, he picked up Cathy's arrowhead. He rolled it between his fingers and felt warmth from the hand that made it, the hand that had sliced it from its shaft.

The old man turned to the west window and, bowing

respectfully, touching the arrowhead to his forehead, he whispered to the Ojibwe, "Thank you."

He turned his gaze again to the east window. Now a streak of pink pastel colored the sky near the horizon.

In the tag alder swamp, Split Toe closed his eyes. He imagined one more trip to the river. A last trip. One more lesson. He pictured himself trotting out of the gravel pit toward the grandfather tree with a shadow beginning to take away the sun. Split Toe could feel the age-old limp in his rear leg. His enormous antlers weighed heavily upon his head.

He knew he was slowing down.

Perhaps he could walk the rest of the way and let the eclipse welcome him into the next place. Let the spirits help him step up the riverbank on the far side, guide him through the curtain of large ferns and bring him into the pool. Where knowledge would be revealed in its completeness. Split Toe's tail twitched in tired excitement.

Soon, Split Toe whispered in his mind. He sensed it.

He would go there and wait for the boy.

"**Ol' Split Toe, my dear friend.**" He remembered the boy's voice floating on the breeze. "**One more thing. This spirit pool ... it is a great place. Go well, my friend.**"

Split Toe opened his eyes and looked at snow lining each thin branch of the thicket surrounding him. He felt the pull.

A drop of rain.

AUTHOR'S NOTE

The rich history of North America's forests starts thousands of years ago as the last ice age glaciers receded. A time when frozen landscapes gave way to barren ground, open for soil development in which trees would someday take root. It is a tale of slow transformation brought about by changing climates and geography, the migration of plants, insects, and animals, and the impact of nearly two hundred years of modern human civilization. It is a story of a continuously changing world and repeated cycles of regeneration.

Michigan is a good place to follow the saga.

Now, more than 11,000 years after the most recent ice age, the oldest known trees still living in Michigan are a few scraggly cedars growing on the white limestone cliffs of Lake Michigan's northern shoreline. They are no more than 1,400 years old.

A few remaining stands of trees that are thought of as "old-growth" white pines evoke the nostalgic forests that towered over much of northern Michigan before the logging era of 1860–1910. Hartwick Pines State Park near Grayling and Estivant Pines Nature Sanctuary near Copper Harbor protect such trees. But

AUTHOR'S NOTE

these *old trees* are only between 300 and 430 years old, a relatively recent generation of the forests that grew before them.

The real backstory to Michigan's forests has to do with the resilience of nature. It is more a story of repeated rebirth than it is a story with a beginning and an end. Each rebirth brings an adaptation to new conditions. Each generation is slowly born into a world that may be somewhat different in temperature, air quality, soil condition, and wetness. These differences bring about variations in the entire food chain, with plants, animals, and insects all adapting. New habitats are, at birth, already reaching for another equilibrium.

But to humans—those reading this book— what I hope captures your attention is the natural timescale of a single tree's whole life, from the time it sprouts as a seedling until it finally decomposes into soil again. And the timescale of a whole forest of trees, with all the birth and death of individual trees taking place within it.

It is easy to think of things in nature only in the context of one human lifetime: your own lifetime, or perhaps a multigenerational lifespan that includes your parents, your children, and your grandchildren. It is also easy to think of natural things as permanent. But even the oldest trees we know of in Michigan are recent and short-lived when considering all the trees that grew naturally over the Michigan landscape since 9,000 BC.

Since the most recent ice age, many rounds of forest destruction and regeneration have been the work of Mother Nature. But during the past two hundred years, human treatment of the forest has profoundly disturbed patterns of natural forest life cycles. As Mother Nature reaches for balance, she addresses human impacts in her own way and according to her own timescale. Mother Nature's solutions are rarely in sync with the desires and expectations of humans.

The human challenge—perhaps, human dilemma—is to walk softly upon the earth. To use no more than we need. To waste little. To create without destroying. Like the forest, to adapt continuously to an ever-changing planet.

For the sake of humanity, humans would be well served to embrace the natural world that we are each a part of. To understand it. To treat it with care. To realize that we share our space with other living things. Living things that are important to our own survival. Mother Nature, who has built resilience into the natural world with her action-reaction process, provides a self-maintaining redemptive solution for the planet. Humans, however, will need to be receptive to change if they are to fit in. They will need to adapt to the changing future world. A world that is at the same time adapting to the behavior of humans.

ACKNOWLEDGMENTS

In preparation for writing this book—and to understand more about the entire life cycle of the forest, including the events that a forest experiences of both natural and human cause—I set out to read the books listed on the References page. I would like to acknowledge the value that those books offered me, rounding out my understanding of nature, trees, the forest, and the experience of early pioneers who came to Michigan's white pine forests when the trees still covered much of the state.

I have spent many years as a forest advocate, including plenty of time living off-grid in a simple kind of forest solitude. Yet despite a life of much first-hand communion with nature, two books caused me to believe that I took trees and the forest for granted. They are: *Finding the Mother Tree: Discovering the Wisdom of the Forest*, by Suzanne Simard, and *The Hidden Life of Trees: What They Feel, How They Communicate—Discoveries From a Secret World*, by Peter Wohlleben. After reading these two books, I was particularly struck by how vastly different the timescale is for the lifespan of a tree compared to that of an animal, particularly a human. It was something I knew, but did not think much about. Something I understood, but did not feel.

Though *Ol' Split Toe* is written as fiction, many of the situations, settings, stories, and time periods are accurate, often taken from firsthand accounts, and adapted into characters and settings described fictionally in the book. My paternal grandparents were both born at the beginning of the twentieth century in small frontier farming conditions in mid-Michigan.

Some of the stories that take place in this book during the time of my grandparents' early lives are based on what they told me as a young adult about their own lives on small family farms they and their parents carved out of the Michigan woods. I thank them for patiently trying to satisfy my curiosity about those things.

Thank you to Harry and Karolyn Martin who sat at their kitchen table and described to me how they lost their dairy herd during Michigan's 1974 PBB contamination. They loaned me their copy of Edwin Chen's book, *PBB: An American Tragedy*. Much of the PBB part of the story follows Harry and Karolyn's firsthand experience.

Thank you to those who read this story in its draft forms, providing feedback, encouragement and coaching: Catherine Kwantes, Angela Nikka, Crystal Wright, Hannah Terry, Rebecca Ellens, Jacqueline Ellens, Jerry Friends, David Martin, Julie Traynor, Patricia Powell, Bill Gleason—*The Tree Man*, Annie Gottlieb, Helen Klonaris, Michael Gabrion, Garrett Bowman, Eli Stanesa, Theresa Cole, and Hart Cauchy. Thank you to Misha Neidorfler and the entire team at Mission Point Press, who helped to turn my manuscript into a book. You are all remarkable people. To all of you, my sincere gratitude.

REFERENCES

Chen, Edwin. *PBB: An American Tragedy*. Prentice-Hall, 1979.

Dempsey, Dave. *Ruin and Recovery: Michigan's Rise as a Conservation Leader*. University of Michigan Press, 2001.

Egan, Dan. *The Death and Life of the Great Lakes*. W. W. Norton, 2017.

Ibuse, Masuji. *Black Rain*. Kodansha International, 1969.

Jager, Ronald. *Eighty Acres: Elegy for a Family Farm*. Beacon Press, 1990.

Lithen, J. August. *The Road to Marion Town: The Settlement of Osceola County, State of Michigan*. Parkhurst Brothers, 2018.

Livesay, Nora, and John D. Nichols (editors). With the University of Minnesota's Department of American Indian Studies and University Libraries. *The Ojibwe People's Dictionary*. Ojibwe.lib.umn.edu.

Marsh, George Perkins. *Man and Nature: Or, Physical Geography as Modified by Human Action*. Charles Scribner, 1864.

Pielou, E. C. *After the Ice Age: The Return of Life to Glaciated North America*. University of Chicago Press, 1992.

Rawlence, Ben. *The Treeline: The Last Forest and the Future of Life on Earth*. St. Martin's Press, 2022.

Shaw, Anna Howard, with Elizabeth Jordan. *The Story of a Pioneer*. Harper and Brothers, 1915. Reprint: Okitoks Press, 2018.

Simard, Suzanne. *Finding the Mother Tree: Discovering the Wisdom of the Forest.* Vintage, 2022.

Winslow, Kenelm, B.A.S, M.D. *The Home Medical Library.* The Review of Review Company, 1911.

Wohlleben, Peter. *The Hidden Life of Trees: What They Feel, How They Communicate—Discoveries From a Secret World.* Translated by Jane Billinghurst. Greystone Books, 2016.

Contact the author at:
danellensauthor@gmail.com

ABOUT THE AUTHOR

Dan Ellens is an outdoor enthusiast who is passionate about connecting people with nature. He spends nearly half of each year in an isolated, electricity-free treehouse on Winterfield Pines Nature Sanctuary with woodstove heat, handpump water, and oil lamp lighting.

Dan has written four nonfiction books intended to inspire adventure, promote self-sufficient lifestyles, and connect people with nature.

While not in the wilds, Dan and his wife live in the small community of Salem, Michigan.

www.ingramcontent.com/pod-product-compliance
Lightning Source LLC
LaVergne TN
LVHW090413120526
838202LV00093BA/53